I0556785

Chronosphere

A. SCOTT HOWE

Third Revision 2024
Plug-in Creations, Beaverton, Oregon, USA

Copyright © 2013-2014 A. Scott Howe

All rights reserved.

ISBN: 0-9850765-5-0
ISBN-13: 978-0-9850765-5-9

DEDICATION

This book is dedicated to the Howe brothers, who have had more real and imaginary adventures than anyone I know.

ACKNOWLEDGMENTS

I would like to acknowledge the encouragement of my wife Ingping Chia Howe.

PROLOGUE

Dr. Reuben Drake and his two assistants struggled up the faintly marked path. The route was not particularly steep, just that any slope is always harder to negotiate in an environmental suit, even at one-third gee, and they were carrying equipment. As Drake neared the top of the slope, he could hear himself breathing in the narrow confines of the helmet, almost overwhelming the sounds of life-support fans working to keep his faceplate defrosted.

Drake let his gaze wander over the reddish rocks ahead of him, trying to get a glimpse of what lay beyond. He took the last few steps as the distant valley began to reveal itself over the top of the eclipsing ridge -- it was one of those breathtaking views that were so common on Mars, framed by towering stone and icy cliffs of enormous scale. Reaching the highest point of the climb, he paused long enough to catch his breath, but kept his eyes on those far away low lands that he had come to see. There was a city down there, or the wreckage of what used to be one.

"*That's Novissima,*" Mei-Hua said through the helmet com as she came up beside him, "*no one comes out of there alive.*"

What happened out there, he wondered. Drake looked around and found a good boulder to sit on, and the two women did likewise. The environmental suit was a lightweight alloy, highly articulated with hard sections and pressure-assisted joints to allow for maximal movement -- even while sitting. To his left, Tina took out the journaler and began to record video and textual impressions of the scene below. Drake thought he could detect something different about that landscape -- did those far away ruins of Novissima have a strange shimmer about them?

"*What could be down there? Is it some kind of radiation?*" Drake asked, thinking about the explosion -- or something -- that had occurred just the previous Sol-day and left not a soul alive ('Sol' was the term that referred to a Martian 'day').

Mei-Hua, looking at her instruments replied, "*I'm not sure. I don't seem to be getting anything out of the ordinary.*"

The surface of Mars was already bathed in galactic cosmic radiation anyway, Drake thought. He was a little irked that his team had been asked to interrupt their research and survey the scene, only because they were operating just over the ridge. But all those people -- some of his friends must have been affected.

He reached up and switched into augmented mode and immediately an image from the helmet detector array was overlaid on the scene. He could zoom in at will. As he focused on portions of the landscape, artificial outlines illuminated various distant shapes and small descriptive text flags popped in and out in front of his eyes seemingly in mid-air -- rock type, spectral data, surface temperature, etcetera -- the sort of information a field scientist would be interested in. But this time between the broken walls he could see crumpled shapes that could only be bodies scattered by some violent event. 'Unknown organic compound,' the flag read, not sensitive enough to analyze human flesh unprotected to the Martian elements.

There must have been dozens of them.

"*Hasn't anyone moved in to help?*" Tina's nervous voice sounded in Drake's helmet com. The girl had paused in her narration of a video recording.

Mei-Hua pointed off to the left and exclaimed, "*No! There they are!*"

In unison Drake and Tina followed her indication -- there was a vehicle all right, well outside the apparent circle of damage -- a stalled pressurized rover parked off to the side. Drake zoomed in to look for what he did not want to see -- more bodies collapsed where they had disembarked from the rover. These were fully clad in pressure suits similar to him. The would-be rescuers hadn't gotten more than five meters from their transport.

Drake gradually began to flip through the electromagnetic spectra while slowly panning back and forth. Ghostly shapes replaced crisp visible outlines as the various filters revealed information only available on that wavelength. Infrared showed typical contours with no hot spots out of the ordinary, and a quick scan through microwaves and radio bands revealed mostly static background noise.

"*I'm not getting anything on the longer wavelengths,*" he said out loud.

Mei-Hua, who had also gone into augmented mode replied, "*There's nothing at the high frequency range either.*"

Drake adjusted the filter down past ultraviolet and suddenly saw a scattering of flashes.

Mei-Hua gasped at the same time, "*X-rays!*"

There was no doubt about it. Drake looked from left to right -- an abnormal level of x-rays was smothering the valley below.

"*But it doesn't make any sense! Any EVA suit would protect against that level of x-rays.*" Mei-Hua referred to the well-used acronym meaning Extra-Vehicular Activity clothing, or in other words 'space suit'.

"*I've got to go down there.*" Drake said calmly.

Tina protested, "*No! We don't know what happened to those people. We should wait for help.*"

The doctor was undeterred, "*Don't worry -- you can see a boundary of sorts.*" he paused and traced out a swath with his arms as if he were painting on the landscape, "*Look, it's more intense inside the line. I'll stay well outside that area.*"

All three of them looked down in augmented mode, the scene overlaid with data from the x-ray band. It was true there appeared to be a clear demarcation of where the contaminated area ended, as if some x-ray source spewed particles straight up from the surface entirely missing the ground next to it. *Even so, those x-rays still can't be very strong,* Drake thought.

Tina continued to voice opposition, but Mei-Hua eased the girl's mind, "*I'll stay with him. If anything happens, I'll tow him out.*"

Mei-Hua pulled out a coil of cable and clipped one end to her harness, smiling through the helmet as she held up the other end for Tina to see. The Asian woman was plenty strong enough to pull the doctor out in partial Mars gravity, having trained on Earth before the home world had become off-limits. Though the name 'Mei-Hua' meant 'beautiful flower', the girl had a roughness about her that belied her name.

Drake stripped down his equipment to the bare minimum, and took the cable end offered by Mei-Hua. After attaching the end to his harness, he began to descend the gradual slope leading down into the valley. Mei-Hua allowed the cable to run taut, then followed him down. Tina stood on the edge with the journaler, pointing the video camera and narrating the recorded scene.

"*Com check,*" Drake paused in his descent and listened for the replies of the two women.

Both the women's voices came back full quieting, so the doctor continued working his way down the hill. He looked up occasionally and tried to toggle the augmented x-ray filter back and forth without losing his footing.

The doctor got all the way down to the bottom and began crossing the plain. He turned around and saw Mei-Hua a dozen or so meters back, and Tina cut a tiny figure up on the shelf. "*Com check,*" he repeated.

Mei-Hua's voice came in loud and clear, but Tina had a little bit of scratch, "*Be careful Rube, I don't like this at all,*" she said.

"*It's okay, we're not flying into this blind. We have the right instrumentation on our side.*" Drake consoled.

The doctor turned and looked out over the plain in augmented mode. Somehow the x-ray flashes seemed a little closer than he had thought he remembered the line to be. He took more readings, and relayed them back up to Tina's journaler. No matter how many measurements he took, the x-rays just didn't seem strong enough to take down a man in an environmental suit. He continued toward the line.

"*Doctor Drake,*" a static-filled voice echoed in his helmet. "*Go ahead Tina.*"

The girl was getting hard to understand through the interference, "*It seems . . . spreading.*"

Drake couldn't quite hear the middle part, but understood the gist of what she was trying to say. Yes, the x-ray field did seem to be advancing. He stood still for a moment and had the suit computer run through some calculations comparing advancement over time, based on several augmented readings. The answer came back soon enough -- a man could easily outrun the pace with a brisk walk, even in a pressure suit. He was not going to find himself run down by a mysterious x-ray emittance.

Drake got a little closer and took another reading. It looked like weak x-rays, not enough to image a skeleton in a doctor's office. Again, he relayed the data back to Tina's journaler and continued walking closer to that fuzzy boundary.

". . . *back!*" Tina's voice barely cackled through the helmet com, "*Come back!*"

Drake turned to face Mei-Hua who was standing a few dozen meters back with her gloved hands grasping the cable.

She said, "*Maybe we ought to turn back, doctor.*" Even her voice began to have a little static in the transmission, and had a worried tone.

"*Okay, but first let me take one more reading.*"

Drake toggled augmented mode and did a slow left to right scan. The x-ray flashes were very close together now, and not too far off. For the last time he relayed the readings back to the journaler, intending to turn around and head back.

It was at that point that Drake realized his mistake. He needn't ever have been concerned about the x-rays -- something far more dangerous was advancing across that field. Suddenly he looked down and the ground seemed to be eaten away. A hazy stain swallowed his leg and caused him to collapse on the ground. He began to lose air as he watched his hand disintegrate. Warnings flashed on the heads-up display and the suit went into self-preservation mode. Internal baffles inflated around limbs to keep the torso and vital organs safe. Drake felt his right arm and leg go numb as they were constricted, and barely registered the countdown readout screaming out for him to get help within x seconds or he would lose those limbs.

Drake felt a powerful tug and knew that Mei-Hua was reeling him in. But the damage was too great. He was still losing air and the suit supply apparatus was trying to maintain a minimal pressure to keep his blood from boiling. More warnings flashed on the heads-up display saying the air supply was running low.

"*Help me . . . Mei . . .*" Drake scratched out in a hoarse voice.

Mei-Hua stared in horror as Drake's suit shut down only five meters away. She had been monitoring his vital signs right up to the last second and knew it was too late. She would not have enough time to cross that short stretch of soil and hook up an emergency air supply from her own suit. She scrambled to release the cable clip as the wall of x-ray flashes lit up the background. Mei-Hua screamed when she saw the metal of Drake's suit, and the ground around it decay right in front of her eyes. She had never seen anything like it before, and that confounded cable would not release! Somehow the clip gave and she backed away staring in horror as the indefinable decay crept toward her across the ground.

There was not even time to see the warnings as her chest seemed to melt away. The suit faithfully continued to give unheeded lines of text flashing red on the heads-up display, but the air leaked out suddenly and the poor girl was already gone. The signals continued to relay back to the journaler until the circuits decayed to non-functionality.

Up on the bench, a horror-struck Tina backed away hugging the journaler, and ran down the hill with tears in her eyes as she put as much distance as she could between herself and that advancing wall of death.

CHAPTER 1

Tom Hildebrandt woke up early one morning with a start. The phone was ringing.

"Hello?" he groggily asked.

A man's voice was on the other end, "*If you're ever in real trouble, remember me.*"

Click.

What the heck, Hildebrandt thought, *a crank call*. He checked the source -- Burning Boat Pub in Novissima. Why would someone be calling him from a pub so early in the morning?

I'll check it out later, he thought -- another problem to solve. But he forgot about it. He couldn't have known at the time, but that insignificant phone call would someday save his life.

Tom's problems started long ago, well before the Novissima explosion. It was true that he was owner and operator of a large manufacturing operation, and managing all that talent had its challenges. But Tom's biggest difficulty might have been his courtship with Murphy's Law -- that age-old adage that claimed anything that could go wrong would go wrong.

He used to think that technology could solve everything, like the machines that dug out the caverns their cities were built in, or rockets or vehicles or power plants or accelerator magnets. *The only way to defeat Murphy is through sound engineering,* Tom thought.

But he was about to change his mind.

With the early morning wake-up call, Tom headed down to Hildebrandt Engineering to start the day. He was the hands-on type -- even though he could have sent out a deputy, indeed, even his deputies could have had underlings out there to fix things -- he needed to go and take a look for himself. As often was the case, Tom would try to jump in and get his hands dirty, but his staff would never let him do anything critical because of old Murphy.

On this particular day as he rushed onto the factory floor, he almost ran into one of the most beautiful women he had ever seen. It wasn't that she was particularly well dressed -- in fact she wore the rugged coveralls fancied by pilots and rover operators. But something about her mannerism captured him for a moment. Apologizing, Tom courteously made sure the woman was okay, and picked up the journaler she had dropped. Unfortunately, in his nervousness, he didn't wait till she had a complete grasp on the unit and it clattered to the floor once more. He tried to pick it up again but her boots caught his attention -- the subtle feminine pink-edged fasteners briefly distracted him and the unit slipped out of his hands. Scrambling to grasp the journaler, his knee pushed the device and caused it to skid across the floor. Finally, Tom was able to retrieve the unit and successfully sent the dumbfounded lady on her way. Still looking over his shoulder, he brushed himself off and went to continue his errand.

Unfortunately, Murphy had a firm grasp by then. No sooner did he turn around than he ran right into a pipe column. The pain was agonizing. Tom winced, spun around slowly, and saw the whole factory floor looking his way in amusement. Tom's enthusiasm endeared him to the workers, and several of them stepped forward to see if he was all right. But perhaps even more painful was the face of that woman --

she had stopped in her tracks to see what had happened to the idiot.

Stupid, stupid, Tom thought. Okay well, then there are women -- maybe engineering doesn't always keep Murphy in control.

Later in the afternoon Tom headed to the Hildebrandt nano lab, which was one level down. The nano lab was purely experimental, and he hoped the work would add a successful new dimension to the company. Generations of engineers had tried to produce universal assemblers that could both reproduce themselves and also build other things, but no one had successfully done it yet. The problem was just too complex, and unforeseen quantum-scale engineering challenges always crept in where friction and kinematics took on new meanings. Finally, it had been determined that the nanoassemblers already found in nature were the best approach -- take base stock from bio-organisms like *rinorea niccolifera* that had a limited capacity to deposit metal, and modify genes from *hymenopterous* insects that use metal to harden mandibles to create bioengineered metallic deposition processes. Tom didn't understand it very well, but essentially it meant that some bacteria would be able to multiply naturally and poop out metal.

The challenge had been to figure out how to keep the bioengineered nanoassemblers in a confined area, supply it with the right intake, and control where it deposited the output metal. In order to manufacture human-scale products, many billions of them would need to be depositing metal in parallel or the process would take too much time to be practical. Hildebrandt engineers had just begun experimenting with wireless control of the latest generation of engineered organisms, and had even branched out from metals to plastics, stone, and other materials.

Tom found the nano lab empty since the engineers had been out for the day. All the nanoassembler cultures were carefully organized or running automated deposition tests.

Unfortunately, Murphy sometimes showed up even when no one was around. By chance Tom saw some uneven shapes underneath one of the desks. He kneeled down to get a closer look, and the first thought that ran through his mind was, *why would mushrooms be growing on the furniture?* Soft, billowy forms firmly adhered to the cracks and corners between the cabinets and the wall.

Tom reached over and grabbed a set of calipers and proceeded to poke one of the rounded objects. Contrary to what he had been expecting, the white blob was firm and unyielding. Mold! Tom's countenance sank -- he had heard all the nightmare stories of runaway mold in enclosed space environments. Entire outposts that couldn't get mold under control had to be evacuated and torched because the stuff would literally take over.

Gotta get rid of this now, Tom thought. He stood up and looked around, trying to find something that could scrape off the mold. All he could see lying on the workbenches were precision instruments and tools. In a desperate mood, Tom rushed out of the lab and headed for the catchall equipment closet they affectionately called the 'Hildebrandt Bunker'. Switching on the light, rows of shelving lined the walls carrying decommissioned hardware, spare parts, unfinished prototypes, and broken tools. It was magic land. Tom fondly remembered the background of the various pieces and thought back on those happy times of brainstorming and development. But there was no time for reminiscing. Tom quickly grabbed a scraper tool and shut off the light.

Just then an acne-faced youth strode by. Seeing the big boss, the young man almost jumped out of his skin.

Tom grabbed the intern's arm and implored, "Arden, go find an incinerator bag and meet me in the nano lab."

Arden Tuttweiler was still high school aged, participating in the Hildebrandt educational work program. He helped out with odd jobs, but had really built up an impressive understanding of Hildebrandt projects and operations. The nervous fellow veered off to find the item while Tom rushed back downstairs.

When Hildebrandt once again looked under the desk he was surprised -- the white growths somehow seemed to be twice as big as before. Tom donned a mask, brought out the scraper, and wondered if he was imagining things. It didn't take long to scrape the clumps away and collect them all in a pile on the floor. He ran over to the sink and washed the residue off the tool.

Just then Arden walked in with the incinerator bag, and stopped in his tracks.

"Arden, clean up this pile and throw it in the incinerator." Tom indicated the broken-up molds on the floor.

"But sir, that's --" Arden began.

"Do you remember last week they found bodies in Novissima drained of blood? Well, this is worse!" Tom interrupted with a dramatic ghost story.

Arden might have been skeptical, but his face looked like it had drained of blood too. Reluctantly, Arden went over and cleaned up the pile and left. Tom took special care to disinfect the area, and then picked up the scraper to return to the Hildebrandt Bunker.

By this time most of the human employees had gone home leaving the digital assemblers and numerical control manufacturing machines on automatic. Somewhere on the floor a piece of equipment was making a horrendous noise. Tom walked down the main aisle and peered into the various work areas to see what was going on. As he turned a corner, he got a shock. There, floating about a meter above the floor was the Toshige hoverpallet making all sorts of racket from the noisy cooling fans. A heavy power cable almost as thick as his arm snaked from the unit over to a panel on the wall. The hoverpallet was of course one of the latest gadgets top engineers Kitamura and Hughes had been tinkering with. What Tom didn't expect was to see that coverall-clad woman testing out the remote steering controls.

"Uh, hello." Tom ventured.

The woman, intent on the jittery, sideways 'crabbing' motion of the unit, reacted quickly to keep it from drifting too close to the work bench. She didn't even seem to notice that Tom had said anything.

Tom waved his hand and said a little louder, "Hi!"

Again, the woman didn't look up but sent her hands swiftly across the control panel. Such dexterity -- Tom saw the focused hand movement as choreography in an exquisitely beautiful dance or the playing of an instrument.

Finally, Hildebrandt intended to yell a greeting loud enough to overcome the cooling fans, but Murphy stepped in. Somehow Tom changed his mind at the last instant and instead of saying 'hi' mistakenly merged it with 'hello'. Just as the woman powered down the fans, Tom's voiced boomed through the silence across the entire factory, "Hyellow!"

Tom froze as the woman stared at him in mild shock.

"Carry on," was all he could say, and then escaped to his office without waiting for a reply.

Stupid, Tom thought, *why can't you get it right?*

It was several hours later, Tom having been interrupted by late-working engineers, that he realized he had left the Bunker open and the lights on. The factory was running on automatics with no one around. He shut off the lights and went home. Thus was the life of Tom Hildebrandt as he daily battled with old Murphy.

*****

It wasn't hard for Earth-borns to get used to the Martian Sol, which was roughly 24.5 Earth hours. Nevertheless 'day' and 'hour' sometimes could have multiple meanings depending on context. The next Sol-day Tom made another early start down at the plant. It was a good thing, because Murphy had been making mischief.

"Tom, all the drains are stopped up." Masamune Hughes caught Tom as he walked through the door.

What now, Tom thought. Toilets were plugged, sinks wouldn't drain, and one shower had overflowed a bit. Folks were standing around wondering what to do. The office staff called in a plumbing crew that began putting robotic snakes into the traps. The team worked its way down the branch lines until finally everything was flowing smoothly.

Tom stood waiting with some of the engineers and interns as the plumber pulled out the last snake. He opened up the sample catch and pulled out a white substance.

"This is it. This is what got in your drains." The plumber explained.

Tom looked closely at the substance then turned around to face the group milling about. He locked eyes with Arden Tuttweiler the intern, who nervously shrugged.

"Sir, I tried to tell you yesterday," Arden shyly began, "that wasn't mold we cleaned up, it was an offshoot nanoassembler colony."

Tom stared back with an incredulous look on his face. *Oh great, Murphy -- nanoassemblers in the drains*, Tom thought. With their ability to take various inputs, the minuscule biotech devices may be highly corrosive, eating into whatever environment they happen to find themselves. Later, Tom called the chief nano lab engineer who was still offsite, to see if he could find anything out.

"*That prototype escaped and seeded itself behind the desk,*" the chief began, "*for some reason it would go through unexplained growth spurts. We let it grow in place until we could figure out what caused the super growth.*"

And Tom washed some of them down the drain! This was definitely not turning out to be a good day. He spent the rest of the afternoon worrying whether they had actually gotten rid of the little devices, knowing that even a few survivors could build up another healthy colony.

Another Sol-day was coming to an end. Tom was a bit drowsy as he made his way to the main floor to help close up shop. He came to immediate wakefulness however, as he almost ran once again into that swanky female pilot. Tom's face turned crimson red as she took his breath away.

"Ah Tom, there you are," mechanical engineering chief Masamune Hughes said from the side, "I'd like you to meet Carrie Johnson our new equipment operator. Carrie this is Dr. Hildebrandt."

Tom almost blushed again as he thought of all the effort he had gone through to break the ice, when Hughes jumped in and took care of it in five minutes. Carrie was staring back at him as if she had a new level of respect. *You mean this is the big boss*, her eyes seemed to say.

Reigning in old Murphy, Tom stood back on his heels in dignity and replied, "Hello Carrie, welcome to the team."

It was several Sol-days later when news of the Novissima explosion would change their lives forever. Tom was at one of the underground construction sites run by Kajima Corporation, this time inspecting the big shield tunnel boring operation connecting Power Plant Nine with the rest of the complex. The shield borers were huge cylindrical behemoths that had diamond-tipped excavators spinning along the front. As the big cylinder progressed, debris would be carried backward on Hildebrandt robotic rubble carriers, and a continuous supply of precast concrete panels would be set in place to line the tunnel. In effect, the big machine 'extruded' a finished cylindrical concrete tunnel as it inched forward.

Suddenly there was a low rumble. The walls began to shake and klaxons sounded. It was the low-pressure alarm -- deep though the tunnel was, somehow there had been a pressure breach with the outside, and Grindavik's atmosphere was escaping out the hole. Several Kajima employees rushed Tom back along the tunnel to the emergency containment partitions that spanned the tunnel. By the time they reached the air lock, Tom's ears were starting to pop.

Hildebrandt watched piped-in video as operators remote-controlled the massive shield borer machine in reverse. Pressure-suited inspectors climbed into the narrow gap between the excavation head and the scarred rock face and began sweeping the surface with ultrasound detectors and video cameras.

Just then the news came in -- a massive explosion at Novissima had been the cause of the quake. They had felt the tremors halfway around the planet!

Thinking some fracture of rock was the culprit for leaking air, it came as a great surprise that ultrasound readings showed a perfectly straight bore hole down from the surface. Someone in times past had taken a core sample deep into the ground and the shield machine happened to intersect the shaft the very instant the southern explosion occurred.

Very strange, Tom thought -- he had no idea Murphy could be so clever. A video image showed a perfectly round opening about eight centimeters in diameter in the rock, with suited inspectors swarming about taking measurements.

"*There's something down here, seems artificial.*" Tom heard the inspector over the loudspeaker.

The operations control replied, "*Can you retrieve it?* "

Radio traffic went back and forth and Tom watched folks go in and out through the airlock. Intrigued, he spent the next hour watching video of ungainly clad team members sticking a variety of instruments down the hole to try to pull out whatever had been lodged inside. Finally, there was success as one long rod gently pulled upward emerged with a cylindrical capsule attached -- a plain, off-the-shelf document canister.

One of the suited figures carried the canister out while the rest shot foam up the hole to seal the breach. Tom watched as the Kajima chief retrieved the canister from the airlock and took it to a nearby table. With a little work, the lid came off and out spilled an old sheet of Mylar, like a lithographic negative from fifty years previous. Printed on the Mylar was a message with the exact date and time the Novissima explosion had occurred.

"Grindavik devils! Hope you enjoy the end of the world," was all it said.

CHAPTER 2

The hum of automated machinery was in the air as round-the-clock manufacturing characterized the Hildebrandt Engineering shop floor. But it was nearing the end of another work-Sol for the human employees.

"Hey guys I'm outta here." Masamune Hughes called over to a group of workers gathered around a workbench.

A complicated assemblage of mechatronic components was clamped to the table, and engineers were poking, prodding, and testing connections. Behind the white-clad group were countertops scattered with small parts, tools, and articulated task lights dangling from overhead racks.

Nine-year-old Sally Averman, who had the best soldering skills of the bunch glanced up and said, "Bye," before returning to her delicate handy work. Tom Hildebrandt also briefly looked up and smiled before turning to his work -- the poor fellow had a lot on his mind lately, with those escaped nanoassemblers and all.

One Asian fellow stood up and reached over for a rag to wipe his hands. Masamune's best friend Jiro Kitamura separated himself from the group and walked over to where Hughes was removing his own lab coat. The Kitamura's lived in the same ward in Grindavik as the Hughes family and were quite close. Masamune had named his own second son after his friend, but the boy had passed away only a few years previous.

"Dancing tonight, eh?" Jiro asked.

Hughes groaned, "Yep, Sachiko found this place that has trundling lessons before opening up the dance floor."

"You don't sound too enthusiastic."

"Well, whatever makes her happy, you know. At our age she still wants to drag me along, as if I could learn the tosses and whirls." Hughes modestly explained as he hung the lab coat up in his locker at the end of the room.

Masamune was well into middle age, already graying a bit around the edges -- some say he had a grandfatherly look, even though he was still the father of younger children. He had mixed Japanese-Chinese features for the most part, but had the Hughes family nose, which seemed to have clung on from several generations back.

Hughes turned around to face Jiro with a smile, "Why don't you and Beth join us later, for dinner?"

Jiro frowned, "Maybe, if I can get this power assembly back together again. Tom says they can't put the attenuators on until we are working and in place."

Kitamura was a bit younger than Hughes, but was balding on top. Still, he had a lean, handsome look that the women seemed to prefer.

"Call me later, guy."

"Will do," Jiro said and turned back toward the group.

Masamune walked through the vast Hildebrandt Engineering works past lathes, digital routers, and other manufacturing equipment, some of which had workers lingering nearby but for the most part were cutting / building parts unattended. It was a state-of-the-art rapid prototyping and design facility. In one area there were assembly stations with various generations of quantum plasma superconductor magnets under production that had been the main product of Hildebrandt of late. In another area Hughes walked past the

Toshige hoverpallet that they were working on for another client.

Young Arden Tuttweiler tended a machine automatically spitting out plastic built-up parts.

"Go home Arden. Don't you have a girlfriend?" Hughes jeered as he walked by.

Everyone knew Arden had a one-way crush on a girl over in materials, and he always tried to sit by her during the various student lectures. Their education system was set up as a hands-on merit-based process that put the young folks right in the middle of things as they proved themselves capable. They encouraged the inexperienced ones to move around a lot until they found something they liked, but teenagers were teenagers, and one couldn't blame a fellow for following a girl around.

"Very funny Dr. Hughes," Arden answered.

Hughes smiled as he sarcastically added, "You're very smart Arden -- don't let all those brains go to your head."

Arden waved the older gentleman along with a chuckle and returned his attention to the work.

When Hughes rounded the corner, he glanced up at the big observation windows. Neither his wife nor daughter were there, so he aimed for the side door exit -- they were probably working late and he would have to head down to the accelerator facility to meet them, he thought.

Hildebrandt Engineering was a tightly run, efficient organization located in the subterranean industrial section of Grindavik Colony. Streets and boulevards had been carved out of the native stone to protect the community from the radiation that bathed the Martian surface. There was a lot of activity about, and Hughes had to avoid several transports loaded with materials destined for some factory.

Passing along a corridor, Hughes paused long enough to peer through a small observation window that faced outward onto the wide Grindavik Crater basin. Several layers of thick clear panes set into the tool-scarred crevice held back the pressurized atmosphere of their fragile home and framed the massive cliffs and canyons beyond. Even after all these years it was still hard to imagine how such a pleasant sunlit landscape could actually be so hostile to human life. Hughes briefly scanned the line of Chinese made antimatter reactors marching across the dusty crater bottom, sufficient to power dozens of cities (or high-powered physics experiments), and worriedly glanced up at the sky. There were clouds forming there, something that was hard to contemplate in Mars' thin atmosphere. Hughes couldn't imagine what environmental effect could possibly cause such a dark billowing, so different from the typical dust storms. Nevertheless, he was sure it had to do with that strange x-ray storm out on the southern polar cap. The x-ray storm, or whatever it was, seemed to be getting bigger and no one knew why.

"Living up to your name, eh?" he said out loud -- he had grown up using the Japanese word 'Kasei' for the red planet, which meant 'fire star'.

At the end of the corridor Hughes took a lift down into a series of pressurized underground voids that made up the accelerator facility. Sachiko had been spending the last few years smashing atoms, and their daughter Teresa had turned out to be a chip off the old block, spending more and more of her training hours down in the lab.

The first set of doors on the left after the lift was where most of the action happened. Hughes looked into the big plate windows at a cavernous room filled with catwalks and scaffolding cradling pressure chambers and collision detectors. A large diameter conduit, which was a branch off the 36-kilometer superconducting accelerator ring, came out of a tunnel to the left. On the right the conduit emerged from the scaffolding and split into several branches that each went off into its own tunnel.

There were white lab coats at various stations on the scaffolding, and even a few young people were working late on some project. Toward the top of the structure Hughes spotted ten-year-old Teresa who had been helping one of the physicists calibrate instruments. Teresa saw her father and enthusiastically jumped up and waved her arms. Hughes smiled and waved back as he opened the door and stepped inside. Teresa came bounding down the cascading ship ladders.

"Hey Tou-san! Kaa-san says they may be able to run a test tomorrow!" Teresa used the informal Japanese terms for 'father' and 'mother' that their family had adopted.

Masamune grinned, "Well that's great sweetheart -- I'll bet you helped a lot."

Teresa beamed and led her father into one of the branching accelerator tunnels. Confined by the narrow rough-hewn red rock walls, Hughes could see ahead several massive plasma superconducting magnets placed at regular intervals along the conduit. The magnets were Hildebrandt products that had been installed several years previously, and Hughes recalled all the work that had gone into designing and manufacturing super-cooled helium capillaries that kept the units a few degrees above absolute zero.

They only walked a little way before the tunnel opened up again into another high-ceiling chamber. In the middle of this large volume sat another piece of hardware he had helped build -- the machine consisted of a large toroid frame standing upright with complex bundles of smaller super-cooled Hildebrandt plasma magnets placed around its perimeter -- in effect, a small accelerator in itself. The middle of the torus, where the hole should have been, was a spherical vacuum chamber with multiple cameras and other sensors protruding from it. It was the Hyperaperture Mark I, a device that, if all went well, would generate a stable window into another universe.

Hughes didn't understand all the details, but apparently the accelerator team had succeeded in forming a series of artificial singularities -- mini 'black holes' -- in the main viewing chamber. Particles accelerated around 113 kilometers of circular conduit are brought together with tremendous energy. By aiming the beam, they found they could control spin, feed particles, and actually observe the dragging effect of spacetime around the intense little gravity wells. Quite by accident, they noticed that sometimes two or three singularities would form for a few nanoseconds before combining and then evaporating away. Depending on the co-dependent orbits and spin, light cones could be tipped until they overlap to theoretically create closed time-like curves. It was thought that a single black hole would scramble all information at the event horizon, whereas an orbiting pair might theoretically counterbalance each other and perhaps allow recoverable information to pass through intact. With a little fine-tuning, they got two of the singularities to orbit each other before they collapsed in on themselves. That was where it had all started -- just before the collapse one of the instruments had recorded a flash of light ejected along the rotational axis of the orbiting pair, which no one could explain. They repeated the flash several times and realized that the light may have been coming from outside the observable universe. It was coming from another dimension!

Hughes remembered how his wife had justified the construction of the Hyperaperture unit: "A fellow named Vandevender theorized that micro black holes could behave like atoms indefinitely, with regular matter orbiting them. I think that under the right conditions we could keep a pair of them stable without evaporating."

It was enough to get the facility director's attention, and even the colony leadership and Mars Interim Government jumped on board. The team came up with the design for the Hyperaperture which would be capable of holding the two singularities apart indefinitely, allowing for lengthy observations through what they supposed would be a stable 'wormhole'. The construction of the device had engaged much of the colony's industry, and Hughes' specialized mechanical engineering capability at Hildebrandt had been one of the critical inputs.

So, it was finally ready, Hughes thought. If, as Teresa had said, the team intended to fire up the device, Masamune thought it was good news indeed.

Immediately Hughes sensed some sort of tension in the white-clad knot of technicians off to the side. Typically, there would be folks all over the equipment, doing adjustments, assembly, or calibration, but the entire group was gathered around a view screen listening to an announcement. Sachiko saw them and walked over with a grave look on her face.

Hughes reached over and gently patted his pregnant wife on the belly where their next child was coming up on the first trimester. "What's up dear?" He asked.

"There's been no contact with Bonestell, Perepelkin, or Aktaj. Maybe even some of the farther colonies," she explained.

Sachiko was a petit pure blood of Japanese descent -- not particularly beautiful, but with a sort of brainy attractiveness that comes with being a nerd. She was usually quiet, only speaking when she had something significant to say.

"Nothing new about that. They're probably ignoring us again." Hughes countered.

The Mars culture consisted of multiple colonies that had been settled by all sorts of groups from the mother world. Some of the communities had been commercially motivated, others had left Earth for political reasons, and yet others had sought isolation on religious or philosophical grounds. Masamune and Sachiko were employed by Lawrence Livermore National Laboratories and had early on found themselves transferred to the Grindavik science and technology colony where they had remained ever since.

The colonies barely tolerated each other for the most part, and for reasons that Hughes could never quite understand, Grindavik was held in contempt by many of their neighbors who were intimidated by science. Kasei was still governed by the 'Mars Interim Government' because of all the turmoil and strife among the colonies -- some of who didn't even recognize the authority of that governing body. Progress was at a standstill. It would not surprise Hughes at all if communications and intercourse had been dropped for a few

Sols-days because of some real or imagined dispute. *If they want to ignore us, good riddance*, Hughes thought.

Sachiko remained concerned, "They all went silent at once, apparently, and from about the same time the x-ray storm began."

That was alarming, but Hughes couldn't help but think that it was likely a coincidence, "We'll probably find out they're just being reactionary. Remember how they blame us for every solar flare or meteorite even when we're only giving them the courtesy of advance notice from our telescopes?"

Sachiko brightened a bit, "You're probably right. But I do have some good news -- we're going to do a test run of the Hyperaperture. We'll need Hildebrandt folks standing by."

Hughes nodded, having gotten advanced notice from their daughter.

Sachiko continued, "Come on let's go. We have to pick up Sabby on the way out."

Saburo Hughes was their six-year-old son who was too young to have any training hours yet, but attended school learning the basic R's, reading, 'riting, and 'rithmatic. They found him doing addition and subtraction games on a series of transparent pipes partially filled with liquid and ball bearings. Hughes noticed the same games not only gave the children math skills but also taught them intuition about volumes, diameters, viscosity, and fluid surface tension, and also gave them opportunities for hands-on precision assembly.

Teresa went in and shepherded her brother away from the engaging contraption, "Come on Sabby, Tou-san and Kaa-san have a date tonight."

The four of them made their way out of the learning center, which was located some tunnels away from the acceleration facility, and took a lift up to the promenade deck. They emerged from the elevator into a multi-story volume filled with shops, restaurants, and crowds of colonists of all ages going about their various business. This portion of the promenade nearly circled a quarter of the crater rim, broken only by pedestrian locks. Brightly lit ceilings arched high overhead like a great, coffered conduit partially filled with bisecting floor decks. Hughes couldn't help but recall back to when the voluminous promenade caverns had been hollowed out and the mall construction began. Sachiko led the group past crowded storefronts toward the quieter streets where commuters were on their way home. Rounding a bend, one of the pedestrian locks gaped open only a dozen meters in front of them.

"Run, quick kids!" Sachiko called out and began to rush through the crowds toward the massive metal opening.

The four of them just barely made it inside before a warning sounded and the heavy, automated pressure doors swung shut. Hughes looked around the crowded lock and saw impatience etched on the faces of the commuters as they stared blankly ahead. The lock took a good ten minutes to pass through, and they were lucky to catch one open -- they could have been stuck waiting for the next cycle. Once the doors had sealed themselves, the pressure began to drop slightly as the cabin equalized with the space beyond. It was not enough to get 'the bends', but Hughes had to work his jaw until his ears popped. Soon the pressure stabilized and the opposite set of doors opened slowly. He had always thought it amusing that the two sections of Grindavik had somehow been designed with only a few tenths of an atmosphere off from each other. They had separated the city into manageable volumes for safety's sake anyway, so no one had bothered to unify the ambient operating pressures once the built-up portions of the city had merged. It was of course common to encounter a whole range of internal pressures on Kasei-Mars, where different manufacturers, standards, and operating procedures for modules, rovers, cabins, cockpits, and outposts often required locks to pass between them.

A wash of green light leaked in and bathed the interior of the lock as folks began to slowly move into the next section. Hughes held his son's hand as he moved past the threshold and saw the elegantly landscaped park and hydroponic gardens stretch out of sight in front of them in the vast, multi-tiered volume. Pools of light revealed the locations of diffusers in the high, vaulted ceiling, and fed by fiber optics -- that was radiation from good ol' Sol. In his minds' eye he could imagine all the collectors up on the top of the cliff pointing high in the afternoon sky as they tracked the setting sun, sending all that light deep underground. But what a pleasant sight! Hughes loved the various pockets of green scattered throughout the underground labyrinth, contrasting with the frozen desert above them.

Masamune and Sachiko took the children up the lift to the residential levels. Their oldest son, sixteen-year-old Ichiro, was already home, having arrived early from the hospital where he was fulfilling training hours. The parents made sure the kids were settled for the evening then headed back down to the promenade deck to catch a tube train.

Just as the pair stepped out of the lift, Masamune got a call from Kitamura. Hughes pulled Sachiko out of the flow of commuters onto a Sol-lit patch of grassy turf as he took the call.

"What's up?" Hughes asked.

"*Hey Mas, things are looking good here -- we're tightening up the last set of bolts on the power assembly,*" Jiro's tinny voice sounded through the phone.

Hughes nodded to Sachiko who was watching intently to see if their plans for the evening were going to change.

Jiro continued, "*Where was that place you were heading tonight?*"

Hughes looked questioningly over at his wife and covered the mouthpiece, "He wants to know where the trundle place is,"

"It's the Jetman's Lounge, out near the space port." she replied loud enough for Jiro to hear.

There was a short pause, then Jiro said, "*You'll have trouble getting out that way -- didn't you hear?*"

"What do you mean?"

Jiro explained, "*There was an announcement this morning --
'uchimawari' is closed at Wendover to repair a leak in the tube. They're
walking people through unless they take the long way around on
'sotomawari'.*"

Hughes paused for a moment. 'Uchimawari' was
Japanese and meant 'inside around', referring to the
counterclockwise pneumatic tube train loop that circled
Grindavik crater rim. Conversely, 'sotomawari' meant 'outside
around' for the clockwise tube. Hughes, Jiro, and the entire
Grindavik Japanese community had informally borrowed the
colloquial reference to Earth Tokyo's Yamanote train since
the loop lines mirrored each other.

The pneumatic tubes worked by building up the air
pressure behind the passenger carriages and using the
difference to speed the magnetically levitated train along. In
order to get the system to work in a loop line, airlock baffles
had been constructed in sections, and the high-pressure air
was shifted back and forth between tubes in an ingenious way
to save energy. If part of the tube at Wendover were shut
down, they would stop the carriage and have the passengers
walk the maintenance tunnel to the other side of the blocked
portion. Once the carriages were empty, they would move
them over to the 'sotomawari' tube to switch directions.

"We can't do 'sotomawari' -- it will take too long. I think
we should walk it." Hughes replied.

Sachiko was itching to go dancing and agreed.

"*That gives me an idea -- wanna have dinner first?*" Jiro asked.

Sachiko, who heard the electronic voice, nodded a silent
'okay'.

"*Beth and I heard of this fantastic place in Wendover we've wanted
to check out, but it's not connected.*" Jiro proposed.

"What do you mean?"

Jiro paused a moment then explained, "*It's outside, on the
surface, on the cliff overlooking Chryse plains!*"

For an instant Hughes was confused. To go outside you
had to have some official business to attend to, or access to a
rover or pressure suit. Not everyone had EVA suits just

hanging in their closet -- with a price tag in the hundreds of thousands of dollars such luxuries were hard to come by even on Kasei. There were rentals of course, but Kitamura was likely talking about something else . . .

Then it hit him -- Hughes brightened and smiled, "The Chryse Mining Company!"

Sachiko also looked excited at that name -- they had all read about it. The Chryse Mining Company was a recently established restaurant out on a promontory that had taken over the old diggings of the same name. The place had developed quite a reputation for great food and fantastic scenery. They all quickly agreed to meet in Wendover in half an hour.

The tube ride was uneventful and took only fifteen minutes. As Jiro had warned, the counterclockwise carriage they rode was stopped just short of the locks and passengers were disembarked. To their surprise Beth and Jiro were waiting right there on the platform, having arrived on the previous train. The passengers were all herded toward a maintenance door that opened onto a tunnel rough-hewn out of the raw Martian red rock, almost claustrophobic in its narrow width and low ceiling.

By Hughes' estimation the group of passengers were marched several hundred meters or so through the slightly curved passage. At one point metal doors and a maintenance way station interrupted the tunnel. The passengers were herded into the chamber and had to wait until all were in before the opposite door could be opened. Hughes and the other three wandered over to an observation viewport that overlooked Grindavik Crater, while Sachiko filled Beth in about her latest work in the accelerator lab.

"The accelerator was constructed out on the shelf between Grindavik and Calahorra Craters. A straight spur branches off, bored through those rock piles out there," she explained.

The four of them stared through the thick glass at the undulating cliff line beyond, with each crack and canyon depositing massive piles of debris and rocks sloping down to the flat crater floor. The early settlers had chosen the twelve-kilometer diameter crater with the intention of eventually building a dome over it to hold breathable atmosphere, but the city occupants had just found it easier to bore new underground passages. Hughes tried to imagine roughly where the conduit tunnel might be located under all that rock.

"We're going to run a test tomorrow. Our Hyperaperture installation should allow us to peer through a hole in the fabric of spacetime." Sachiko explained.

"A hole -- that means there must be something on the other side," Beth considered, "what do you expect to see?"

The group began moving toward the opposite set of doors when Sachiko shrugged, "Nobody knows. We've already observed brief flashes of light coming from somewhere, but who knows where that might be. Some of my colleagues say the hole opens to another part of the universe, but I can't imagine how we can just open a door here with all that generated power, and find some other door out there already waiting to let light through."

"Is it some natural process? What if it was the heart of a quasar or black hole? Wouldn't that be dangerous?" Jiro offered from behind as they stepped into another rough-hewn maintenance tunnel.

Sachiko, who walked ahead of everyone, made frequent turns of her head as she explained, "We don't think that's the case because the measured flashes were too weak, but we'll ease into it anyway. We wouldn't want to open a hole into vacuum, for example, unless we have vacuum on this side already. If there were any unbalance at all on either side of the aperture the forces would try to equalize."

"Like creating a wind or rush of air if one side has lower air pressure than the other." Jiro suggested.

"Or a waterfall if the other side were under water," Hughes threw in.

The group walked on silently for a few minutes, apparently each in deep thought imagining their own scenario of unbalanced environments on either side of Sachiko's 'gate'.

Beth, a rover pilot by trade, was not even an armchair physicist but her imagination was piqued, "Or, could there be someone, or something else out there, also trying to . . ."

Beth had a somewhat stocky build, and like Masamune had a mixed heritage where she maintained her Asian features. The woman could operate anything that flew, rolled, hovered, floated, or crawled, and had quite an impressive resume chocked full of flight experience. But sometimes Hughes thought she could get out there on the edge, always dreaming up exotic explanations for mundane things.

Hughes saw a brief look of worry cross Sachiko's face, but his wife didn't elaborate. The second tunnel was much shorter than the first one and they had already arrived at the exit door. The tube attendant directed everyone through onto another platform -- 'Wendover Breaks' the sign said. They had completely bypassed Wendover proper due to the pneumatic tube maintenance.

The train attendant showed some of the passengers to the set of carriages waiting to carry them on their continued journey around the 'uchimawari' inside track, "For those of you heading to Wendover, the office deck two levels up has a continuous indoor passage back the way we came."

Hughes started to walk toward the lift when Jiro stopped him.

He said, "Wait, I think this is the right station. I don't think the Chryse Mining Company is in Wendover itself."

Sure enough, Hughes saw the sign just as Jiro said it -- pointing off to a side tunnel, along with other advertisements for restaurants and hotels. The four walked several hundred meters passing storefronts and the gathering night crowd before reaching the Chryse Mining Company waiting lounge.

It was at that point that Hughes realized why the media said the restaurant was disconnected. The lounge was simply a front for a large boarding airlock that serviced a pressurized shuttle rover. There were several guests waiting in the lounge for the next shuttle ride which was still minutes away, so the four of them walked over to the heavy plate windows to watch out for its arrival.

The sky beyond showed a deep crimson as the sun began to set. Hughes noticed the strange storm clouds over the dusty plateau he had seen earlier and briefly wondered what the latest news on the x-ray storm might be. Then suddenly in unison all four of them let out a gasp at the sight of the rover coming their way -- it was no ordinary Mars buggy! Extremely lightweight and sleek with wheeled outriggers, the vessel tacked a zigzag course pulled along by a massive billowing sail. Hughes immediately thought of those old early science fiction tales by, was it Bradford, or Bradbury? The colorful sail showed the Chryse Mining Company logo that snapped clear and clean after the wind caught it on each turn. Soon the other guests in the lounge crowded against the windows and the wonderful sight kept their eyes glued until the vessel (for indeed 'vessel' was the right word) let down the sail and backed into the lock on electric battery power.

Hughes followed as guests piled in to a tight, narrow cabin where one had to duck in order to get into one's seat. Once the door was sealed, he could hear various motors and winches sounding through the hull, moving them away from the docking port and out onto the open sand. What followed was an exhilarating ride where the craft often tipped up sideways at an angle as they rode the wind to their destination.

It didn't take long before the vessel was pulling up to The Chryse Mining Company air lock and lobby, which Hughes noticed consisted of vintage pressure modules docked in sequence -- the kind that used to be flown from Earth packed with food and equipment for early astronaut explorers on short missions. The modules were half buried farther along, and interfaced with the actual diggings and tunnels that had been abandoned so long ago. The whole restaurant ambiance was set up like a museum, showing early prospecting robots, digital excavators, and Spartan living quarters for the human crew. Even the tables and booths used vintage machines and equipment to create eating surfaces, seating, and privacy partitions. Hughes was delighted that the architect had taken pressurized cockpits and pilot cabins of some excavator or other vehicle and refitted them as semi-private dining areas and booths.

By the time their party had been seated for dinner Hughes was so enamored by the museum tour that he had forgotten their main purpose for being there was to have a meal. They sat awestruck looking out the massive plate glass windows across the twilight Chryse plains toward Oxia Palus. They ate in high spirits and later in the evening, to Sachiko's delight, the restaurant staff moved some of the tables off to the side to form a dance floor and she forgot all about Jetman's. Even though his wife was expecting, the low-gee environment allowed Hughes to whip her around and do all sorts of flips, swings, and spins that were so popular on the trundle. He wasn't the greatest dancer, but the mood allowed him to ham it up a bit in the partial gravity.

Late in the evening, like in a dream, they rode the sail rover back to Wendover Breaks station. There had been no repair work needed on the 'sotomawari' outside tube, so the next train to come along would send them home without any delays.

"Why don't you guys come watch our test firing tomorrow?" Sachiko offered as they piled into the pneumatic carriage.

Jiro indicated he would be there of course, since their crew had been instrumental in the manufacture of the Hyperaperture magnets.

Beth considered a moment but declined, "I can't -- I'm scheduled to drive to Trud in the morning with a load of fabrics. You know, down by Pathfinder Monument."

Sachiko nodded and aimlessly let her eyes wander about the cabin -- they were all dead tired after the long event-filled evening.

Suddenly Sachiko came alive with alarm, "Isn't Trud one of those colonies that they lost contact with?"

Beth was surprised, "I didn't hear about anything like that."

"Yes, I'm sure Trud was on the list," joined Hughes, "but it's nothing to worry about. Apparently, we lost contact with several colonies about the time the x-ray storm began, but it's probably one of those protests."

Sachiko's face revealed she was not convinced, and Beth too began to get a little worried.

"What would cause an x-ray disturbance like that, anyway?" Jiro asked.

Sachiko couldn't even venture a guess, and something seemed to be troubling her. The mood remained somber until Jiro and Beth got off at their stop.

"Take care -- I'm sure the com thing will turn out to be nothing," Sachiko said in parting.

Hughes could see his wife was feeling guilty for causing her friend to be so nervous.

"Call me!" Sachiko said as the door shut.

Sachiko remained a bit stressed the rest of the way home and the next morning as well. Hughes asked her what the matter was several times but his wife just shrugged it off. He and Teresa followed in her wake as she determinedly fought her way through the early morning commuters down to the accelerator lab, dropping off Sabby along the way.

Hughes went to Hildebrandt in the morning but followed Jiro and the power team back to the accelerator lab sometime around mid-morning to do some tests. It was in the afternoon when things started to get exciting -- crowds of scientists and engineers had set up their equipment in the observation room and were already capturing telemetry streaming in from the Hyperaperture Mark I machine.

When the countdown reached T-minus 15 minutes, off to one side there was a disturbance -- a group of well-dressed men and women walked in and sat down in the VIP viewing area. Eva Landerman, accelerator director was there, as was Dr. Jacob Harrison the Hyperaperture Principal Investigator. Hughes also recognized one of the men to be Howard Statner, Grindavik Colony President himself, accompanied by members of his staff and several other high-ranking community leaders Hughes didn't recognize.

When the instruments powered up, a series of monitors overhead showed the scene inside the Hyperaperture chamber in various wavelengths, including visual and infrared. Other means for reading the incoming data could also be seen, including oscilloscopes, real time updating graphs, and digital readouts, but Hughes had no idea what most of it meant.

"*T-minus ten, nine, eight . . .*" a voice droned over the speakers and echoed through the high bay chamber as the countdown wound down.

Several technicians scrambled away from the machine and stood back to watch. Hughes observed the screens intently waiting for something to happen. He remembered the conversation from last night and began to imagine all sorts of strange environments suddenly trying to equalize through the spacetime hole -- vacuum, energy, and even water rushing through.

"*. . . one, zero -- main breaker on,*" the voice repeated steps as they were accomplished, such as powering up the magnets, firing the accelerator and such.

First, they had to use the entire 36-kilometer main accelerator to create the little black holes. Upon achieving the target mass, the test particle would then be sent off into a branch tunnel to arrive at the Hyperaperture unit. Minutes later the crowd applauded when there was an announcement that a single sustained singularity had been formed. Looking at the monitors Hughes could not particularly see anything other than some sporadic flashes of weak light bounded by a black background.

"*Fine tuning the accelerator aim,*" the loudspeaker voice announced, then minutes later, "We have achieved a second singularity."

Again, the crowd applauded. The main accelerator gradually was powered down, leaving the Hyperaperture Mark I torus running on its own to contain the orbiting pair. Hughes watched as the device slowly stepped up the alternating charge on and off in the magnets to increase the orbit rate until the spacetime dragging effect could be observed.

On the overhead screens there began to be a steady glow. Scientists and technicians alike stared in awe as a rippling effect showed through a series of quick flashes and dark shapes. Somehow, Hughes had the impression of a vast space -- a hole in the fabric of spacetime.

Then it was all over -- the ripples and the vast space disappeared as the pair of mini black holes was slowed down to a sustainable orbit inside the torus. They had achieved what would eventually be called a Singler Gate, which meant simply a 'hole to who knows where'. In a Singler Gate scenario, the investigators had control over the aperture on their side, but had no idea about where or what the spacetime tunnel connected to if anything at all. Again, the crowd applauded, and the VIPs stood up and walked out of the room, congratulating the chief scientists and investigators who followed them out. Hughes and the rest of the technicians brought their subsystems down to maintenance status -- the test was over.

It was another hour before Masamune could get Sachiko away from the apparatus. Jiro was closing up shop, and Teresa had finished her tasks for the Day. Sachiko came over excitedly, and began to take off her lab coat.

"Air," was all she said.

"What?" Hughes was startled.

Sachiko elaborated, "Air -- there's comfortable, warm air on the other side of the aperture."

Hughes and Jiro looked at each other with perplexed expressions on their faces. The other end of the universe had air too?

Suddenly the chime on Sachiko's phone rang indicating an incoming call -- it was Beth.

"Hi Beth -- our test was an overwhelming success. No quasars, no neutron stars, no . . ." Sachiko began but suddenly stopped, a concerned look on her face.

Hughes and Jiro could hear the distressed voice of Beth carried to them through the earpiece, but it was not enough to understand what she was saying. To Hughes, it sounded like the poor woman may have been crying.

"Say what!?" Sachiko blurted out, "There's nobody where?"

They waited as Beth went through a long monologue on the other end of the line and Sachiko gave occasional nods. Finally, it was over.

"Yes, he's here -- I'll tell him." and she hung up.

Sachiko first looked up at Jiro, "Turn your phone on -- Beth has been trying to reach you."

Jiro remembered he had turned it off during the morning tests and switched it back on. Both he and Masamune looked to Sachiko expectantly, waiting for an explanation.

"Beth arrived at Trud and there's nobody there." she said.

Hughes looked at her with a puzzled look on his face, "What do you mean there's nobody there? Are they hiding from delivery trucks too?"

Sachiko returned his stare with a deeply concerned expression, "No, the entire colony is deserted. The lights are on, and the automatics are running, but there's not a soul anywhere to be found."

CHAPTER 3

"This is where Tina took her video recordings, I think," Carta Randall said as she stood on the edge of a bluff overlooking the Novissima valley.

Carta was highly ranked, a brunette down-to-earth (or should we say down-to-Mars) practical woman who had never been interested in marriage, preferring to advance her career instead. Part of the reason for that were her stern demeanor and the fact that she was quite plain in her looks.

Carta's partner, Phoolendu 'Lenny' Chopra stood nearby in his orange anodized pressure suit, running through several filters in augmented mode, "*No sign of x-rays that I can see.*"

Carta carefully searched the valley floor, zooming in at locations of interest. Suddenly she had a gut-wrenching reaction as she spotted the two suited bodies she had been looking for -- there was Mei-Hua, and a little further on Dr. Drake was sprawled out with limbs arranged at impossible angles.

"Right where Tina's videos showed them to be," Randall whispered half to herself.

Carta and Lenny had responded immediately after receiving word from division headquarters of the Mars

Interim Government Investigation Bureau. They had flown down as quickly as they could on a Planetary Resources shuttle, to see if they could talk with Tina before visiting the site. The poor woman had been picked up only two Sol-days previously and was nearly out of her mind with fear.

"What do you think it was, Tina," Lenny had gently asked, introducing themselves as government investigators.

The girl shook uncontrollably and had just mumbled, ". . . deteriorated, they just deteriorated. . ."

The medical staff took her away somewhere.

The two investigators had viewed the data over and over again, played back telemetry from Drake's and Mei-Hua's suits, and still couldn't figure out what had happened down there.

"*Didn't the regionals say the x-ray storm was expanding?*" Lenny asked, the final syllable popping through the helmet com in his Indian accent.

Lenny had quite handsome features and the dark brown eyes of his ancestors. He sported a close-cropped beard that didn't interfere with helmets or any other variety of headgear. He was quite smart, and Carta always thought that if it wasn't for the man's insatiable desire for fieldwork, he might have made a good professor at a university somewhere.

Carta continued looking across the valley at the ruins, and those distant cliffs of ice and stone. It was as peaceful appearing as ever. If not for those grisly remains down there she could have believed it to be a typical polar landscape.

Chopra lifted his suited arm and made a sweeping motion, "*Is that some kind of discoloration?*"

Randall looked closer -- yes, there did appear to be some darker stain in a wide swath that reached from the ruins off to the horizon. Zooming in, the ground and rock surfaces had an odd speckled appearance.

"It's clear, let's go down," Carta said finally.

The two gradually made their way down the slope, stopping frequently to take readings. There was no sign of abnormal x-rays. They snapped stills of the scene as they approached the boundary of the dark stain -- were those black specks holes in the ground? Randall fixed her eyes on the pattern, which strangely appeared three-dimensional as her perspective changed.

Up ahead, the bodies of the two scientists lay undisturbed as they had fallen only Days before, several dozen meters inside the discolored rocky ground.

"Stay back here, Len. I'm going to take a look at the ground up close." Carta held her arm up to block Lenny from going any further.

As she got closer to that dark boundary, it became apparent that the texture of the rock was different there. She snapped still after still, sending them back to the rover. It was not until Carta stood right on top of the boundary that she fully understood the nature of the discoloration -- the rock was riddled with small, straight holes like Swiss cheese. The entire area was misshapen and pockmarked with cavities, as if someone had set off powerful explosives and pulverized the natural wind-torn surface.

"This -- it's impossible!" Carta gasped.

She picked up a small rock and dropped it into one of the holes, and watched it bang back and forth until it disappeared into the darkness deep below. The hole was perfectly round, and bored straight as if a giant drill had pressed from above deep into the Martian landscape. She looked around as Lenny walked up, to count hundreds, thousands of them, all oriented straight down into the rock.

"*I wonder how deep they are,*" Lenny ventured after looking around and letting his curiosity get the best of him.

Both the investigators snapped stills right and left. Lenny took out a ruler and photographed several holes with the ruler lying next to them. The two carefully made their way over to where the bodies lay on the ground, careful not to step in any of the holes.

Randall never enjoyed this part of investigative work -- the documentation of foul play, or nature's power gone out of control. Fragments of what used to be a living, breathing soul, torn apart by some unknown cataclysmic force. They crisscrossed the scene, photographing, measuring, and canvassing for evidence. It was apparent that whatever caused the holes in the rock had also been responsible for the scientists' deaths, like unknown projectiles catapulted out of the ground to pierce metal plating and tear apart flesh and bone.

Except that something was strange. Projectiles generally tore away at their targets, ripping away material tossed to the side as the ballistic core forcefully and instantaneously moves it aside. These were different -- there was no displaced material, no craters, no torn away edges. Rock, metal, flesh, and bone simply revealed crisp perfectly circular cutting planes as whatever had passed through simply annihilated the material that used to stretch between. It was completely gone without a trace.

"*Some sort of particle beam?*" Lenny asked.

A scattershot particle beam covering dozens of acres all at once? Carta shrugged.

After documenting the scene, Lenny reported back on relay to the coroner's office. A crew would be out later to take care of the remains. If only there had been just two victims . . .

Carta and Lenny made their way across the rotten ground toward the ruins of Novissima. As they carefully picked over the cavity-strewn desert, Randall again wondered how deep the holes went -- none of the instruments they had on hand could measure it. Was the rotten rock upon which they trod still strong enough to hold without collapsing? She imagined a sinkhole suddenly opening up below, the remaining rock between holes shattering in sequence like a zipper.

The town of Novissima had mostly been a mining town, gateway and bedroom community to the various outfits that extracted water and volatiles from the ice in the polar cap. For the most part, the town consisted of hundreds of modules buried in trenches or gunite-lined shallow caves. There were homes, stores, commercial supply depots, restaurants, and even schools and community centers to accommodate the seasonal work crews and their families. Carta recalled there had also been a fairly high-end research facility -- was it Stillwell? No, Stockwell Institute, that mostly worked on advanced new mining techniques, such as mass drivers, electrostatic separation, superconductive material handling, and particle beams.

Particle beams! Could something have gone wrong here?

Carta glanced up at the ruins as they approached the north side of town. There was wreckage scattered all over the place, and mounds tracing out buried volumes revealed the old passages and chambers as they had been laid out by the early miner colonists. She could see the speckled telltale pattern of holes that must have permeated and eaten away every isolated pressurized compartment in the town. It didn't look like they would find any survivors. If some industrial disaster had occurred here, they would likely find its source farther on, where the Stockwell laboratories had been located.

From up on the ridge, it had been possible to see other victims piled up between the ruins, but that had been farther on. At the near edge of town there were none such visible, leaving Carta to believe any victims in this part of town may have been trapped inside.

The pair made their way to the line of structures. A wrecked vehicle sat several dozen meters ahead between them and the first modules. Carta noticed the pressure hull full of holes, clear and crisp with no buckling of the metal skin. She dreaded what they would find as she skirted her way toward the short stair that mounted the heavy track treads. Behind her, Lenny worked his way to the front of the vehicle to see if he could look inside the thick windshield. Her gloved hand gripped the grab bar on the side of the pressure hatch and she made a deft hop and climb up to the narrow EVA porch. Hesitantly Carta tried to get her clear bubble helmet close enough to allow her to peer into the small circular window set in the middle of the door. The airlock beyond was empty. Using the manual controls, she released the lock and pushed the door to the side. She tried to peer into the window of the inner hatch but all she could see was darkness, with perforated holes in the ceiling letting in a minimal amount of daylight. There was obviously no pressure inside, so she closed the outer door to allow the failsafe inner lock to reset itself and opened the hatch to the cabin interior.

There was no one inside.

Carta sighed with relief and went back outside, meeting up with Lenny who had walked one circuit around the caterpillar rover. The two of them made their way to the nearest entrance to the buried modules, which appeared to be a maintenance garage. A large gaping door was framed by two berms on either side -- a haunted gate to an underground city of the dead.

Carta switched on her helmet lamp as she passed into the dark garage. She could see tools lying around as if the mechanics had just left them sitting where they lie as they went off for lunch. The mysterious holes could be seen everywhere, and once or twice Carta spied a tool handle bored clean through without disturbing the alignment of both halves.

"You first Len." Carta indicated the small airlock door in the back.

Chopra knew the drill -- they both entered the airlock on manual, and made their way to the outpost interior. Again, Carta dreaded what they would find -- she imagined crews and families asphyxiated as the precious nitrogen-oxygen mix rushed out to be replaced by poisonous Martian atmosphere.

There was no one in the offices immediately adjacent to the garage. Carta and Lenny walked down corridor after corridor, checking in each room as they went. No one was there. Three or four times they had to go through pressurized bulkheads as they slowly made their way through a deserted town -- not a soul to be found. Realizing they didn't have enough air in their suit life support systems to check all the rooms, the two investigators finally made their way topside again to relay a report back to their rover.

Unfortunately, they knew there were more victims, because they had seen them from the top of the cliff.

"Let's go toward Stockwell Institute. If something went wrong here, that might be the center of things." Carta pointed out.

The two investigators made their way between berm mounds and past dark openings. Wreckage on the ground became more prevalent. Each time they came across a shard of metal or twisted structure they would photo-document it and go through the standard procedure of placing it in the investigation scene for later reference. It wasn't long before twisted metal heaps became so large it posed a difficulty for the two to maneuver around.

Lenny commented, "*It didn't look that bad from up there.*"

"Yeah, I wonder what these folks had in their lab that would generate so much junk."

Some parts of wreckage were recognizable, while others were totally foreign.

"*I've never seen that model before.*" Lenny said, as they walked around the wreckage of what was obviously a small self-propelled space vessel.

It wasn't long before the two were halted altogether. Below them was a blast crater of massive proportions, with metal slag melted into wicked shards and drop holes -- all sorts of traps that would threaten to puncture an environmental suit.

"*This is it -- this is where the explosion occurred.*" Lenny commented as she took stills and panoramas to capture the evidence.

Carta agreed, "Yes, and I also think we've found the center of Stockwell labs."

The two of them continued to document the crater for a few minutes, then began to work their way around counterclockwise to find a clearer path through the wreckage -- they would need to record everything. Unfortunately, the amount of wreckage they had been able to see from the bluff was only the tip of the iceberg -- it soon became apparent that perhaps there was more twisted metal out there than could be accounted for. From the top of a small rise, the two investigators could see a debris field stretching several kilometers through the canyon toward the horizon, with no end in sight. Carta estimated at least several hundred thousand tons of metal, and perhaps much more -- way beyond what the small town or research outpost could have held.

"It didn't occur to me earlier, but I haven't seen any of those bore holes since we left the blast crater." Lenny pointed out.

Carta had been mechanically recording everything she saw since the beginning. Yes, Chopra was right -- there were no holes to be seen. It was the strangest thing -- a blast crater, wreckage to one side, mysterious beam holes scattered in the other direction. What could have happened here?

Carta and Lenny made their way down the slope to where their augmented instruments showed concentrations of organic matter -- on the harsh Martian landscape a sure indication of human remains. There were no boreholes here, just twisted piles of wreckage and blackened gunite ruins. Carta wound her way through broken shards reaching up like teeth toward the sky, when suddenly she found them -- several dozen heaps of mostly unrecognizable body parts. Carta held back the urge to vomit and turned away -- it was the most gruesome sight she had ever seen.

The two investigators documented every scrap of organic matter they could find. Occasionally there were intact bodies staring up into the sky with lifeless eyes, skin ruptured in places by the relatively low atmospheric pressure.

"Look at this one here," Lenny noted, *"He looks identical to that one over there, same clothing and all -- twins maybe?"*

Exposed and out in the open, it was apparent that none of the victims had been wearing any sort of protective clothing. Had settlers been faced with such horror as to drive them outside -- or was this the remains of folks who had been blown out by the explosion? Or, remembering the strange wreckage of the small space vessel and unfathomable quantity of twisted metal strewn across the dusty canyons, had something crashed from outer space?

Carta was given no time to contemplate the answer, because an urgent message was coming over the rover relay.

"Randall, you need to get your people out immediately! We've tracked the x-ray storm and it's heading your way again."

CHAPTER 4

Masamune Hughes made oatmeal for breakfast one morning. After preparing the meal, he opened up one of the kitchen cabinets and slid the container of oatmeal back into its slot. The radio frequency tracker chip imbedded in the package registered its contents on the house computer inventory list, and electronic scales calculated how much of the contents had been consumed. Finding the remaining oatmeal less than what was typically eaten by the Hughes family in a week, the house computer automatically put in an order for another package of oatmeal.

Hughes saw a notice on the control screen that oatmeal had been ordered, but since the cereal had been designated as a household staple item, he didn't give it a second thought. An automated warehouse deep in the mountain retrieved a package from the correct aisle and delivered it to the shipping department via robotic arms and moving belts. A pneumatic crate was waiting with its lid open, and the oatmeal package dropped right in. The sealed crate shot through a series of pneumatic trunk and branch lines using high-pressure air, and arrived at the restocking cavity behind the kitchen shelves. A robotic re-stocker arm pulled out the new oatmeal container from the pneumatic crate and set it on the shelf behind the partially empty one.

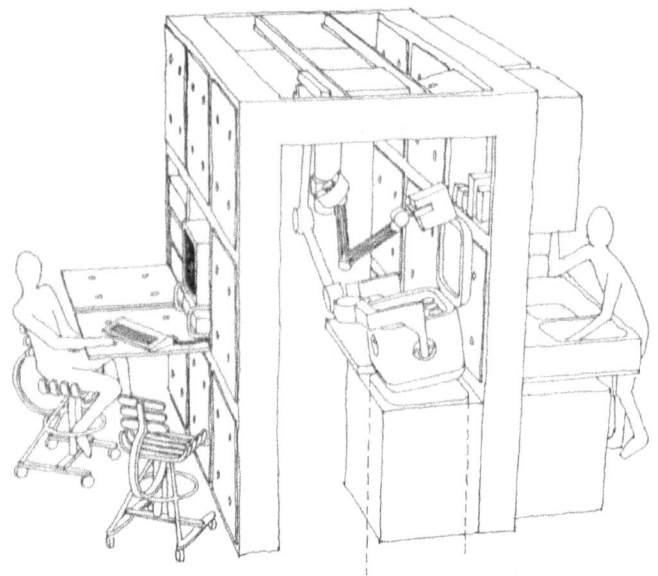

The Hughes account was charged for one package of oatmeal. Since oatmeal had been in unusually high demand of late, the automated warehouse registered low stocks and triggered an increase in the number of new oat seedlings robotically placed in aeroponic greenhouse planters. The seedlings would be on track for an accelerated growth cycle, to be harvested, processed, rolled, and packaged to bring the stock levels back to normal. Then the whole system reset itself before Hughes even sat down at the dining table.

"Okay, we know that light is coming from somewhere. Can't you just take a picture of the source through the hole?" Masamune asked Sachiko over breakfast.

Teresa stared up at him with an incredulous look on her face, as if it were a dumb question.

"It's not that simple Mas," Sachiko explained, "The two singularities orbit each other so fast that they begin to drag along the very fabric of space. When spacetime gets warped enough, a hole is formed. Do you realize how convoluted the paths of light would be coming out of there?"

Hughes was still confused, "Can't you just make a hole big enough and stick the camera lens through?"

"Think of the tremendous pull of gravity formed by those black holes -- any old lens would just buckle as the molecules tried to follow the currents of gravity. It's like a whirlpool of gravitational forces in the middle you know," Sachiko returned, "If our models are correct, we may be able to untangle the light a bit using software and post-processing, but that's about as far as we could go without some super strong tube that shields its interior from those extreme gravitational forces."

Everyone finished their meals and left the dishes on the table. The bowls, plates, and silverware were all standard housewares, so they all slid into a sorter as the table folded up into the wall. Trash and paper products came out the end and were redirected to the recycle dump. Each of the dishes ended up in its unique slot in the cabinet, which doubled as a dishwasher. First, a high-power water jet cleared out remnants of food that were washed to the compost dump. Then the wash cycle began, ending with air-dried dishes in their proper place, and every single drop of precious water recycled. It never even crossed Hughes' mind that somehow the housework got done, except when he had to wash the special ceremonial Japanese plates by hand after New Year's celebration.

The conversation went back and forth as the four left the apartment. They dropped off Sabby and made their way through the underground tunnels toward the accelerator lab.

The discussion had mostly worked its way dry when, without warning, Teresa blurted out, "Tou-san, you could do it, right? You could build something strong enough to float through the hole."

Hughes stopped in his tracks. Teresa was right -- he suddenly knew how to get instruments through that hole, and the answer was sitting that very minute on his shop floor.

After seeing the two females to their lab, Hughes hurried on to Hildebrandt with a new agenda for the day.

Rushing onto the factory floor, Hughes made a quick glance off in the corner at the prototype hoverpallet as if to verify that it was still there hooked up to all its massive power cables. He only hesitated a moment or two before hurrying over to where Jiro Kitamura was working on bigger and newer laser plasma magnets for the Hyperaperture. His friend was due to deliver the new units that very afternoon and had already started loading some of them onto the transport.

Jiro was busy at the moment, so Hughes studied the magnet and tried to guess what the new diameter of the torus would be. He traced his fingers along the C-shaped section that would define the outer curve of the donut. *Interesting*, he thought. The new magnets when put together would resemble a tire without a rim -- there was no apparent chamber at the hub.

Jiro came up behind Hughes and slapped a hand on his shoulder, "It will be open in the middle. You'll be able to throw a rock through the hole," he said.

Hughes thought about Sachiko's gravitational whirlpool and imagined a rock aimed for the middle getting flung off to the side to who knows where, "No, we're going to get Toshige's hoverpallet through there," he countered.

Kitamura looked at Hughes a moment before the concept registered and he broke into a grin, "Brilliant!" was all he could say and turned back to what he had been doing.

The rest of the morning Hughes pored over the Toshige pallet specs and had the mechanical team do some brainstorming. At one point he was able to get Dr. Hiroyuki Toshige himself on the phone to ask him about the pallet's propulsion system.

"What if the gravity is pointing in all directions at once?" Hughes asked.

Toshige's voice on the other end was silent for a moment, and then the other said, "*The hoverpallet works by essentially achieving neutral buoyancy in the gravity field -- it bends or deflects the waves slightly.*" Toshige explained, "*Then you can simply push the pallet here or there and it will stay motionless until you apply force to it again. If gravity waves were coming from all directions, you would have to have the hovercoils pointed around the side and upward as well.*"

Hughes told the doctor about the orbiting pair of black holes, "We can't just make a strong tube because the gravity waves penetrate through materials. We need something that will actually bend the gravity waves around so it won't damage what's inside."

"*That is an interesting challenge. The shareholders would go wild -- go for it Mas.*" Toshige encouraged, then added, "*But we haven't figured out the power problem. It takes so much energy that it must always be attached to the ol' extension cord.*"

Hughes got the mechanical team to work configuring coils around a tube-like geometry. But the excitement of the new project was interrupted just before noon -- two young interns came running in telling everyone to look at the news. Technicians working on various projects gathered around the small number of monitors mounted on the walls.

"*The x-ray storm is circling the planet in a spiral,*" the announcer said, "*It appears to have begun in or around Novissima, and precisely matches the 24-hour Mars rotation, circling the pole and coming back around again once a Sol-day.*"

Spiral? Hughes wondered what sort of natural phenomenon could get an x-ray source to travel in such a precise curved line. The colonies had mostly adopted Kasei hours and minutes, stretching the Earth-reckoned 24-hour and thirty-some odd minutes into a clean 24 divisions, like the early probe and robotic rover missions. If the storm followed a perfect spin of the red planet -- could the x-rays be some bombardment from space?

The announcer paused to look to the side where an animation of Kasei's southern hemisphere was showing. A narrow swath began tracing a circle around the south pole, following at nearly the same latitude all the way around. However, when the complete circle came back to the starting point it was slightly off, to the north of Novissima. The animated path wrapped around the pole several more times, coinciding with the number of Sol-days since the incident began -- each time it eased northward a bit in a gradual spiral.

"*The x-ray storm devours everything in its path -- it leaves behind thousands of small holes in the ground and everything else in its path too.*" the videos showed pictures of pockmarked rock and lacerated habitat modules.

"*Our sources say that if it continues on its current pattern the spiral path will gradually move toward the equator like peeling an orange, leaving devastation in its wake.*"

There was murmuring and gasps as the crowd looked at each other in surprise. Some strange phenomenon was happening down in the southern hemisphere, but Hughes could see most of them didn't connect the event with themselves -- it was just a curiosity. Hughes certainly had it in the back of his mind that some scientists somewhere were working on it and that the phenomenon would be explained soon. *Oh, that's nice, what a strange universe we live in,* he thought. It was odd that some habitats and outposts had been harmed because of the phenomenon -- did everyone get out safe, he wondered. He even took a few minutes to call around and see if he could find anyone who had heard more. Did the scientists know what was causing the storm? No one knew.

At noon he got through to Sachiko, who had a number of things on her mind to worry about. Not only had more abandoned colonies and towns been discovered, but also the data coming in from the Hyperaperture was going in an unexpected direction.

"*Take a look at your monitor, Mas,*" she said.

Hughes watched as Sachiko streamed him a video of the latest observation through the spacetime hole. The ripple effect he had seen the first day appeared, and again flashes of light in what appeared to be a vast void. This time the ripples smoothed out and the bright spots seemed a little clearer, as the software boys must have untangled the light rays in post processing. Some of the lights migrated toward each other and annihilated, but others remained steady. Suddenly, as if disgorging meals, some of the bright spots burped out dark objects one or two at a time until the vast void had dozens of them. It was still too blurry to tell, but most of the objects seemed similar to each other, randomly floating near and far.

Hughes gasped. One thing was clear -- those objects were all machines! In that vast space beyond the aperture, artificial shapes drifted in various orientations. Then, as suddenly as it all began, the aperture closed and the video ended.

"*I'm not sure what this means, Mas.*" Sachiko confided.

Hughes was speechless. How could a machine be out there when they had just opened the wormhole? It didn't make any sense.

"*I'm worried, Mas. I've never been so scared in all my life,*" Sachiko added.

Hughes could tell his wife was visibly upset. He tried to come up with something to say that would console her, but all he could think of was a jumble of x-rays, deserted colonies, and floating machines -- everything seemed to be coming at them at once. Confusion reigned for a minute or two, until he remembered the Toshige hoverpallet.

"Dear, I think I can get a camera through your gravity whirlpool," Masamune described the concept where superconducting hover coils mounted around a cylinder could protect any sort of payload inside.

Sachiko listened intently, but shook her head on the phone monitor, "*Mas, I'm really scared. Some unknown intelligence is out there traveling through wormholes. What if they saw our machine and came to investigate?*"

Unknown intelligence! He hadn't considered that angle before. The thought sent Hughes into a wild mental tempest where every science fiction story he had read on alien conquest came haunting him. The tempest was over as soon as it had begun however -- *how intriguing*, he thought.

After lunch Hughes briefed his mechanical team and had them redouble their efforts. Toshige had a shipment of hover coils sent over right away, and since the Toshige Enterprises warehouse was almost next door, the parts arrived only a few hours later. Jiro Kitamura diverted one of his engineers and two trainees to begin working on the power problem, and young Sally Averman came over to solder all the leads. They christened the modified hoverpallet 'APP' as an acronym for Aperture Penetration Probe.

"I need to hit some balls," Sachiko told Hughes that evening.

Hughes knew his wife was struggling with some things, but when the balls thing came out, he knew it must be really bad.

"Okay, I'll have Teresa take Sabby home and let's go." Hughes returned.

The place Sachiko liked was halfway around Grindavik Crater. They took the 'sotomawari' pneumatic tube train to Delaware Heights and pushed through the street crowd toward the golf range. There were actually several ranges in Grindavik Colony, but all the others were inside some hollowed-out chamber. The Delaware Heights range was unique, and definitely what the doctor ordered for frustrated wives.

After paying the fee at the reception desk, Masamune and Sachiko climbed a narrow spiral stairway up a round chimney bored out of solid rock. There must have been about a dozen coils of the stairway, but Sachiko was taking it like a workout. When they got to the top, they found themselves in a domed cupola up on the top of the ridge. Hughes could look up through the thick glass and see those amber-colored storm clouds.

An attendant welcomed them and took a few measurements -- body height, chest size, etcetera -- then guided them into a room lined with various sizes of pressure suits.

The attendant showed each of them the rack containing their size and said, "Pick one you like."

In fifteen minutes, they were struggling to put on the pieces of the suits in numerical order, careful to follow the checklists. It was no easy task since the suits were all hard components that needed to be threaded correctly to protect the multiple o-rings. Hughes was glad Sachiko was not very far along in her pregnancy because there probably wasn't a unit built for pregnant women. There was no need to do any pre-breathing with the hard suits -- the internal suit pressure matched the atmospheric pressure of the living spaces. None of the dangers of decompression sickness, gas mixtures, or oxygen percentage existed like there had been with the old soft suits. When all the pieces had been assembled, airflow tested, temperature controls verified, and com units checked, the attendant gave each of them a club and bucket of balls, and put them through the airlock.

"The only rule is to not hit anything artificial." the attendant said with a smile.

The airlock opened out onto a stone apron that stretched all the way to the cliff edge. Two rows of gigantic magnetic coils protected customers from the more dangerous galactic cosmic radiation from overhead, but other than that clients were free to pound the little things wherever they saw fit, most choosing the cliff edge as the most logical target.

Sachiko set herself up near the edge and began swinging away, completely oblivious of her husband. Hughes could not believe how far each of the golf balls went -- first of all it was intimidating to just stand near the cliff edge, being quite high. But adding a drive at one-third gee must have taken those things a good kilometer at least. Hughes hit a few balls himself, but ended up donating the rest of his to her -- it was definitely more entertaining that way.

It was a few Sol-days later when the APP team thought they had a machine that could be tested, and several Sol-days beyond that before the Hyperaperture Mark II was ready with the new magnets. The x-ray storm had made several spirals around the pole and still no one knew what caused it or how to stop it. Hughes stood in the Hyperaperture observation room and surveyed the scene out on the main floor. Technicians were scurrying back and forth doing last-minute software checks as they were about to test the new machine. The second generation Hyperaperture stood tall, with its gaping donut hole some two meters wide. A catwalk had been erected on both sides of the hole, and technicians were routinely moving through it as they made final adjustments on the magnets. That hole would frame a gate to another part of the universe.

To his right, the new APP unit stood ready for insertion -- a half a meter wide tube chocked full of cameras and other sensors -- cantilevered out horizontally on a set of rails. Hughes recalled his amusing thought of the rock thrown through the hole and chuckled to himself -- they were going to play it safe and roll the stand directly into the center of the hole. After all, what would happen if the APP were slightly closer to one side or the other -- would the powerful gravity fields of the two orbiting black holes wrench the unit off in some unplanned direction?

Hughes watched as they counted down to the first test that would be without the APP. He switched on his journaler and captured last-minute scrambles of technicians removing catwalk sections away from the hole. A set of appendages began to spin around the torus, generating an air curtain. Crowds of white lab-coated technicians stood back in anticipation.

Jacob Harrison the Principal Investigator dropped his arms and the main accelerator worked in concert with the Hyperaperture to form two singularities quickly in succession. The powerful laser plasma magnets drove the orbiting pair faster and faster around the torus until the donut hole began to shimmer and the back wall of the chamber, clearly visible only moments before, faded as scrambled light beams were scattered by the tremendous whirlpool of gravitational forces.

Suddenly the background faded away and on the other side of the hole a group of anxious faces peered back through. The two groups stared at each other from each side of the doorway, with incredulous looks on their faces. Dr. Harrison went into a panic, waved his arms about, and motioned to shut the thing down, whereupon the faces on the other side vanished, the background returned, and the flickering spinning appendages slowed to a stop again.

Hughes stood dumbfounded. What had they just witnessed? Technicians were animatedly talking to each other, and Hughes overheard a number of voices postulating about this and that, trying to understand what happened. Was there another group somewhere running a similar experiment? Had they connected with Sachiko's unknown intelligence?

It was quite a bit later in the evening when Sachiko herself postulated a reason behind those faces on the other side of the hole.

"All I can think of is that the gravity forces achieved a standing wave and what we saw was a reflection of ourselves looking back at us," Sachiko explained.

Hughes, Sachiko, Teresa, and Sabby walked along the restaurant district on the promenade level -- they had decided to eat out that evening to celebrate. Their eldest son Ichiro Hughes stood outside one eating establishment and flagged them down.

"Kaa-san, you mean that was us on the other side?" Teresa confirmed.

"Yes, it's strange -- I never would have guessed it could have happened this way, but some folks have theorized some kind of mirroring might occur. When you get powerful gravity fields, all sorts of things could happen," Sachiko said as they took their seats at the table Ichiro had reserved for them, "For example, if in a closed universe you were able to fly fast enough to outrun expansion and get to the outer edge, some folks say the space is so curved at the boundary you would find yourself heading back in."

Ichiro who was studying medicine spoke up, "I had a physics teacher once who said some famous guy (Wheeler was it? Or Feynman?) postulated that the reason electrons all have the same charge is because there's really only one, and it bounces back and forth between a big bang and a big crunch, zigzagging back and forth in time for eternity."

Sachiko smiled, "All sorts of interesting ideas -- I think that one only works if there are equal amounts of matter electrons and antimatter positrons, because positrons are really electrons traveling backward in time."

Sachiko peered around the table at the puzzled looks on the faces of her family, and realized she may have gone too deep again.

She said, "At any rate, we'll find out more tomorrow when we do the APP tests through the aperture. Sabby, what did you do today?"

There was a haunting tone to her voice, as if she were worried about a lot more than what she let on. At least superficially, the issues bothering her were quickly swept away when dinner was served. The family enjoyed themselves over the meal, and the subject of wormholes and physics didn't come up again that evening. But Hughes knew his wife well, and Sachiko kept a nervous note as if she were trying to forget something.

That night more disturbing news came over the media. Another x-ray storm was discovered near the north pole, spiraling south. That was much closer to home! *What the heck is going on*, Hughes thought. X-ray storms spiraling in from both poles? Would someone be able to stop it before it got to the larger colonies? Hughes still didn't connect the danger back to Grindavik. *The government must be working on it*, he thought.

The next Sol-day Hughes and Sachiko were on station at the Hyperaperture bright and early with Teresa. The first test was to be a quick one, mainly to see how the APP worked and to take a quick picture.

"Are you sure you can dip in and out that quickly? I'm really scared Mas" Sachiko confided.

Underlying her tone was that concern over 'unknown intelligence' and whether all those machines they saw on the other side posed some kind of a threat.

"I'm sure it will be alright. We'll get our picture and shut it down before we attract any attention." Hughes consoled.

"But what if they're waiting? What if they know we'll open up again and pounce quickly?" Sachiko countered.

Hughes didn't know what to say. All he could do was smile and embrace her, giving her as much physical comfort as he could.

Fortunately, the tasks required for the test began to take up everyone's thoughts and the Hyperaperture chamber was a bustle of activity. This time Masamune and his team were on the floor getting the APP ready. Hughes caught the expressions of some of the technicians that walked by and saw the same concern on their faces -- were they due for a visit from hostile neighbors?

When the countdown finally began, however, Hughes was also beginning to feel a little nervous. Technicians cleared the area and the air curtain appendages began spinning around the torus as the electromagnets fired faster and faster. The shimmering began and the rear wall faded away. Strangely, the reflected image of the room didn't occur this time, as the machine pushed right past to reveal a dark bottomless void -- a gate to a distant universe. Suddenly Hughes' team was on center stage -- it was time for action.

Hughes looked over to Carrie Johnson who was at the controls and watched her power on the APP device. On the back side of the APP tube a thick umbilical of power and control cables snaked off to a power panel, and for an instant Hughes considered that all the raw power needed by both the

APP and Hyperaperture could have easily exceeded that required by the entire colony of Grindavik several times over.

The APP moved slowly on the set of tracks as it approached the center of the hole. He could tell that the tremendous gravitational forces had already started working on the device, but the coils held true. Carrie pushed the remaining controls and the APP slid right through and stopped, while dozens of technicians around the room took readings, snapped pictures, and gathered data from all the instruments. It only lasted a few seconds before the APP was quickly pulled back on the rails and the Hyperaperture shut down. They had achieved what would eventually be called a Singler Gate (**Figure 1**).

It was over, and nothing menacing had followed them through. Hughes glanced over to his wife across the room and she flashed a greatly relieved smile in his direction.

The photos that came back however opened up a whole new set of questions. Hughes looked at the shots and was admittedly shocked at what he saw -- multiple bright spots with identical machines poking through. Those weren't any devices from some unknown intelligence -- Hughes recognized the cluster of hover coils and nose cameras on each of the objects. It was their own APP unit protruding from dozens of apertures at once!

"I don't understand it!" Jiro said, "Does everybody in the universe design the same Aperture Penetration Probe?"

Carrie Johnson just shook her head, and Tom Hildebrandt and the other technicians sat dumbfounded. The mumble among the workers became deafening as each one discussed this and that, or put forth their own theories. Finally, Dr. Harrison the Principal Investigator called everyone to order, and gave the floor to Sachiko who had a theory.

"It must be some kind of mirroring, like yesterday," Sachiko proposed, "The strong gravitational fields may be reflecting back our own machine from multiple directions at once. I think I know a way to test it -- can Hildebrandt Engineering rig a set of lights that can blink?"

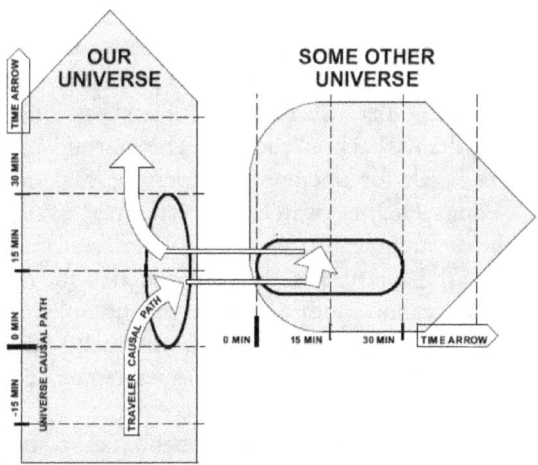

Figure 1: Singler Gate Wormhole: an aperture passage to some other universe. In the diagram above, a continuous ribbon pointing upward in the time arrow direction represents our universe. The aperture connects to some volume that exists outside of our own universe, and therefore has an arrow of time of its own, represented perpendicular to our universe.

Hughes was relieved that his wife was not so nervous as before -- there were still the x-ray storms and abandoned colonies, but at least there didn't seem to be some unknown hostile aliens out there.

Jiro Kitamura sent someone over to the Hildebrandt Bunker to look through the collection of odds and ends. They brought back some simple lights that could be made to blink at will. In the next test, instead of still photos they would run live video, penetrate the aperture, and make the lights blink. If, as Sachiko theorized, all those other APPs were mirror images of their own machine, they would see them all blink the same pattern at once.

It was just after noon when the 'Christmas tree', as the light system had been nicknamed, was ready to go. The Hildebrandt experts were all present except for Tom, who had to excuse himself because nanoassemblers had once again clogged the drains back at the lab. The starting power-up countdown began for opening the aperture, and the video started rolling. Hughes watched as the rear wall visible through the donut hole faded away to blackness. Carrie eased the APP into the aperture as everyone stared at the monitors lining the observation room. He could see multiple flashes of light, many of which moved toward each other and disappeared on contact. But some flashes remained and he could see the nose of the APP begin to emerge.

"Give a quick two blinks now!" Sachiko called out.

Their own unit blinked twice, but there was no immediate mirroring from any of the other APP units. Then, in delayed reaction, one of the other APPs blinked three times. Everyone gasped and the Principal Investigator called the experiment. They pulled out the APP and shut down the aperture.

It was not like anyone expected. The whole room exploded in conversation again and Dr. Harrison had to quiet everyone down. Again, he ceded the floor to Sachiko.

"No one knows what's happening out there," she began, "It's been a long day, but I suggest we do one more test. Let's go for a longer period of time, say ten minutes."

Hughes looked out on the group of scientists and engineers and saw curiosity on their faces. *There was nothing going to stop this bunch from getting more answers*, he thought. He could even imagine some of them not being able to sleep tonight wondering about what sort of physics could result in what they were seeing.

Sachiko saw the looks of approval, "Okay let's get to it - - ten minutes!"

Little did any of them know that those ten minutes of video would haunt them for months to come.

Once more Hughes watched the monitors as the aperture was fired up, and the APP moved into position. Again, there were multiple flashes, and identical APP devices poked their nose through multiple apertures against a black background. Without warning, one of the APP units out there blinked twice.

Sachiko, on impulse called out, "Give three blinks back!"

Their own unit blinked three times, but the other machine backed into its aperture, which abruptly shut and disappeared. The scene continued to unfold. All kinds of blinks were visible now in a variety of colors and intensities, as if each machine out there were trying to express a unique signature. Hughes thought he could feel a storm brewing beyond, but wasn't sure about what he was looking at -- billowing clouds and lightning strikes, or something. APP units continued to extend further through their respective holes until Hughes noticed some machines broke completely away and were free-floating through the void! There seemed to be an air current that disturbed all the machines, like a gust of wind blowing them toward a distant aperture. Electric arcs seemed to spark between some of the holes. As he studied the scene, Hughes began to notice other devices or vehicles of a design he had not seen before. What seemed like a whole fleet of machines began to fill the entire void, moving this way and that, going in and out of dozens of apertures. The gusts of wind continued and all the machines struggled from being drawn toward that distant aperture. The arcs of lightning intensified.

Suddenly amidst a blinding electric firestorm a massive machine or structure emerged from that distant wormhole, and one of the other smaller machines was captured and sucked through to disappear. The distant aperture shut again and the wind and arcing stopped, leaving dozens of smaller machines dwarfed against the large one, all drifting serenely through the void. Ten minutes were up, and the Principal Investigator called the experiment.

No one stirred for several minutes. Hughes tried to process what he had seen. He knew it would take weeks to figure it all out, and they would replay those ten minutes of video over and over again.

Sachiko came up to his side, and said, "I have no idea what's going on out there, but one thing is sure. Did you see the other APP out there blink twice? That was us from our last experiment -- we answered ourselves with three blinks. Some or all of those machines out there are us doing future or past experiments! Each time we open the aperture we start the clock all over again!"

CHAPTER 5

"Lenny, what do you suppose they used this space for?" Carta Randall's voice echoed across the vast empty hall.

Her assistant looked up and around at the bare walls and ceiling, his footsteps barely reverberating on the hard surfaces, "I'd guess it was some sort of dance hall or community center."

The whole facility had been stripped bare of anything significant, but the lights were still on and the environment was pressurized.

"Let's rest a while. I think we've seen at least five of these already." Carta pointed out.

"Yes, housing, schools, community centers, farms, manufacturing -- enough for three or four million people. I thought Becquerel was a small outpost." Lenny Chopra replied.

They had been exploring deserted neighborhoods all day, hollowed out of the Becquerel Crater wall. There was not a soul to be found.

"What I don't understand is why did they build all this if there were so few people living here?" Carta sat down on the floor near one of the walls in the vast hall.

Lenny looked skeptical, "I think there was a full population here, Carta. Look at all the trash and junk they left behind. The bigger mystery is where they all went, and why we didn't notice it!"

True, Carta thought. This was definitely a thriving population until recently -- all the signs were there. Suddenly the population of Mars had swelled more than nine times and nobody knew about it. It was just like what they had found in Novissima -- spacious underground caverns deserted of all inhabitants. Perepelkin and Bonestell were the same, and Carta would bet six months' pay that Trud, Aktaj, and a half dozen other supposed smaller colonies that had lost communication would also be found to have large deserted communities.

The only difference was the impact crater in Novissima. Something massive must have crashed there and left behind all that wreckage and bodies. The Bureau still couldn't determine if the crash and x-ray storm were related or not. Fortunately, whatever happened, the Novissima occupants had long gone before the catastrophe struck. But where?

Carta slipped through a side exit into a service corridor followed by Lenny. There was a freight elevator and Randall wanted to see what was down at the bottom. They rode the elevator down six levels to a scuffed-up elevator lobby. Carta walked across the space and pushed the 'up' button on a large roll-up door. It was another vast space veiled in darkness.

Lenny found a bank of light switches and quickly moved across it shoving them all into the 'on' position. Overhead, industrial light fixtures lit up several at a time to reveal a high bay chamber with bare red rock walls and floors, scarred and scraped by heavy equipment. Three of the walls had a number of roll-up doors, and along the entire fourth wall was a deep trench about five meters wide and a few meters deep. At one end of the trench there had been a small explosion or something, with broken pieces of metal and electronics scattered where they had been thrown. Carta looked down in the hole and saw the remnants of anchor bolts and foundations, as if there had been heavy equipment mounted there.

Lenny walked up behind her and pointed to the rim, "Look at that -- it looks like some big equipment drove right over the edge."

Carta saw tread marks and scars from caterpillar tracks on the red stone as if dozens of vehicles had driven over the edge onto whatever equipment had been mounted in the trench. Several meters beyond, another set of tracks drove over the edge, then beyond that another and another. Four heavily traveled roads set equidistant from each other came from large roll-up doors across the vast high bay and ended at the trench.

"Some kind of ore crunching equipment?" Lenny asked.

Carta shrugged. It was common in all the colonies to have underground garages for digital excavators and such, and new tunnels were constantly being opened. Carta wondered how long it would take for an army of numerical control excavators to dig out caverns for several million people like that. If they had time, someone might have been able to take those blown-up remnants and try to see what sort of machine had been mounted there -- but such an effort wouldn't have been worth the time.

"All right, let's survey that last block of offices and call it a day." Lenny suggested.

Going back up the elevator, the pair moved through deserted corridors and underground avenues, lined with untended hydroponic vegetable gardens. The automatics on the pedestrian locks worked fine, so they passed through a bulkhead into another pressurized sector of town. This was where the colony administration offices were, Carta supposed.

The passage they entered was wide, and had crowd control queue barriers enough to manage large numbers of people in parallel lines. *Curious*, Carta thought. She and Lenny followed one of the lines to the end as it wound around corners and snaked its way back and forth inside large halls. The queue ended at a blank wall, along with all the others.

There were identical scars on the floor at the end of each queue which, along with trash and discarded screws, anchor bolts, and other odds and ends hinted that some installation there had been hastily removed -- some booth or equipment that people had been willing to wait in long queues to interact with.

Lenny wandered off into a nearby corridor while Carta leaned down to collect evidence. She could see folks lined up in her mind's eye, waiting in line to . . . to what? Somehow it must have been significant, but she couldn't put a finger on what it could be.

"In here!" Lenny called out from somewhere down the corridor.

Carta stood up and followed Lenny's voice until she found the Indian in a long hallway looking at photos on the wall -- a string of dozens of portraits showing smartly dressed men and women.

"How long did you say it was since Becquerel was established?" her assistant asked.

Carta thought for a minute or two. She had just read the factoid recently and passed the trivia on to Len.

"I think it was started around sixty years ago by some religious immigrants." she said.

Lenny stood there and looked at her with his mouth wide open, "Not according to this. Look, these show the Becquerel governor succession."

Carta started at one end and walked all the way down the line. Under each was a plaque listing 'circuit number' and span of years as governor, explaining how the person had taken over from the previous governor. 'Shot her fair and square' read one; 'took over from his father' read three in a row -- apparently father, son, and grandson.

"What is a 'circuit' anyway?" Carta asked.

"I'm not sure, some district or rank?" Lenny suggested, "but add them all up."

Suddenly it hit her. The immigrants had settled there only sixty years previously, but the succession of leaders up on the wall showed that the colony had been in operation for over 380 years!

CHAPTER 6

"So, each of the machines we see protruding from other holes is us performing future experiments?" Tom Hildebrandt asked.

It was the beginning of a new Sol-day and Jacob Harrison the Hyperaperture Principal Investigator had called a floor meeting for all heads of departments. Tom had brought Masamune Hughes and Jiro Kitamura with him to represent Hildebrandt Engineering. In the background, the ten-minute video taken through the aperture was playing in a loop.

Sachiko explained again, "What we have here is a bubble, if you will, a hyperspace continuum. The bubble is formed when two or more apertures are opened. Since the continuum is hyperspace, it does not relate to our universe at all, neither in time nor space -- that is why apertures from different times can link together to create it."

Harrison added, "The continuum is finite. It is formed the moment we open the aperture. It's like a bridge of spacetime between all the apertures."

Some of the scientists around the table showed understanding, but Tom could see that Hughes, Jiro, and some of the others were not completely getting it. It could

73

have been a case of not understanding the physics, but Tom knew the crew was feeling a bit discouraged over the news they had gotten that morning -- funding cuts due to the x-ray storms. The Mars Interim Government was redirecting all the resources it could to try to figure out what was happening and try to stop the phenomenon. Hyperspace bubbles just didn't hold enough priority anymore.

"Can you explain it a little better?" Tom requested.

Sachiko who had experience explaining complex physics to her family replied, "Okay, let's say there are two holes, one today, and one tomorrow. For some reason we don't quite understand the holes try to connect to each other and make a tube or tunnel of volume between them. When we add holes next week and next month, they become new doors in the tunnel between the first two, only they all open at once -- they create a big bubble between them all. Anything that comes out of those doors gets all mixed up in that bubble."

Tom looked at the faces of his engineers and thought he saw understanding there.

Jiro wondered, "So explain the blinks. What happened there?"

Harrison explained, "When we did our first experiment, we started the clock at the beginning of the bubble. We blinked twice. Then when we did our second experiment, we also started the clock at the beginning of the bubble formation, and therefore were concurrent with the previous experiment -- we then blinked three times to answer ourselves."

A murmuring occurred around the table. *It was fantastic*, Tom thought -- no matter how many days, or years, apart the aperture is opened in this universe, over there it starts at the same instant, at the beginning of the bubble. Which meant . .
.

Tom asked, "So in the first experiment we could see forward in time?"

"Exactly. In fact, we can see way forward in time, because we see all those other experiments." Sachiko affirmed.

Another murmur went around the table.

"But what about paradoxes? What if we decide not to do any more experiments?" Tom wondered, thinking they were almost begging for Murphy to come along.

"Yes, interesting thought." Dr. Harrison returned, "I think we have an interesting opportunity here. We've achieved all our main objectives so far. Can we come up with experiments to answer some of those age-old questions?"

Tom noticed that Hughes was perplexed about something. The mechanical engineer was squinting and almost unperceptively moving his fingertips as if he were trying to spatially organize a set of facts.

"What is it Mas?" Tom prodded.

Hughes began, "Well, most of those future APPs came completely out of the aperture, without a tether -- they floated around on their own power."

Sachiko thought she saw where he was going with that. It was the old gravitational whirlpool problem again.

She said, "Remember, anything that goes through the aperture must be protected from the tremendous gravitational forces from the singularities -- you can't just have a power cable be exposed to that, it would get severed unless it too was shielded."

"I think he knows that," Jiro stepped in, "What concerns him, and me too, is that the hover coils on the APP consume tremendous amounts of power, maybe even similar to the total power the entire colony of Grindavik uses at any given time. It's one reason Toshige hasn't been able to market the thing yet -- we're trying to solve that problem for him. We don't have the kind of power density to fit in that package that would fire up the APP for even a millisecond."

Now the scientists were confused.

Hughes explained it in simpler terms, "We don't have batteries that powerful -- I don't think batteries that powerful are even theoretically possible!"

Jiro nodded. Again, the table erupted with a murmur as those present considered the new dilemma. First, it was clear that somehow their future selves had figured it out. Now they were expected to perform something they didn't even know was possible.

Hello Murphy, Tom chuckled as he sarcastically noted, "Looks like you might be able to test the paradox by default -- if Hildebrandt doesn't perform . . ."

But the scientists at the table were dumbfounded. Something Hughes and Jiro said caught them completely off guard.

Harrison enlightened the engineers, "I think you just illustrated an answer to an age-old question -- can information be provided from the future? The debate has been whether information from the future could have causal effect in the past."

Tom and the others were confused, "Please explain." he said.

Harrison continued, "Well, what if a time traveler goes back in time with a wristwatch and gives it to her grandmother who is a little girl. The grandmother grows up, has children of her own, then gives the wristwatch to the granddaughter, who in turn goes back in time."

Hughes understood, "The wristwatch gets in a causal loop -- who made the wristwatch?"

"Yes," Harrison confirmed, "However our situation is fundamentally different. We are not taking the APP from our future selves to use it just the way we find it. Instead, we are observing future information and are producing something based on that inspiration. There is causal resolution to all physical particles. Only there doesn't seem to be a resolution to the information that inspired it."

Sachiko piped up, "Wait -- maybe there is. If you think about it, do we know how the thing works? We actually don't know anything. All we have are impressions on what we think we saw. And consider this: if we see a ball drop, we reach out and catch it before it hits the floor. If we are calculating backwards from the future event of catching the ball, there is reverse causation that makes us reach out. It requires 'intelligence', but for some reason we don't quite understand, 'intelligence' is able to respond to future events."

"You are right," Harrison agreed, "The particles and forces must all have causal resolution, but 'intelligence' puts a whole new spin on things -- it is able to read the environment, so to speak, and influence future events in ways that favor itself."

Another scientist whom Tom did not know suggested, "But somehow, when you break down the neurons and quantum processes there must be a deterministic solution."

"That's not necessarily true." countered Harrison, "Remember that for every radiation problem there is both an advanced and retarded solution. The advanced one is usually ignored because it doesn't agree with causality. But remember the work by that 20th century physicist Cramer who proposed the 'transaction effect' or some such, where the advanced solution helps bind the future and the past. Essentially, that means every event creates a splash in time with waves going out forward and backward."

"Yes," Sachiko broke in, "It may be that quantum processes in neuron microtubules become antennae for advanced radiation, allowing 'intelligence' to pick up the future event, or many possible future events and choose among them."

Interesting, Tom thought, *sort of like guiding someone in the past through emotions, in order to get around the causal loop problem.*

The entire table became quiet as each person reveled in his or her own thoughts.

Finally, Harrison broke the silence, "Okay Tom, see if your folks can solve the power problem, or at least come up with possibilities. Since we have to keep track of our APP once it gets out there, find a way to follow it through a unique code system or something." then Jacob's face lit up in a way Tom had never seen before, "We'll work on a set of experiments that can test the new technology. Also, I want some kind of metric for placing holes we observe on our timeline -- can we predict which hole is from the future, and which are behind us?"

Everyone relaxed, the relief was almost palpable -- that was the signal that heavy physics lectures were over. Tom looked at the time -- it was already noon, time for lunch. When the group broke up he invited Jiro, Masamune, and Sachiko to a meal for an informal discussion. The four of them made their way up to the Promenade level and looked for a good restaurant.

The public street was quite crowded. Tom briefly wondered if all those missing folks from the deserted colonies had somehow secretly entered Grindavik and joined the population. He quickly dismissed the thought however, because there were supposedly millions upon millions of missing persons -- a troubling mystery. As they walked down the street with storefronts on both sides Tom saw Hughes reach over and hold Sachiko's hand. She was in the early stages of pregnancy, and it pained Tom to see them so happy. He had not been successful with women and was still single. There had been a few girls in his life here and there, but the right one just hadn't come along yet.

Jiro found a good cafe that they had all eaten at before, so they went inside.

Tom brought up the subject that was on everyone's mind, "Have you heard the latest about the x-ray storms? Is the government seriously thinking about evacuating a whole planet?"

"I don't see how it could be done. First of all, we don't have enough ships, and where would we go?" Jiro wondered as they sat down at a table.

Hughes was not happy, and Sachiko had a withdrawn look on her face. Tom wondered if they were talking about a subject that upset the woman.

"It's too bad Earth is off limits," Jiro continued, "With all that orbital debris from the satellite wars we can't even get a radio signal down there."

"Or there are no more antennas to get a signal. The war went on you know. Earth's surface could be uninhabitable as far as we know." Tom speculated.

Jiro was calm -- whatever was happening at the poles couldn't affect them at Grindavik, it was too far away, "I'm sure the scientists will figure it out. Evacuation is ridiculous."

Tom suddenly looked like he'd seen a ghost, "You know those troubles we've been having about nanoassemblers in the drains. I have a horrible feeling about this. What if the assemblers have somehow evolved past their programmed feed material and are eating into the bedrock?"

Jiro's eyes opened wide, "You mean those x-ray holes!"

Hughes also appeared shocked, "*Our* escaped nanoassemblers chomping away at all those colonies?"

The Drexler 'gray goo' scenario with runaway replication -- maybe Mars will end up completely consumed unless we can figure out how to stop them!" Tom frowned.

"Red goo," began Hughes, but didn't finish.

"You know, I've been thinking," Sachiko broke in -- she had not been listening at all, "How small could you make the hover coils? And Jiro, so far we've been trying to get the Hyperaperture magnets bigger and bigger, but how small could you make them?"

"The super-cooled quantum magnets can get very small, even micro-sized, the coils too." Kitamura noted.

Hughes looked questioningly at his wife, "Why, what are you thinking?"

Sachiko paused as if gathering her thoughts, then said, "You remember seeing lights at the beginning that draw to each other and merge, then disappear. I'm wondering if there's a way to uniquely link only two holes to each other permanently, for a custom tunnel between two points."

Tom thought he got the general gist of what she was saying, "I like the idea of a tunnel between two fixed points, but how do the migrating lights relate?"

"Well, it looks like we can't just make a hole in space and expect it to go nowhere. It always has to connect with some other hole at the other end. If we just create a hole with our equipment, it goes right to the bubble because no partner is specified. But maybe when two apertures are purposely paired right at the beginning, they kick themselves out of the hyperspace we observe and form their own private wormhole between them. They're not connected to the bubble anymore. I'm thinking that's what we are seeing." Sachiko explained.

An enlightened expression came onto Hughes' face, "I see! A wormhole tether! So, you're suggesting we create a dedicated wormhole tunnel with two end gates, and string power and data cables through them."

Jiro also understood, "Yes, you aren't kidding! That would give us a cable only a few centimeters long. Talk about power efficient. But will that work once we get through the Hyperaperture?"

Sachiko gave a simple explanation, "Yes it will. A wormhole permanently connected would have zero distance between the two exits if you pass through it, but in the real universe the tori that contain the exits could be taken as far apart from each other as you wish, light years even. In fact, the two openings don't even have to be concurrent in time."

Tom and the others didn't quite understand that part, but at least they had a working plan for how to get the APP independent and free flying.

"The small tori would be completely portable themselves," Hughes pointed out, "continually open and drawing off the power coming through the micro wormhole. No wires! But they'd still be very heavy if they're carrying micro black holes."

Tom suggested, "Hughes, we'll call our Self-Contained Aperture Penetration Probe SCAPP for short. You two get on it."

Sachiko Hughes explained her idea to Jacob and the others and it was agreed that the team try to create a pair of connected gates. They restarted the old, smaller Hyperaperture Mark I device that had the observation vacuum chamber in the middle of the donut hole.

"Somehow we have to make sure the pairs of black holes stay entangled. If we make four singularities, then alternate the magnets to draw them apart in pairs, what do you think?" Sachiko proposed.

Harrison agreed. Creating both apertures at the same time proved to be the right trick for making sure the exits stayed connected to each other. It had been theorized that two entangled black holes drawn apart would create a wormhole, but such an arrangement would not allow any intact information to enter the tunnel mouth because of the presence of the singularity. That's where two sets of two came to be useful -- each set balanced a tunnel opening in pairs such that the heavy mass was offset from the tunnel mouth. Each set constituted a single system, and if you entangle two sets with each other it allows a traversable wormhole. The physicists got right on it, and several Sol-days later the team had a confirmed exclusive wormhole between two orbiting pairs of micro black holes. What would eventually be known as a Dualer Gate was formed (**Figure 2**). Where the Singlers automatically connect together in a big common bubble, Dualers are given their mate from the start and never even open in the bubble at all.

Jiro delivered micro tori that could contain each pair of black holes separately, and they drew the artificial singularities out of the main Hyperaperture unit using a timed firing of the magnets through a side port. It was only a week later that Toshige delivered some micro hover coils ready for testing tiny shield sleeves. Again, the visionary doctor had already been working on miniaturization. The APP team permanently installed the shield sleeves in each of the little tori, and performed a test stringing cables through the wormhole.

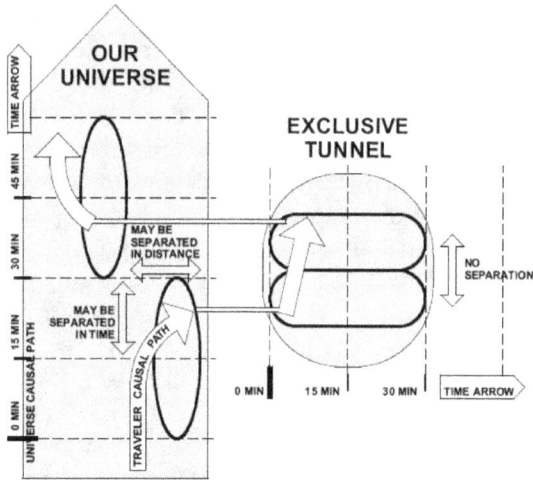

Figure 2: Dualer Gate Wormhole: a tunnel that connects two apertures in an exclusive wormhole. Apertures can be separated any distance in space, and can be separated in time as well. In the diagram above, a continuous ribbon pointing upward in the time arrow direction represents our universe. The tunnel formed between the two apertures is a volume that exists outside of our own universe, and therefore has an arrow of time of its own, represented perpendicular to our universe.

The holes in the little tori were about 10 centimeters in diameter, so Hughes got an idea.

"Jiro, wheel that toroid into the next room and watch the opening." Hughes suggested.

The two little tori sat side by side in the middle of the room. The devices though small were still too heavy to lift by hand and had to be wheeled around on a cart. A cable connected to a nearby power panel kept one of the tiny units powered, but the second unit sat isolated away from anything. Instead, it got its power through a short 20-centimeter wire poking through the hole of the first, traveling through the unseen wormhole tunnel to emerge from the hole of the second -- it was free to be relocated as needed. No matter how far away they separated the two units in real space, the power cable through the wormhole tether would never exceed 20 centimeters. Jiro obediently pushed the portable toroid into the next room leaving the other one where it was since it had to be located near the power source. As Jiro wheeled the unit away, Hughes leaned over and peered closely through the little wormhole. He could see a strange sort of optical illusion -- he could follow Jiro's progress out the door and into the corridor through the small circle, almost as if a camera on Jiro's unit were transmitting its video back to a screen on the stationary one. When the motion through the hole came to a stop, Hughes slowly lifted his right hand and pushed it through the opening. There was a slight tingling sensation but other than that, his head reeled at the thought that his hand was protruding from the hole in the other room! Hughes heard Jiro whoop and holler, and his friend grasped the hand in a firm handshake -- a first ever!

Tom Hildebrandt found himself in the Hyperaperture observation room sitting next to Carrie Johnson. There had been opportunities to work together lately, but he was too nervous to approach her, especially since Murphy had done so much damage already.

"Are we ready Carrie?" he casually asked.

Tom was certain the girl had no idea he was interested in her.

"The SCAPP is ready, sir. We removed the rails yesterday, and have full control through the wormhole tether." she said.

Tom looked over to the right and saw the machine hovering at about eye level. It stood completely detached from any visible power source or rail support. Hughes was over there standing next to the unit, doing last minute tests on the compressed air propulsion system. At the last minute they had snaked a compressor hose through the wormhole tether that allowed them to add all sorts of pneumatic actuators, including thrusters to push it along and steer it with puffs of air.

Tom could see that the countdown had already begun, and the Hyperaperture donut hole was getting hazy.

"Where do you usually eat dinner?" he suddenly asked.

Carrie looked embarrassed and self-conscious -- she was talking to the big boss, "Excuse me?" she asked.

"Um, I mean, if this is successful, where should we take the team to celebrate?" Tom recovered.

"Oh, well, I guess we could . . ." Carrie began, but Hughes, her immediate supervisor, had just finished his work on the SCAPP and walked back into the observation room.

"Get ready to do a quick steering test, Carrie." Hughes said, completely oblivious of any romantic electricity that might have been there.

"Yes sir," Carrie replied.

As Hughes called out the commands, spin left, spin right, nose up, sideways crawl and such, Carrie operated the joysticks and the SCAPP answered with bursts of compressed air. The machine handled perfectly.

Tom was hoping Hughes would go away, but instead Jacob Harrison came in too. It was getting crowded in there.

"We're almost ready for you. Remember on this test you drive through the aperture, go through various maneuvers, and come right back out." Harrison confirmed.

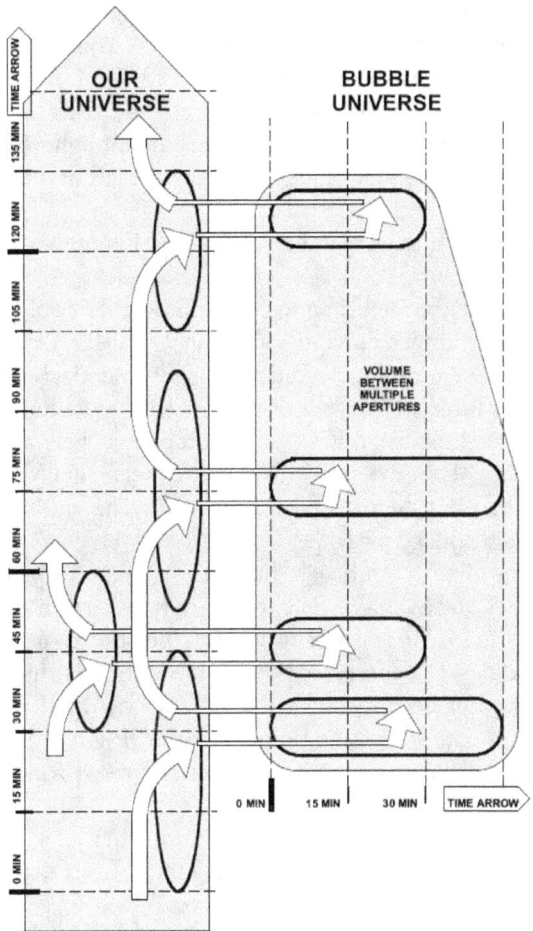

Figure 3: Bubble universe: the volume between multiple Singler Gate apertures connect to become a common volume outside our universe.

Then Sachiko walked in, "Jacob, we have a series of tests to try next."

Jiro came in with two trainees and began to set up their monitoring equipment. *What was I thinking*, Tom thought, *I'll never get a free moment alone with her.*

The test went off without a hitch, and the crew began setting up for the next test. Right when he thought the whole place was going insane, suddenly everyone left and there she was, by herself at the controls.

"Um, what does that do?" he said, pointing to a lever off to the side.

Carrie earnestly began to explain how they could use the lever to set different codes for the SCAPP, for tracking purposes. Since they expected to observe identical machines from their future or past selves, they needed to make sure *their* unit had a unique address every time they performed an experiment. Tom extended his arm and accidentally brushed Carrie's hand as she reached for the lever. The girl looked up at him as he pulled away.

"I um . . ." Tom began, but they were interrupted again by Hughes and Sachiko. The team ran several more tests, sending the SCAPP farther away from the hole to observe the surroundings. Carrie steered the machine around other vessels out there, but began to complain about how hard it was to keep it on course. At one point the SCAPP got a direct zap from one of the electric arcs, which overloaded some of the detector circuits.

"Remember in the first ten minutes there are some air currents." Hughes advised, "Just stay away from that distant aperture as the large machine comes out."

The team was watching the monitors seeing all sorts of machines of various designs pop out of their respective wormholes in the bubble universe (**Figure 3**), and the as of yet unidentified humongous structure or machine, or whatever it was, came out amidst electrical fireworks.

"It looks like a building," Sachiko remarked.

Hughes shook his head, "It's much too big even for that. I'll bet it is at least as long as Grindavik crater is across. Look at the size of that thing!"

Their SCAPP unit wove back and forth but couldn't keep a straight line. At times it seemed as though it were being drawn toward that distant aperture. Twice more the SCAPP got direct strikes from lightning.

"I'm really having trouble guys," Carrie pleaded.

"Just get her back for us." Hughes returned.

One of the strangely designed smaller vessels got too close and slipped into that distant hole before it shut again. Then the struggle to control their machine ended -- the air currents had stopped.

"It seems like all the air is rushing out that distant aperture -- when it closes the currents stop." Hughes remarked.

Their SCAPP cruised right back and came out their own aperture, ending another successful test. Again, most of the crew went back out to tend the machine, leaving Tom and Carrie alone.

"So how do we keep track of which machine is ours?" Tom asked.

Carrie again pointed to the lever and said, "We reset the code each time it goes out, so there is no confusion. Also, the wormhole tether stays connected to our control system, even though identical tethers are on all the other machines."

The beautiful woman stared at him for several uncomfortable moments.

"Um, I ah . . ." Tom stumbled, but Carrie got up and hungrily pinned him against the wall with a passionate kiss.

She could read him like a book.

That evening Tom watched the news. The x-ray storm at the north pole had plowed right through one of those deserted colonies. It was sobering to watch those formerly pressurized living spaces completely lacerated with holes -- no one would ever live there again. But Tom could not think of anything other than a beautiful SCAPP pilot.

The next Sol-day Harrison got everyone together and announced, "Today we're going to collaborate with our future selves."

Everyone looked at each other with quizzical looks on their faces. Tom was thinking, *what if they don't want to cooperate?*

Harrison continued, "We're going to do a three-hole time sortie -- open three apertures an hour apart from each other. From our perspective, we'll see a SCAPP go in and out each of the three times we open an aperture. But each time we will swap with another device in hyperspace and see a SCAPP come out from a different group of experimenters. The apparatus will have travelled forward and backward in time."

A roar came from the crowd as everyone applauded. Harrison pointed to a diagram showing what he was proposing. A wide oval stretched across the page at the top, representing the hyperspace bubble. Across the bottom was a timeline in real space, and three narrow necks an hour apart showed where the apertures would be.

A weaving line showed the route of travel the SCAPP would take, going in the first hole, out the second, in the third, then backward to go out the first, in the second, and out the third again, ending up in real space.

Tom studied the chart (**Figure 4**). By the looks of it, as soon as their own SCAPP entered hyperspace, a version from two hours later would immediately emerge.

"How do we find the right hole to exit once we are inside?" Hughes asked.

Harrison returned, "We color code the holes, red, green, and blue. When our SCAPP pokes through the first hole we have a red light on the nose advertise that this is the red hole. Then our SCAPP will navigate toward the green hole and exit. An hour later, we'll mark the second aperture with a green light and so on."

The room was full of grinning technicians as they contemplated the interesting tasks ahead -- they were about to realize time travel!

Harrison added one more thing, "Sachiko is going to put a splotch of colored paint on the nose of each machine that leaves here, depending on the color of the hole at the time. After the third hole closes, we should have a SCAPP with all three red, green, and blue paint marks."

The group broke up and went to their various stations. The countdown began, and the Hildebrandt team readied their SCAPP to enter red hole as soon as the gate opened. Sachiko pulled out a paintbrush and can of red paint and put a splotch on its nose.

Carrie sequestered herself into a corner in the observation room and started up the apparatus. When the aperture opened, Carrie had the machine enter, pause partway through, and shine the red light for whoever might be watching out there. Then she was supposed to head for the green hole to exit. Unfortunately, that's where the first snag occurred.

"Dr. Hughes! There are two green holes!" she exclaimed.

Tom and Hughes rushed over to see what the SCAPP was streaming back onto the monitors. Sure enough, there were two green-lighted noses right next to each other, protruding from the holes. *What can go wrong, will go wrong,* Tom thought. But as he looked down at Carrie, he was sure Murphy might be on the way out. The two SCAPPs from the green holes continued out and separated themselves from their apertures leaving both holes free.

"Um, well, pick one. Maybe they're mirror images of each other or something." Hughes advised.

When Tom looked around, he saw not only two green holes, but two each of red and blue as well. It seemed as though the other versions of Carrie operating the other SCAPPs were all hesitating as well, wondering which one to choose. Finally, they all sorted each other out and a SCAPP exited from their red aperture as planned.

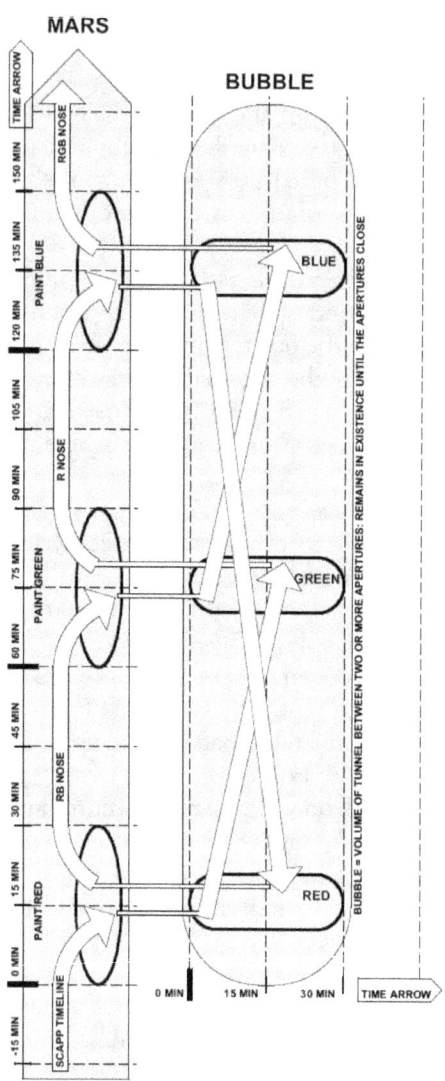

Figure 4: Three-hole Time Sortie experiment

The technicians stood around the machine in awe. On its nose were two splotches of paint already -- red and blue -- the red one matching the unique dot Sachiko had just painted on their own SCAPP. The machine had come from two hours in the future!

As the clock ticked down before green hole was to open, technicians pored over the device to see if time travel changed it in any way -- no, everything normal.

"But why does it have a blue mark? Sachiko only painted red on it." Jiro wondered.

Sachiko explained, "You're not thinking four dimensionally. The future me at blue hole two hours from now painted that before it went into blue aperture."

The second hang up came when they prepared to open green hole. Carrie discovered that she couldn't control the machine that had returned to them. It took a few minutes for everyone to realize what was happening.

"Your wormhole tether is connected to a machine in our future. The two ends of the tether are offset in time." Harrison explained, "Since you exited green hole, the device at the end of your tether is waiting to enter blue hole. You're going to have to drive it while watching the monitors."

Tom stood behind Carrie and gave her a gentle squeeze on the shoulder, which she answered by reaching up to touch his hand -- they both stared intently at the monitors above them which apparently was broadcasting back the view of the Hyperaperture chamber from about an hour in the future. Hughes, Jiro, Sachiko, and several others rushed in to watch as well.

Sachiko advised, "Okay, just assume you are driving something here and now, and follow the time schedule. I'm sure the future Carrie at blue hole will do the same for us."

The countdown for green hole ended and the aperture opened. As planned, Sachiko put a splotch of green paint on the nose of the machine from the future. Somehow, the future

Carrie drove the machine using monitors and entered green hole, turning on the green light as it poked through.

In the observation room a more interesting scene played out. Up on the screen they could see a future Sachiko bring up a couple of cans of paint -- one blue and one yellow. The future Sachiko seemed to argue with her colleagues, but eventually took the blue paint and dabbed some onto the nose of their machine. Carrie drove their machine into the future blue hole and turned on the blue lights. According to plan, her next destination was red hole.

Again, there was some confusion as to which of the double red holes she should enter. Somehow it worked itself out and she drove the machine through one of the red apertures. On the monitors, a crowd of her colleagues from the earlier red hole could be seen gathering around her machine astounded that it had come to them from two hours in the future. Déjà vu.

In their own Hyperaperture chamber, like clockwork a SCAPP exited the green hole that had only a red dot on its nose. The team had one hour to open the final blue hole and finish the experiment.

Suddenly Tom had an idea -- he was going to hunt Murphy down. He made a quick trip over to the Hildebrandt Bunker and switched on the light. Finding a can of yellow paint, he made his way back to the accelerator facilities where Sachiko had set the three cans of marker paint and snatched up the blue one, leaving the yellow one in its place. He was about to take the blue paint and hide it somewhere when Sachiko caught him.

"What are you doing!" she demanded angrily, picking up the yellow can.

She snatched the blue can away from him.

Tom replied a little shyly, "Trying to make things a little interesting."

Sachiko eyed him for a few minutes, not knowing what to say. Tom could tell she was weighing the implications of trying to change causality. They had both seen the machine come from the blue hole with a blue dot on its nose. And they had both seen a future Sachiko paint a blue mark. Were they in control of their own futures? Would fate somehow force that blue mark to appear? Or could they, through free agency, paint a yellow one instead?

Tom was proposing a paradox. If they painted a yellow spot at the blue hole, how could that machine from two hours before have come out with the blue dot?

"Tom, what you are proposing is extremely dangerous. What if spacetime unravels in the collision between causality and free will?" she asked.

Hildebrandt knew she wasn't serious. Silently he reached for her hand, took the blue can, and gave her the yellow one again. He smiled as he walked away toward the supply room. *She's as curious as I am*, he thought. He left her standing wrestling with her physics demons.

Jacob Harrison was also using that last hour to their advantage. Tom walked back to the observation room just as the doctor walked in with accelerator facility director Eva Landerman. Not only her -- Tom involuntarily straightened when he saw Grindavik President Statner, and Mars Interim Governor himself, Stephan Wang, followed by a large number of dignitaries.

Suddenly his little prank with the yellow paint didn't seem so smart. Maybe the universe was conspiring to get that blue dot after all. Tom couldn't do anything about it at first. Harrison went through the introductions, and as one of the main contractors Hildebrandt was expected to be present. Sachiko was there too, but didn't have as high a ranking as he. Tom tried to catch her attention a number of times, and finally succeeded -- he flashed his eyes toward the paint cans and motioned with his head for her to go get the blue can back. But she just ignored the gestures as if she hadn't seen them. Finally, the short tour brought them close enough to the cans for him to see for himself -- red, green, and . . . blue! *Ah*, he thought, *she must have chickened out and swapped them again*. Tom finished the rest of the tour with a feeling of relief.

Then the time to open the blue aperture was upon them. The countdown ended and the aperture began to form. Tom looked back at Carrie who was driving some other SCAPP who knows where in time. Another Carrie somewhere in the past got the machine in front of them moving toward hole blue. Then Sachiko went over to the paint table, grabbed a brush and opened the blue can. Horror of all horrors, the paint inside the can was yellow! Sachiko quickly dipped the brush, and put a mark where the blue one was supposed to be before anyone could stop her.

The dignitaries didn't really understand why Harrison, Hildebrandt, and several others jumped up and cried, "No!" in unison. But the action was too late -- the yellow painted SCAPP headed inside, paused a few seconds to turn on its blue lights, then disappeared into the hole.

Time seemed to stop -- Tom was suddenly aware of all his surroundings, as the details impressed themselves on his mind. Tick, tick, tick -- a slow echo, probably in his imagination, seemed to count out the milliseconds. The whole universe stood still. Then after what seemed like an eternity another SCAPP came out and the blue aperture shut down. It was over.

Tom wondered what could have just happened. He recalled all those corny entertainment videos produced by ignorant directors where something changing back in time suddenly changes the here and now like instantaneous ripples, as if there were no time gap between the two events. Or other scenarios where a change back in time erases the memory and all records of what used to be in the timeline, swapped by the new thing. But Tom still had his memory -- he still remembered seeing the blue mark come out of the red hole. He still remembered the video of Sachiko painting the blue spot on the nose of the machine. And he still remembered where minutes ago a different Sachiko had painted a yellow dot instead.

Alarmed, Tom looked over at the SCAPP that had just exited the hole, to be forever theirs, regardless of who it

belonged to previously. On its nose were three paint marks --
red, green . . . and blue!

CHAPTER 7

"I need to make another trip to Novissima. But I want you to go to the north pole to this location." Carta Randall handed Lenny Chopra a disc with coordinates on it.

Carta continued, "Bring two agents with you and set up this white tarp exactly according to the instructions."

Carta pointed over to an ultraviolet-resistive white fabric folded up on the floor.

"You'll need a global satellite phone and two-way local radio." Carta grabbed one space-hardened radio from a pair sitting in the charger and tossed Lenny the other one.

Lenny looked confused, "Carta, we'll be on opposite sides of the planet. Why do we each need one radio from a paired set? These can't do anything better than line of sight."

Carta flashed her angry eyes at him, "Just do it!"

Then Carta picked up two satellite phones and kept one for herself. Lenny let out a sigh of relief.

That evening Carta lugged her bag to the Bureau's hopper port. A metal ramp led to the departure deck, where a central equipment staging area was surrounded by a dozen or so pressurized boarding doors. Carta went straight for her locker, and tagged the crate holding her government issue environmental suit for loading on the H6 multi-terrain hopper. A robotic arm detached itself from the ceiling and grabbed the crate, carrying it off to one side. Carta casually followed behind it with her bag on the shoulder, looking around to see which other ports were in use. A number of boarding doors were open and led into the cramped cabins of the hopper vehicles. Carta followed the robot arm as it plugged the crate into H6's EVA platform in such a way that she would be able to don the suit right out of the crate through a small suitport hatch in the bulkhead. Two flight crewmembers were already onboard and welcomed her. To one side, four tight bunk compartments laddered up the wall. Carta tossed her bag on one of them and took a seat in the passenger section. She signaled for the vehicle to shove off.

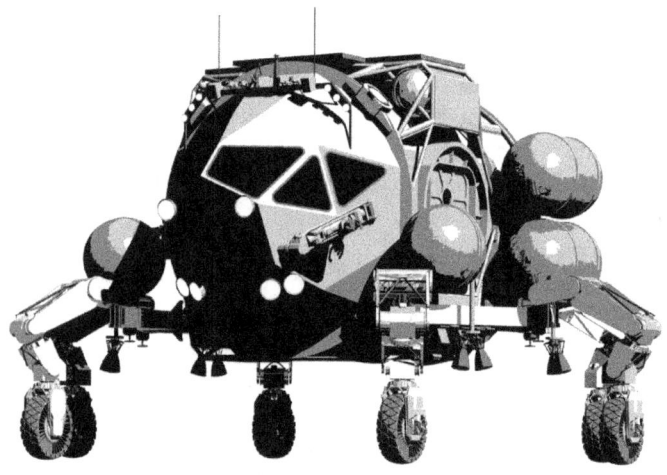

The hopper had its rear end mated to the docking fixture. One of the crewmen closed the boarding door, then made fast the vehicle hatch before patting the side. Carta could hear the fixture disengage, and the entire cabin shuddered as it pulled away from the building.

Outside the window, Carta could see other parked hoppers ready for action, secure in their docking fixtures. *Beautiful machines*, she thought. A small cabin surrounded by propellant tanks and Vertical Take-Off and Landing (VTOL) thrusters was mounted to a suspension ring with six articulated legs. At the end of each leg was a wheel, so the vehicle could roll across flat ground, step over rocks, or make short hops depending on the terrain to be covered. The heavy All-Terrain Hex-Limbed Extra-Terrestrial Explorer (ATHLETE) mobility system invented by NASA Jet Propulsion Laboratory back in the previous century was still the most versatile way to go cross-country where there were few roads.

Carta watched the parked hoppers slide past as their own vehicle built up speed. Soon she could see Redstone city center, which was a cluster of liquid filled transparent dome shells protecting lush gardens and lacy structures. After a while the pilot adjusted their travel vector and all they could see was the endless terrain of reddish cliffs from which the city took its name.

Several times they passed unattended machines with tall sunflower-like solar arrays constructing surface structures. Like spiders on roller skates, the Freeform Additive Construction System (FACS) machines melted local soil and regolith and Contour-Crafted the mixture into thin layers to gradually build up walls one centimeter at a time. It was like building a house with homemade lava. Anyone could create a CAD model of a remote outpost, FAX it to the other side of the planet, and let the machines print the designs to completion before the occupants even arrived.

The flight lasted overnight, alternating between a rolling ground travel where possible, and the quicker hops that took them over the rougher valleys and canyons. More than once the machine stopped at an automated ISRU methane refueling station, and Carta listened as the pilot used an agency account to make payment for the fuel. 'ISRU' stood for In-situ Resource Utilization and was a term that meant 'living off the land' extracting metal out of rocks, or in this case making rocket fuel from thin air. The ISRU unit literally drew in carbon dioxide from the Mars atmosphere, combined it with breeder hydrogen, and the resulting methane mixture was captured into tanks. They met up with an overland paved road at one point running north and south, and Carta knew the road would normally take them south right into Novissima, had large portions of it not been destroyed by the x-ray storm's passing.

Carta directed the team to fly straight to the coordinates that directly opposed the point she had given Lenny in the north. It was an isolated spot, having just been visited by the x-rays the previous Sol-day.

Carta got the automatics to prep her suit. The crate deployed itself on the exterior of the vehicle, and an indicator light showed that the suit was ready to board. From the inside of the cabin, she opened the suitport hatch to reveal the suit cavity ready to jump in. Carta did a quick glance out the helmet to make sure there were no obstacles, and then climbed up on the donning seat that stretched across the opening. She let her legs dangle into the back of the suit, held onto the grab bar overhead, and slid right down into the legs. In one smooth motion she aimed her arms into the suit arms, and ducked into the helmet. Behind her the Personal Life Support System (PLSS) backpack closed and clicked into place, sealing the suitport hatch on the vehicle. One of the crewmen inside gave her an okay. She was ready to go.

Slowly Carta moved forward. Behind her the backpack disengaged from the suitport hatch and she could see the man waving through the window. The suit crate had transformed itself into a compact Extra-Vehicular Activity (EVA) porch complete with all the common tools she would need on most any mission. Carta attached the satellite phone to her com output and took the local radio and a high-powered laser. She stepped down onto the pockmarked surface.

Carta consulted her computer through the heads-up display in her helmet. She saw that a communications satellite would pass within range in two minutes, so she counted down the seconds.

"Lenny, can you read me?" she queried after dialing his number.

"Hello Lenny." she repeated a few seconds later.

Lenny's voice came online, "*Yes Carta I'm all set up.*"

"Okay hold on." Carta replied.

Before leaving the vicinity of the vehicle, Carta grabbed a precision leveler. Watching the positioning system on her heads-up display, Carta carefully walked overland, avoiding the larger holes that riddled the ground. When the positioning system signaled the right spot, she took the leveler and mounted it over one of the perfectly round holes, inserting the laser straight down. She turned on the laser and adjusted the leveler to be perfectly vertical.

"Lenny, get on the local radio handheld." Randall said.

She disconnected the satellite phone, and plugged her own short-wave radio into the com output.

"Lenny, can you hear me now?" Carta called over the short wave.

"*Yes, I can! I don't believe it!*" Lenny answered, "*But the sound moves in and out.*"

"Can you see my laser shining on the tarp?" Carta asked.

Lenny hesitated on the other end, "*No. Are you thinking the holes go all the way through the planet? What kind of crazy . . .*" but didn't finish the thought.

Finally, Carta got the hopper crew to lay a grid of sensors ten kilometers wide, moving in rows dropping them out the bottom of the vehicle.

"Okay I'm going to set some charges," she explained to the hopper crew, "Take the readings and run them through the 3D visualizer."

The charges went off in a timed manner, and Carta made her way back to the vehicle. The charges were designed to send shock waves deep underground, to allow them to detect subsurface structures. She backed up to the suitport until the backpack engaged, then went through all the steps to get back into the cabin.

An hour later Carta was on the phone with Lenny again. She was rotating a 3D ground truth image around on the screen, viewing it from various angles.

"Not only do the holes go all the way through the planet, but they all curve slightly in the same direction!" she said.

CHAPTER 8

Jacob Harrison was fuming mad. He couldn't believe Sachiko Hughes would do something so risky that was out of line from the regular research plan.

"Do you realize what we have here?" Sachiko implored, "Look what's happening out there. The x-ray storm is going to decimate our world, and we might have a means that could help stop it."

"You had no right to put everyone in danger like that!" Harrison argued.

The heads of department were in a meeting again, trying to figure out what happened.

Tom Hildebrandt spoke up, "It was me. I put her up to it."

"Hildebrandt? You?" was all he could say.

Hughes had been listening in the background, trying to figure things out. "What exactly happened? How did my wife put yellow paint on the machine going in the blue hole, and it still came out blue?" he asked.

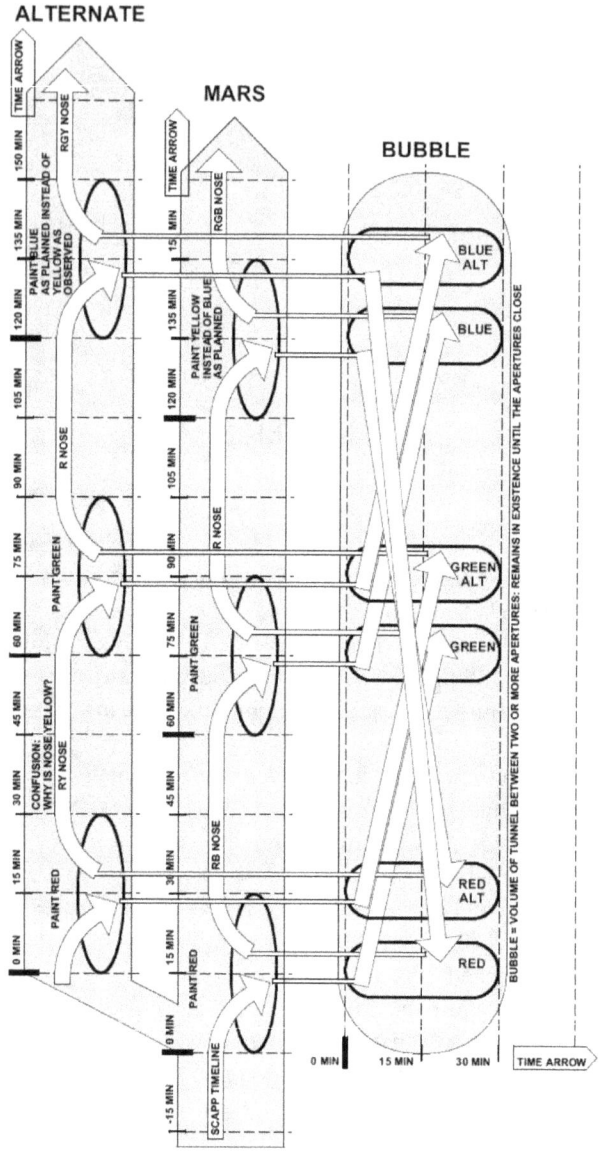

Figure 5: Three-hole Time Sortie: what actually happened

Harrison said, "Hard as it is to understand, Sachiko actually stumbled on something long suspected -- proof of a multiverse. The other set of red, green, and blue holes were from an alternate reality very similar to our own, except for a yellow mark." (**Figure 5**)

Sachiko chimed in, "The two realities continued their individual tests, but crossed over at one point -- in our universe, everyone was shocked that I painted the yellow spot, but in their universe, they had seen the yellow spot come out at the red hole, so they must have been just as shocked when the alternate Sachiko painted it blue. The two got mixed up. Apparently, the hyperspace bubble may have more apertures than what belongs to our own universe."

Hughes was still not satisfied, "Then why didn't we see more copies of the colored holes? It seems as though some alternate Sachiko could just as easily have painted other colors at other gates."

Harrison nodded, "Yes, you've gotten right to the heart of things. I'm angry Sachiko didn't consult anyone before trying her stunt, but we've learned three important things off of this. Apparently, time travel is possible number one; number two we still have our free will and paradoxes resolve themselves as alternate realities; and number three, only the most probable realities actually come into being."

Sachiko added, "You see, folks have been wondering about whether alternate realities meant that all possible permutations are worked out somewhere, like a block universe -- could there have been hundreds of me each with a unique shade of paint? For that matter, not only on the human scale of events, could there be quintillions of slightly different configurations of atoms had I used my left hand or right hand? The permutations are endless."

Harrison jumped in, "But only two scenarios emerged -- improbable events didn't even materialize. Perhaps Sachiko's mind could subconsciously work out two future scenarios and choose between them, giving each an alternate universe to calculate the causal consequences."

Hughes wondered, "So our Sachiko chose blue. Does the universe of the yellow-choosing Sachiko continue forever parallel to ours?"

Harrison shrugged, "Good question. If the yellow universe only existed for the sake of Sachiko's consciousness, to calculate causal options, you would think it wouldn't propagate past what is needful. But with quantum transactions and possibilities, perhaps it needs to go on forever to give the correct outcome here and now. Besides, how would an alternate universe causally come to an end? There's too much we don't know, and even given a time machine we may never have access to the answer."

Just then there was a commotion over by the door. Tom was surprised when Eva Landerman and Governor Wang walked in again with their entourage. The two came straight over to where the meeting was taking place.

"Dr. Harrison, Governor Wang has an important request to make of your team." Eva said.

The engineers and scientists around the table looked at each other quizzically -- it was quite unusual for someone so high up to make such a visit.

Governor Wang jumped right into his business, "As you know, two mysterious x-ray storms have been ravaging the planet, moving away from both poles. We have not yet been able to identify the cause of the destruction, nor how to stop it. It looks like the x-rays will continue to spiral down until every square meter has been affected. The storms surely mean the end of our world."

Gasps came from around the table. Rarely does a government leader speak so frankly about such things. For Tom Hildebrandt, who like everyone else had assumed the government had the situation under control, the news came somewhat as a shock. And he couldn't help but think there might be unstoppable nanoassemblers down there proliferating unchecked.

Wang continued, "After seeing your demonstration today, I think you folks have a means to find a solution."

Jacob spoke up, "How would we be able to help, sir?"

"You have proved that it is possible to go back in time. It may be that we could go back and discover what happened, or even prevent it." Wang proposed.

Hopeful thinking, Tom thought, *he must know the limitations of what we've discovered.*

Harrison shook his head, "We're able to travel back in time as far as the first aperture was created. Respectfully sir, we achieved the first wormhole after the storm had already hit."

Wang was unfazed, "I understand the way the technology works doctor. I have some information that you may not have considered."

Again, the group at the table looked at each other with curious stares. All Tom could do was shrug, and the person whom he thought knew the most about things was Sachiko, who was just as clueless as the rest.

Governor Wang motioned with his hand and one of his aides, Mark Tomes, set an electronic reader down on the table. The aide proceeded into a briefing.

"Similar 'atom smasher' research like that being done in this facility has been going on since the early 21st century, and maybe even before that," the aide began.

"Think back through the literature on experimental physics. Has there not been a time or two when someone somewhere has by chance instantaneously created a black hole? What about CERN or the Large Hadron Collider back on Earth?" the aide paused and looked around at all the faces at the table.

Tomes continued, "Even a century or so ago on Mars when the first colonies were being settled, one of the first things that a new planet would be useful for, it was thought, would be to perform dangerous experiments that might otherwise harm the mother world."

Tom thought back on the first accelerator on Mars, built at No Point -- it had been a disaster, apparently. There had been a big blow-up and not much was heard about it after that. Tom looked up and could see light dawning on the faces of Harrison, Sachiko, and some of the other physicists.

"Yes, you understand what I mean," the aide smiled at the knowing scientists, "There may be more apertures than you previously thought."

Tom looked at the aide a little closer – *surely, he was a physicist himself, retained on Wang's staff as an advisor*, he thought. Tomes was implying that some of those flashes of light observed at the beginning of the bubble could have been historical folks doing high-energy experiments. In the same way their own apertures all connected back to the start of the bubble, those old experiments would also have been like Singler Gates searching through time for a mate, starting at zero in the same hyper bubble universe. If that were the case, and they could figure out how to penetrate one of those older holes, their machine would emerge into a world decades, or even centuries before the x-ray trouble even began!

"We understand those old experiments were quite small in scale. You would have to figure out a way of perhaps prying open a mini aperture to make it traversable. But hopefully some of the classified documents in this reader will help." Tomes concluded.

Landerman thanked Dr. Harrison for his time and escorted the governor and his staff out of the facility, leaving a bunch of dumbfounded scientists and engineers.

Later that Sol-day the teenage Arden Tuttweiler came up to Tom with a frustrated look on his face.

"Dr. Hildebrandt sir," Arden began, always intimidated by the company president, "the toilet in the lab is stopped up again. I tried feeding the snake through the access pipe, but the stoppage might be deeper this time."

Maybe deeper than you know, Tom thought. The two of them headed down to the lab to view the situation. By the time they arrived there must have been close to 10 centimeters of foul-smelling liquid covering the floor. Several technicians in rubber boots were frantically clearing lower shelves to keep all the important equipment above the waterline. The look on Arden's face indicated that the boy knew that no matter how this clog got solved, he was the one that would be spending a untold hours cleaning up and scrubbing floors.

After donning boots himself, Hildebrandt gathered the team together with a potential solution, "Okay let's try poison. There must be some kind of poison that will work on organic nanoassemblers. Try to find something that won't harm the algae in the water revitalization system."

Two Sol-days later Hildebrandt walked into the Hyperaperture chamber to find a distraught Masamune Hughes.

"We've lost the SCAPP!" he reported.

Tom was shocked, "What happened?"

Hughes was trying to get over himself. Tom could see Carrie Johnson shaking in the background and longed to go to her.

"We went off to explore that large thing -- Tom I think it's a spacecraft, with heavy-duty propulsion systems! Carrie almost got caught in the air currents again. She took the SCAPP all the way around -- and boy I tell you," Hughes was getting excited, "that is one humongous vessel!"

"So how did you lose it?" Tom prodded.

Hughes got a perplexed look on his face, "Funny thing -- suddenly we lost video. Then all the telemetry leads went dead. But the unit is still drawing power."

Tom thought a minute then said, "Well, whatever you do, don't shut it down. Maybe we can insert some stereoscope through the wormhole tether and restore functions."

"The aperture has already shut down," Hughes noted, "So if we open up again, the clock will start all over -- there will be an operational lag between the SCAPP and the aperture."

Tom felt somewhat frustrated all of a sudden. They didn't even have a backup vehicle -- why would they be concerned about an operational lag?

Tom pointed out, "Well, just keep your eye on that wormhole tether. See if you can rig something up to peer through it."

Hughes agreed.

Later that afternoon Tom went to check on Jiro Kitamura's team who were working on third generation Hyperaperture magnets. They were huge.

"This will allow a 3m diameter SCAPP to pass through. But the black holes for this unit are much bigger -- they'll be competing with the Kasei --" Jiro corrected himself, forgetting that the non-Japanese weren't familiar with the term, "I mean Mars gravity vector."

"What do you mean?" Tom asked.

Jiro grinned as he explained, "Anyone in that room will feel a sideways tug -- you'll end up standing diagonally on the flat floor just trying to compensate."

Just then Hughes walked by.

"Oh Tom, we put a stereoscope through the tether -- I'm not sure I understand what's happening -- you'd better take a look." Masamune said.

Tom followed him over to where one of the little wormhole tether toroids was bolted to the floor next to a power grid transformer. A fat power cable came out of the transformer and disappeared into the little wormhole, along with dozens of other smaller cables and conduits. The acne-faced youthful trainee Arden Tuttweiler was poking the stereoscope through while looking up at a set of monitors.

Tom and Hughes paused in front of the screens. The internal structure of the SCAPP was visible, along with various avionics, electrical components, and pneumatic manifolds bolted to the crossbeams. Through the cracks Tom could see the edges of hover coils around the outside, and beyond that what should have been the blackness of the hyperspace void . . .

"What is that? Is that a room or something?" Tom squinted as if to see more clearly through the gaps in the structure.

Arden jumped up, suddenly realizing the big boss was watching him work.

Arden apologized, "Sir, there's not much room to get the stereoscope through there -- it keeps bumping into that manifold there."

Hughes encouraged the boy, "Keep working at it. See if you can twist around it."

Arden got back down and continued trying to feed the long tube into the limited gap on the toroid. The fisheye, low-resolution image on the screen jerked back and forth, and the little camera again and again bumped up against the aluminum manifold. Then without warning the camera gave, and Arden pushed it past the crosspieces and hover coils.

The scene that revealed itself on the monitors appeared to be inside a workshop of sorts, but Tom couldn't place it. Hughes and Arden just stared at the screen, dumbstruck. Tom could pick out clamps and tool clips that are normally used on zero-gee maintenance workstations.

Suddenly the image swung upward -- someone on the other end had grabbed the little camera and peered down its lens for an instant before everything went blank. Arden began a tug-of-war with whoever was on the other side, pulling at the stereoscope tube, and finally had to give up because of the other's superior strength. The tube was quickly pulled into the toroid until the control box and power unit hung up on the edge. The tube was yanked through so violently that it separated from the bulkier components leaving them to fall to the floor in a clatter.

Tom didn't know what to do, and Hughes seemed at a loss as well. White acrid foam began bubbling out of the toroid and building up on the floor -- the person on the other side was spraying something through the little aperture into their lab! *Surely that stuff can't be good for our health*, Tom thought.

Hughes must have been thinking the same thing because he yelled, "Shut it off! Shut down the power!"

In the millisecond it took for Arden to reach for and kill the power to the SCAPP and wormhole tether, Tom wondered if it were wise to just shut off the containment of two micro black holes orbiting each other at high speeds. But it was too late -- there was a crash as the toroid exploded and something shot off at blinding speeds through the wall of the workshop like a projectile. Tom heard almost instantaneous echoes of similar impacts as the wayward projectile crashed again and again through walls beyond, until it was too far away to be heard.

Without warning the alarm klaxon sounded signaling a pressure breach. Tom could hear the emergency pressure doors outside slam down and lock into place. *The thing has gone outside*, Tom thought. In his mind's eye he could picture Grindavik commuters stranded in small cells as the colony pressure system automatically evaluated and isolated the leak.

In the end, no one knew where the little black holes ended up. They had apparently continued to orbit each other initially, slowly getting flung apart by the tremendous rotation speed, but held in check by gravitational attraction. The little things sucked up matter as they impacted walls, floors or any solid object they came in contact with, and left perfectly cylindrical holes bored through like soft butter. Fortunately, no one had been in its path -- the investigators traced the holes through solid stone and figured they had flung themselves kilometers away out on the Martian landscape.

The foam turned out to be a fire-suppressant material and was harmless. But the question of who had stolen the SCAPP remained -- no one recognized the face captured briefly on the screen, and the workshop didn't resemble any in memory. Were there others building wormholes in other colonies? Or was that an alternative reality of their own lab? Perhaps no one would ever know. Tom had only one consolation -- whoever it was had the other wormhole tether toroid, and when the power shut off they too had probably experienced trouble. *Serves you right*, Tom thought.

That weekend Tom found himself sandwiched between Masamune Hughes and Jiro Kitamura watching the shuttle races out at the spaceport. Emi Toshige, Hiroyuki's pretty partner wife was there, as was Beth Kitamura the rover driver and pilot Carrie Johnson. The Toshige's had gotten them six prime tickets. Tom glanced over at Carrie and wished he could sit by her, but he had invited her as a business venture and none of the others knew he was interested in more than just engineering. Beth was also pilot rated, and Tom could hear the two women bickering about the finer points of piloting each time a new vessel shot up in the sky.

The six of them were sitting in the pressurized grandstands, looking out huge plate windows at the launching stations strewn over the blackened tarmac. Hughes likely would have brought Sachiko, but it was rumored that the grandstands received a higher dose of cosmic radiation than was healthy for pregnant women so she had stayed away this time.

The billowing dark clouds on the horizon caught Tom's eye for an instant. *Out there somewhere was that confounded x-ray storm, slowly creeping up on us, and nanoassemblers might be gobbling up the planet*, he thought as he stared out the windows at the Mars landscape. And here all these people are enjoying the races -- don't they know what's going on?

But Tom too forgot, as the excitement of the race impressed itself upon him. He couldn't help but thrill as a two-stage rocket-powered capsule launched upward with a deafening roar. The grandstands had been fitted with surround speakers, such that even the sounds passing through the thin carbon dioxide atmosphere outside were picked up and amplified. The purpose of the races was for each contestant to launch, reach orbit, dock with the buoy, and go through re-entry in as short a time as possible. There were extra points for smaller vessel size, fuel efficiency, speed, and several other categories, and demerits also.

Not good, Tom thought. This guy will have to get his first stage down safely as well. In a two-stage system, two rockets are stacked on top of each other -- the first stage on the bottom uses up all its fuel then jettisons leaving the second stage capsule to reach orbit with less mass to carry around. In the shuttle race rules, one couldn't just allow the spent first stage to come crashing down, but had to show it being recovered somehow.

Of course, only a portion of the race was actually visible to the race fans -- the die-hard fans followed their favorite competitors on monitors over many hours, and sometimes days. Fortunately for short attention span spectators like Tom, all the launches took place close together, which was the most fun part anyway.

"You're going to love this, Mas," Emi said, addressing Hughes, "I've been working on it for a year. The only thing that had been missing before was the wormhole tether for power."

A roughly aerodynamic vessel floated out onto the field. There was a cockpit toward the front, but Tom noticed bulk underneath deftly hidden by the design of the control surfaces. In four quarters could be seen rocket nozzles pointing downward that apparently swiveled like Vertical Take-Off and Landing (VTOL) thrusters.

Hughes gave a whistle and said, "Hoverpallet for passengers? What a beauty!"

The announcer's voice reverberated over the loudspeaker, *"This next entry is from Toshige Enterprises, a first-time entrant. The vessel's name is* Back Door Bandit. *Looks a little small for the whole race, so maybe the team wants to just show off their launch technique."*

The crowd around them broke out laughing and Tom could hear some of the folks jeering at the little thing. The Toshige craft was obviously way undersized compared to the other contestants with their massive chemical fuel tanks -- so small that one would think it was a rover or surface transport rather than something that could get to space. Tom felt sorry for Emi, until he looked over and saw her grinning. He knew that look, and knew that the woman had something up her sleeve.

The digital countdown clock got to zero, and a massive plume shot out of the four rocket nozzles catapulting the little craft up into the sky. Four or five gee takeoff, Tom wondered. The crowd watched in awe as the little capsule sustained thrust all the way up the flight path. No heavy propellant tanks, no stages to drop. In less than an hour the little vessel had achieved orbit and was at the buoy.

"They've got to refuel somehow." Tom heard Beth point out to Carrie.

Tom watched the live video of the activities taking place high above their heads. The docking went quickly, because they didn't have to worry whether the small buoy would pick up any momentum or not -- move in, soft capture, and close the gap just long enough for the two surface temperatures to equalize. Once the judges acknowledged docking complete, the vessel oriented itself to give the buoy a shove in the right orbit, and used the momentum to get itself on a homeward vector.

The four rocket nozzles fired, and within minutes the little craft had ridden its jets down to a gentle hover about a meter above the pavement. The clock stopped, and the crowd was completely silent -- even the announcer couldn't say a word.

Finally, the announcer sputtered out, "*It's official folks. Back Door Bandit has just broken the record. I've never seen anything like it folks -- this was not an incremental win -- it was three times as fast as the previous champion!*"

The crowd roared as they cried out their support for their new favorite. Tom looked over at Emi who had that vengeful look on her face.

"How did you do it?" Hughes asked as they walked toward the exit.

Emi who was a propulsion specialist replied, "It's our latest model. We came up with that one right after the wormhole tether was invented," she chuckled, "Remote unlimited hover power, and no need for propellant tanks if you can feed any amount of fuel through the wormhole directly to your combustion chamber."

Tom, Masamune, and Jiro looked at each other with big smiles from ear to ear -- *brilliant thinking,* Tom thought, *chalk another one up for that genius Murphy-conquering Toshige!*

Emi smiled and continued, "She is designed as a surface-to-orbit shuttle, but I thought you could use one."

Tom purchased two.

"We've graduated from probe to platform. I want these fitted out as crewed aperture penetrators. We'll call them Crew Operated Self-Contained Aperture Penetration Platforms, or COSCAPPs for short." Tom said with a chuckle.

A week or so later, Harrison held a meeting for heads of departments. The two COSCAPPs were already well on their way toward adaption as aperture entry vehicles. The scientists had been poring over old records and notes, and had made attempts to map flashes of light in the bubble universe videos with historical high-energy experiments.

"We've found a few early aperture candidates," Jacob began, "There were a few black hole collider experiments done on Earth back in the 21st century, and we think we know which of the hyperspace flashes match up with those."

The engineers and scientists around the table babbled with excitement -- no one really expected such opportunities to actually be found, but there they were, right in the hyperspace bubble within reach.

"Unfortunately, the observation chambers used in those days were quite small. We've had to eliminate them from the list," Harrison was quick to add, "However, the experiments at No Point in the early Mars days used very large chambers. We've done some research, and it might be possible to use hovercoils to expand the holes and insert one of the COSCAPPs."

Tom looked over at Hughes who had a big grin on his face. The poor engineer had been pushing his team well past any reasonable expectation, and they were getting close to finishing one of the crewed vessels, with the second one close behind.

"I would like to design and build a new 'Seed Hyperaperture' that could be carried on board one of the COSCAPPs and installed at the other end on arrival, providing a door back in time 65 years earlier." Harrison proposed, "The 'Seed Hyperaperture' should be a compact, foldable device that fits through the door of the COSCAPP and can be taken anywhere. Just pull it out, set it up, and turn it on."

Tom frowned -- Hyperaperture hardware was massive, and required incredible amounts of power. It would be quite a challenge to figure out how to design some compact, deployable 'seed' unit that could fit through a man door.

But the murmur among the team members quickly drowned out Dr. Harrison as excited speculation passed back and forth. The third generation Mark III toroid Hyperaperture was already under construction behind them in the big chamber, with it's huge donut hole. Tom couldn't help but notice that in addition to a new ultra-thick foundation, all the work platforms and observation room had been outfitted with two-point carriages -- large swinging platforms -- that would be able to passively settle into their own local vertical once the large black holes had been installed into the new device. These things were just getting bigger and bigger. How do you miniaturize something like that?

"Analyzing the video from previous visits, it's clear that some of the machines we've seen in the hyperspace bubble are likely COSCAPP vessels performing various experiments." Sachiko informed the team, "We've even observed what appears to be a COSCAPP entering the No Point aperture from 65 years ago, hinting at our eventual success."

The whole team broke out in applause at the good news.

"We'd better not congratulate ourselves yet -- that may not be us, but a team from an alternate universe. Remember, we still have free will to mess this up if we're not careful." Sachiko cautioned.

The group around the table put on a more sober atmosphere. Nevertheless, it was heartening when Hughes scheduled time on the Hyperaperture the following week, right after the construction was to be completed -- two quick tests of penetration using one of the new COSCAPP vessels.

After the meeting Tom followed Hughes back to Hildebrandt Engineering. Instead of going in through the shop floor, Hughes led him up the short flight of stairs leading to the overlook that the curious public sometimes visited to see what their firm was about. There were large observation windows that looked down on the shop floor.

"Sachiko sometimes brings Teresa and Sabby here waiting for me to get off work," Hughes said.

He pulled out a journaler and handed it to Tom.

Masamune smiled and said, "They've been so busy lately, I want to take a quick video to show the kids what we've got."

Tom began shooting the video as Hughes walked over to raise the shutters on the big windows. Hildebrandt Engineering was spread out below them, with all the lathes, mills, and automated manufacturing equipment working away around the clock. Hughes had gone downstairs and was now standing next to one of the new COSCAPP vessels as it hovered on the shop floor. Toshige had given them two vessels they had named '*Infinity's Breach*' and '*Towa Maru*', the latter of which apparently also had something to do with 'infinity' or 'eternity' in Japanese. Tom zoomed in as Hughes opened the side hatch and climbed inside. A minute or so later, Hughes could be seen waving from the cockpit. What a gorgeous machine! Toshige had designed a double hull that hid the hovercoils covering the outside with a thin shiny metal skin. Tom stopped the video recording and climbed down the stairs to join Hughes on the factory floor.

On the day of the COSCAPP test, a gleaming *Towa Maru* hovered a few centimeters off its sway platform in the Hyperaperture chamber. The vehicle was listing to one side, tipped at an angle. As Tom looked around the room, a queer perspective showed multiple sway platforms all leaning inward so that the people in the room stood at a diagonal at their workstations -- the tremendous gravity from the black holes in the new Hyperaperture Mark III made each person's apparent local gravity vector different from anyone else.

There were no VTOL rocket nozzles on the *Towa Maru* -- the craft wouldn't have fit through the new aperture if it did. Instead, small clusters of compressed air attitude control thrusters were located at strategic locations on the hull, all fed by wormhole tether pneumatic hoses. But the best part was the propulsion system -- in place of chemical thrust rockets, Emi Toshige had come up with a control algorithm that pulsed the hovercoils to take advantage of nearby gravity wells. And with so many apertures available in the hyperspace bubble, there were many of those to choose from -- pairs of singularities at each of the open gates would provide all the gravity points they would need.

Dr. Toshige stood to Tom's left, admiring the team's handiwork.

"So, the nominal crew is four, but it can carry two short term passengers?" Tom asked.

Dr. Toshige replied in the affirmative, "We're hoping to market the vessel not only as an orbital shuttle, but also as a short sortie support craft that can stay away on missions of a few months at a time." he said.

The Toshige's had a film crew inside the vessel making publicity shots of the living quarters, galley, cockpit, and cramped work areas. The company hoped to use these initial flight tests to make an impression on investors. After the coup at the races, the phone was ringing off the hook.

"We've stocked up the galley for the cameras, and will be narrating the whole sequence." Hiroyuki added.

Just then Jacob Harrison called everyone's attention on the floor, "Okay, the first sequence will begin in a few minutes. In the first test, I only want Beth inside at the controls. The other passengers can board later for the second test."

The countdown began, and Beth Kitamura, who had been training with Carrie to pilot the new vehicles, walked in wearing a pressure suit with the helmet under her arm. Two technicians helped her put on the helmet and check out the suit. Tom shook his head in amazement -- that woman would go down in history as the first living flesh to ride through a wormhole into hyperspace -- after Hughes' arm of course.

Beth boarded the *Towa Maru* and the hatch was secured. Tom saw the donut hole of the Hyperaperture start to cloud up and fade, then a velvet black opening stood there, crisp in the artificial lighting. Overhead, monitors showed multiple views of Beth's face, the scene outside the cockpit, the control panel, and *Towa Maru* passenger cabin interior.

When Harrison gave the go-ahead, Beth raised the vessel, aligned it with the center of the hole, and slipped right through. The entire room erupted in applause as history was made.

On the screens, Beth's face showed happy as can be, and she turned the craft around and came right back out again in under two minutes. The atmosphere was gay, but there was still urgency in the air -- Tom couldn't forget the escaped nanoassemblers turning the planet into Swiss cheese, or that x-ray storm that was already spiraling its way halfway to the equator. They would need to redouble their efforts, and figure out how to get large numbers of people through an unknown wormhole sixty-five years earlier . . .

Beth stayed in her seat as the other five passengers boarded the craft. On its inaugural run, Hiroyuki and Emi Toshige, Masamune and Sachiko Hughes, and Beth's husband Jiro would have the pleasure of the first ride -- symbolically three couples showing how the team was working to save humanity -- to be recorded in the publicity videos. Sachiko gave Teresa a hug and stepped aboard, followed by Hughes and the others.

The wormhole opened up again and Tom could see several hands waving through the portholes and cockpit. Monitors overhead also showed the five passengers waving from different perspectives. On signal, Beth again raised the craft and hovered gently through the center of the opening. Tom felt a little melancholic as he watched the tail end disappear through the hole. Little did he realize that he would never see his friends again.

As if in a daze, Tom listened to Dr. Toshige's voice as he narrated the experience for the cameras. It was only three minutes into the test when Carrie caught his eye -- she was wearing headphones at her workstation trying to get his attention. *Not now*, Tom thought, *let's get these folks back safely*.

Carrie persistently signaled so Tom wandered over to her side.

"Tom, there's something wrong." Carrie had long since dropped the formal 'sir'.

Hildebrandt could see everything going okay in the videos -- nothing amiss as far as he could tell.

Carrie looked at her data feed monitor and said, "There's a power drop somewhere."

Beth was flying around other vessels out there, and it was almost possible to see faces through the portholes as identical *Towa Marus* or future flights of the *Infinity's Breach* whizzed this way and that through the void.

Tom looked down at the screen and saw the power dip -- it was the pulse propulsion system.

"Not critical, Carrie, I think you just need to reboot the system -- tell Beth to stay on air thrusters for a while until the reboot finishes." Tom advised.

Toshige's voice could be heard over the loud speakers, "*Strange how all those vehicles seem to go out of their way to approach us -- they wave heartily. It must be in reverence for our milestone first flight.*"

Carrie communicated the problem to Beth, who was using air thrusters anyway, and started the reboot.

Toshige excitedly exclaimed, "*Look at those fellows, trying to send out a harpoon. Watch it Beth! What in the world is their experiment?*"

By the sound of Hughes' voice in the background, Tom could tell he was extremely curious about what happened to their lost SCAPP, "*Beth point over there,*" and, "*Is that our SCAPP?*" and, "*Swing around the big structure and see if our SCAPP is there.*"

Tom knew that eventually, they would figure out where the thing went and which wormhole it had disappeared into because history replayed itself over and over again every time they opened a new aperture.

"*Look at the size of that thing!*" Toshige's voice narrated the flyby of the huge floating spacecraft, or whatever it was.

Carrie looked up at Tom and said, "Beth is experiencing turbulence -- it's those air currents."

Tom advised, "Tell her to get out of there. Come back to our own aperture."

Beth's voice suddenly rang out, "*We're being pulled toward that big aperture the huge spacecraft came out of -- give me my propulsion back!*"

Carrie looked up and shook her head -- the reboot was almost complete, but not quite.

Tom snatched the headphones away from Carrie and yelled, "Get out of there now! Beth, use all your air thrusters!"

But it was too late. The *Towa Maru* slid faster and faster toward the massive hole. Electric arcs seemed to be flying wild. The overhead monitors in the observation room piped back video showing lots of small debris swept up in the air current, with motionless machines floating passively in the background. Suddenly the screen showed the *Towa Maru* slip past the aperture threshold, and all the other vessels could not be seen anymore.

An alarmed Hughes' voice could be heard in the background, "*What the hell is that?!*"

Then there was a bright flash and everything went black -- all the video feeds showed void data.

"Beth!" Tom called.
"Come in *Towa Maru*!" Tom repeated his plea.
Nothing -- no response.

CHAPTER 9

Sixty-five years ago, a white-masked young man peered through a narrow circular opening where a polished conduit stretched off to eternity. In the distance Yu Gao could see a glow, and expectantly waited until he could hear the steady hum of electric motors. A robotic inspector unit slowly approached in a stop-go rhythm as it scanned the walls of the conduit.

"There we go *Little Pang*," Gao called to the machine in Putongwa Mandarin as he reached for the manual control handles, "Come to papa."

Hai Qi, a second masked youth chuckled, "Why do you call it *Xiao-Pang*, it makes no sense."

In Putongwa 'xiao' meant 'little', and 'pang' meant 'obese'.

"He holds everything up around here. Have you ever seen such a small machine with so much ego?" Gao replied.

Qi knew that outside dozens of scientists were waiting for the inspections to end so they could continue with their tests. It was practically the only time the two of them got much attention around here.

Gao turned off the unit and disconnected it from its umbilical. Careful not to damage the side of the conduit, Gao lifted *Little Pang* and was about to place it in the case Qi held out for him.

"Wait! Don't put the inspection device away yet!" Gao heard the voice of Liang Zhou, the head physicist call from outside.

Gao paused with the little robot dangling over the case, and peered into Qi's eyes. *What does she want now*, his expression showed.

Zhou instructed, "Put it through the other side, just a couple of meters."

Qi took the case to the side as Gao tiptoed around him in his 'bunny boots', which were special white foot coverings designed to protect the machines and instruments. Gao twisted himself into the right position and carefully inserted the robot, waiting as the operator outside moved the device back and forth in a few passes through the tube. Finally, the pair were able to button up the operation and put the machine in its case. Qi carefully walked over to the access port and handed it back through to waiting hands. More hands appeared to help lift the two fellows out of the chamber.

Gao looked around the room as he shed his bunny boots. He stood on top of a catwalk that ran the perimeter of the combustion chamber and watched Qi get pulled up out of the hole behind him. The chamber was a large standing cylinder with dozens of instrument ports protruding out in all directions. On the floor below, a crowd of technicians looked up and watched the crew seal the access hatch. It was a high bay with various levels of scaffolding -- much similar to many of the other linear accelerator facilities he had worked in over the years. This facility however was trying to achieve sustained matter-antimatter combustion for power generation. Zhou stood among the scientists on the floor, and instructed some of the technicians to swap out detectors and cameras to observe positron paths from high-speed collisions.

Qi took the *Little Pang* over to the maintenance workstation and began to recalibrate the various scanners. In the background, Gao could see technicians scurrying back and forth as they got the accelerator ready for another test. He stepped outside and walked down the hall to his cubicle, and began to analyze the scanner data.

Just then Xiaoyu Lin walked by and smiled. What a beauty! Gao kept a straight face and admired the petit office manager as she disappeared around the corner -- no one could tell the passion he felt for her, had they been watching.

An hour later Gao could feel the accelerator start up. It was almost as if the room were throbbing with power. He could imagine particles colliding and traces of positrons shooting off in all directions until they annihilated with an electron. Then he imagined sweet Xiaoyu walking toward him with a smile -- gently swinging this way and that. Nature's true power . . .

Without warning, Gao's vision burst. Qi had run in from the corridor all excited.

"Black hole!" Qi exclaimed, "They've formed a black hole!"

CHAPTER 10

The mood was solemn for days after the *Towa Maru* disappeared. Three organizations lost some of their best people -- for such a risky operation Tom Hildebrandt couldn't get over how foolish and overconfident they'd been. Murphy seemed alive and well. And those poor children! Teresa Hughes continued to do her training down at the accelerator, religiously dropping off little brother Saburo on her way and picking him up afterwards. Tom even checked in on the elder brother Ichiro once to see how they were managing at home. The poor family had gone through a lot, losing their second brother years earlier, and now not knowing whether their parents would get back alive.

"What about the 'Seed Hyperaperture' device Dr. Harrison spoke about? Weren't they carrying one of those?" Teresa had asked at one point.

Smart girl, Tom thought. "We're still trying to figure out how to build one of those seed units. Your parents couldn't include one on their mission yet. We can only test one thing at a time my dear."

Then those stormy eyes pierced through Tom as she looked up at him, and they would haunt him many nights to come, "And the wormhole tether?" she asked.

The wormhole tether indeed -- continuing to draw power as if the machine were operating normally, even after they had shut down the Hyperaperture. Carrie Johnson monitored the *Towa Maru* telemetry feeds and reported that she could see patterns of thrustering, propulsion, and maneuvering, but communications had been lost. Tom assumed they were still out there somewhere trying to get back, but he didn't have an answer for the little girl.

After the *Towa Maru* had disappeared, they had left the aperture open for several Days, until all the vehicles in the bubble had returned to their respective homes. One by one the holes shut down until only the massive machine remained out there, floating in a void between two isolated apertures. It was the longest they had ever done so, and eventually they would call the mission Prime A. It was a lonely scene that Tom would never forget.

After that Jacob Harrison sent the *Infinity's Breach* out on several occasions, since each time they reopened the Hyperaperture the clock restarted back at the beginning. Tom himself served on the crew a few times as they watched that fateful trip of the *Towa Maru* and saw it fall into the wormhole again and again. They would do close flybys waving their hands through portholes trying to convince the others to turn back, but all they could do was to watch Hughes and Toshige smile back at them as if it were nothing more than a friendly hello. Once they even tried to harpoon the other craft, only to see the *Towa Maru* dodge the missile and continue on.

In the end Dr. Harrison called off the rescue attempts, consigned to the fact that even though multiple alternate universes may exist, it was likely harder to derail the most probable future than anyone imagined.

Tom continued to mull over the design of a Seed Hyperaperture unit. Since the Mark III was installed and functioning, Hildebrandt Engineering began to put all its work force on the problem -- figuring out how to attach a wormhole tether, fold up lightweight magnets, and get the black hole containment system to work.

It was during this time that the love between Tom and Carrie blossomed. They would go through hours of intense operations with *Infinity's Breach*, and steal away in the evenings to console each other, ending up in an embrace looking out at Mars' stunning sunset behind some glassed-in overlook. It felt like the end of the world -- the x-ray storm was slowly approaching over the horizon causing all sorts of weather anomalies, and even occasional earthquakes (*or should we say mars quakes*, Tom thought). Yet it also felt like a new beginning -- they had hope that penetration of the sixty-five-year-old hole would be successful and they would find themselves in a new world.

Twice Tom watched as the inhabitants of distant colonies friendly to Grindavik had been shuttled in before their homes had been consumed by the mysterious x-rays and riddled with holes. Drexler' goo was coming true right before their eyes. Grindavik had been temporarily overwhelmed as everyone rushed to find housing for the new occupants. The general contracting firm Kajima was hard at work preparing fast-track facilities. Underground digital excavators were put to work hollowing out dozens of new tunnels to provide space for them. Hydroponic gardens and power plants had been hastily constructed to take care of the refugees.

Even if they were successful opening up a gate into the past, how would they be able to evacuate all those people before the x-ray storm hit? Tom even wondered about that in his sleep, dreaming about crowds of people passing through a wormhole without the need of a COSCAPP machine.

As if following his dream, Hildebrandt Engineering partnering with Dr. Harrison's group came up with a deployable walk-thru wormhole and tested it as folks lined up in one room, passed through the aperture, and exited three kilometers away in a warehouse. The new unit consisted of extremely lightweight, folding magnets set in a ring, with a slim-line SCAPP-like fixed tube tunnel to shield folks from the gravity fields incurred by orbiting black holes. The unit could be carried by a small hoverpallet and set up on a smooth floor surface by two persons. All that needed to be done was to un-stack the magnets, stiffen up the support ring, unfold the shield tube and begin the startup sequence. A special wormhole tether provided power, and a pair of black holes ejected through the tether from a containment field in Grindavik were accelerated into the magnets until spacetime warping occurred. If one wanted to set up a Singler Gate that connected with the bubble universe, a pair of unique singularities would be passed through when the Seed unit charged up. Alternatively, if one wanted an exclusive Dualer Gate with only one tunnel to a specific mate, entangled singularities would be passed through. Once mating is achieved between two separated apertures, a person simply walked through the shield tube and emerged through to the other side, wherever that may be. For the first prototype, the team had to scavenge for parts in the Hildebrandt Bunker, and deal with nanoassembler-clogged plumbing. Once the Seed Hyperaperture device design was ready to go, Hildebrandt Engineering began full-scale manufacturing of multiple units.

After the latest battle with the plumbing system, Tom was up to his eyeballs with frustration -- with his former confidant Hughes missing, he had to bring Harrison on board with the nanoassembler issue. He pulled the scientist aside and explained the situation.

Harrison was shocked, "Are you telling me runaway self-replicating nanoassemblers originating from your lab have been destroying the planet?"

The way Jacob's gaze pierced through his soul made Tom feel like a mad scientist who was guilty of mass destruction.

"Think about it Tom," Harrison's expression softened, "Why hasn't Grindavik been lacerated, even if your lab is the source? And how many nanoassemblers do you know of that give off x-rays?"

Tom stood dumbfounded as the scientist walked away. He wasn't sure Harrison understood Drexler's warning -- the world was getting eaten away and nanoassemblers were out there loose. What else could it be?

There has to be some way to stop those things, he thought. Maybe there was some sort of software command they could send to stop the little monsters from self-replicating. Tom made a mental note to check the frequency of the wireless control signal when he got a chance.

"Okay, so let's say *Infinity's Breach* successfully expands the No Point hole and the crew sets up the Seed Hyperaperture unit," Tom began one day at a meeting of all the department heads, "How big was No Point back in those days anyway -- was there enough room for all these people?"

It was Grindavik Colony President Howard Statner who spoke up. He had gotten in the habit of attending some of their meetings with accelerator director Eva Landerman.

Statner explained, "The No Point colony itself was quite small, just large enough to support the Chinese research staff and their families. However, nearby Pointless had more amenities. We're also developing small excavators and seed infrastructure that can quickly be passed through to begin setting up hydroponics, power, and other resources for a large community."

Harrison added, "And remember, we have all the time in the world to set things up once we're there."

"But all these people," Tom protested, "They won't be able to wait that long."

"Tom, you're not thinking four dimensionally," Jacob explained, "Let's say we deliver a Seed Hyperaperture unit and set it up sixty-five years ago at No Point. Immediately that initial team, maybe a small number of specialists, can then take a year or two to construct tunnels, facilities, and infrastructure for additional gates. Let's say they have ten additional gates that they can put online. Over there it took two years, but on this end, we can start up those ten addition gates only an hour after *Infinity's Breach* team penetrates the No Point hole!"

Landerman broke in, "And we don't need to stop there. Those ten gates could bring over major construction crews and excavators to build very big facilities and hundreds more gates, say three years after the first ten come online. So where five years passes on that end, in a matter of hours we could have hundreds of gates operational here for our folks to pass through to ready and waiting new homes."

"But if such a big facility were constructed sixty-five years ago, why don't we know about it in our history books?" Tom countered.

Stanton answered, "There are two reasons. First, the No Point activities were quickly covered up by the government sixty-five years ago -- we haven't a clue about what happened after that. And secondly, investigators have reported vast underground cities capable of supporting millions of people, all abandoned before the x-ray storms began. Some of those underground facilities were found near No Point and Pointless before the storm devoured the region."

"But where did all those people go?" Tom asked.

No one could answer him.

It was only the next week that something happened that would change Tom's perspective forever. He said goodbye to Carrie in the Hyperaperture observation room and gave her a hug. It was going to be a multi-Sol-day mission, where they planned to keep the aperture open for a week of observations. Seed Hyperaperture units were safely under production and Tom had joined the *Infinity's Breach* crew at the last minute to perform long-term experiments setting up distant secondary wormholes.

"I'll be back soon dear." Tom whispered as he walked toward the vessel boarding platform.

Carrie looked up at him with those eyes that he could not resist, "I know, I'll get on com whenever my shift is up."

They embraced, and Tom held the girl tightly as he looked across the vast chamber. The massive Mark III Hyperaperture was confined to one side of the room, the only neatly organized part of the chamber -- construction had already begun on expanding the underground volume, and several new compact Seed Hyperaperture devices were set up. Tom could see dozens of additional sockets waiting for units to be installed, and knew that a lot more were planned in preparation for the big evacuation.

The new units were highly portable, could be pushed around easily using a small hoverpallet, and were designed to slip through the door of *Infinity's Breach. Somewhere*, Tom thought, *dozens of miniature wormhole tethers connected back to the Grindavik grid to power all those remote tremendous loads.*

"It's okay -- not like you'll be out of touch." Carrie pointed out.

"I know," Tom whispered, "I just feel nervous for some reason."

Carrie walked him to the *Infinity's Breach* entry hatch where others of the crew were also getting ready. Tom slipped inside and waved back through the door. There were two Seed Hyperaperture devices all stowed and folded up out of the way. When the rest of the crew boarded, Tom could see Carrie through the porthole as she monitored their flight.

The trip through the aperture into hyperspace proceeded without incident, and the *Infinity's Breach* began their mission. The first task was to find a spot well out of the way, and perform an EVA, or extravehicular activity. Two specially trained crewmembers donned pressure suits and accompanied one of the Seed Hyperaperture units out the airlock in the microgravity environment -- locking their boots onto the hull, the two assembled the unit and created a Dualer wormhole tunnel gate. Technicians in the lab stood near its mate and passed a series of microSCAPP probes back and forth to the suited crewmembers to make sure the tunnel was intact. It was like playing catch between two universes. Then the seed unit was disassembled and stowed back inside *Infinity's Breach*.

They also tested the gravity pulse drives. Emi Toshige's invention only worked where there were gravity wells in the area, either a planet or something else that generated sufficient gravity waves. The small black holes framing each of the dozens of apertures in the bubble turned out to work fine. Surprisingly, the great drifting spacecraft registered as having the largest gravity well of all -- perhaps using black holes in its propulsion system.

Tom communicated back with Carrie whenever he got a chance, and the crew began feeling a bit homesick. It was during one of Carrie's supposed shifts that Tom began to suspect something was wrong. Carrie was acting strange, a little tense as if she were under pressure.

"Anything wrong?" Tom asked.

"Everything is fine sir," Carrie replied formally, as if there were no feelings between them.

Tom played along, "Give me a report of the SCAPP interface."

The SCAPP interface had been mothballed weeks earlier due to upgrades, but Carrie jumped right in and began describing parameters as if the interface were right in front of her in operational mode.

"Okay thanks," he replied.

Tom became quite concerned -- the only explanation he could think of was that someone was there with her and she could not talk freely. Damn you, Murphy!

"Guys, there's something wrong. I think there is trouble back at the observation room." Tom warned the other crewmembers.

All sorts of scenarios popped into his head. Had someone forcefully entered the lab? More than ever, Tom wished they had a phone connection that would allow them to patch into an emergency channel. Up until that point, there had been no real need for any security in Grindavik, since nothing happened other than petty crimes. He recalled a brief news article he had heard about corpses found in Novissima before the explosion, drained of blood. Was Carrie in danger?

"Carrie, I need some more data on the health of one of our magnets." Tom said, trying to keep a conversation going more than anything else.

There was no reply.

"Carrie!" Tom called, but there was no answer.

The rest of the crew was looking at him in alarm.

"Abort! We've got to abort the mission!" Tom cried.

The pilot was already turning around and heading for their own aperture. Tom was sick with worry.

The *Infinity's Breach* exited the aperture and settled in on its loading platform. There was a strange silence as Tom opened the hatch and stepped out into the vast Hyperaperture chamber -- not a soul could be seen anywhere. Tom and the others fanned out looking for the missing technicians.

Two minutes later there was a blood-curdling scream as one of the female crewmembers looked down on the floor behind a desk near the new construction. Tom saw the woman back away nodding her head, and rushed over to see what was the matter.

What happened next Tom would never quite remember. The whole world started to spin and time stood still. He could see the scene unfolding in slow motion before his eyes as blood rushed to his head. His worst nightmare had been realized. There on the floor were three bloodless corpses, and Carrie was one of them.

Tom fainted.

CHAPTER 11

Several hundred years in the future, an interstellar freighter was about to leave a distant star system but something went wrong. What should have been a routine flight ended up with the ship getting lost -- the Navigator had no idea where they were.

"Do you see Bridgestar anywhere?" the Captain asked the Navigator.

The Navigator looked over all his displays. Billions of sensors, arrays, antennas, and cameras funneled untold terabytes of information into an intuitive user interface giving complete situational awareness. The Navigator also knew how to select among the raw data and had attached his own hack piggyback processors that showed more than the original design allowed.

"I see dozens of small spacecraft all over the place, but no Bridgestar." the Navigator replied.

"Spacecraft?" the Captain asked.

The Navigator looked at the readouts, "They look like primitive probes and they all seem to be identical. There's something more worrisome than that -- I can't find any stars at all."

The Captain's eyes widened, "No stars! Any gravity wells at all?"

The Navigator seemed perplexed, "I don't understand this. There are dozens of very weak point sources, nothing greater than a small asteroid. Our interstellar drive is the largest gravity well I can see."

"What about long distance sensors?" the Captain asked.

"That's just it sir," the Navigator began, "there is no long distance. Anything I send out comes back to us again"

"What does that mean?" the Captain had a puzzled look on his face.

"Well, the sensor beams head out and curve back in on themselves." the Navigator checked the readings again, "Sir, I think we are in an enclosed microverse -- it's a self-contained bubble of space!"

The Captain half floated, half leaped over to the Navigator's workstation in the peculiar low gravity of the ship. A microverse?

"Can we play back our approach? We paid the fees -- how did Bridgestar get us here?" the Captain complained.

The Navigator sent the commands through the console, and multiple video displays materialized in midair above the pilot workstation. The entire cabin disappeared and the two men were huddled at their controls in the middle of a vast surround projection.

The sequence from the last few minutes began to replay, including audio from communications. There in front of them was Bridgestar, an artificial satellite around the local sun. From this distance the Captain could only see a bright point of light, but when he magnified the replayed image he could see the constantly evolving, morphing surface. Thousands of modular robotic squares and triangles flip-flopped end over end, tumbling over others of their own kind set into a lattice structure of sorts -- the Captain knew the tumbling modules were constantly updating and swapping out replacements in the lattice, eternally keeping the station brand new and operational, like cells in a body. That distant image was coming on them fast as they approached the station at tremendous speeds.

The Captain listened as Bridgestar asked for their destination. The station was completely robotic, with artificial intelligence responding to their inquiries.

"Mars," he heard his own recorded voice reply.

The Bridgestar artificial intelligence responded, "*Mars is off limits, we cannot create a gate for you to Mars* "

The Captain had expected the answer. Bridgestar held dozens if not hundreds of wormhole gates in its library, each perpetually maintained and connected to distant star systems. An identical morphing Bridgestar space station orbited each of those other stars as well, maintaining the other ends of a complex web of wormhole gates. The gates were preserved at the nano scale, and expanded on demand to allow ships passage quickly between worlds.

"Do you have Mars in your library?" the Captain heard himself ask.

"*Yes, but it is off limits to anyone from this system. The inhabitants of Mars have requested that no one be allowed passage from this system.*" Bridgestar replied.

The Captain and his crew had used Bridgestar to travel to several other stars before, and the answer had always been the same -- no passage to Mars allowed from any of those systems. Their dream of setting up trade with the rich Martian system had been thwarted time and again.

But this time was different -- they now had an interstellar. The Captain had patted the pilot console of their massive freighter and smiled -- an interstellar was independent of the Bridgestar wormhole network. An interstellar drive used pairs of co-orbiting black holes to create a bubble of warped spacetime around the ship, shrinking the universe in front and expanding space behind until the vessel reached its destination. The black holes in the drive were so massive that the ship could never land on the surface of a planet, but had to remain in orbit using smaller shuttlecraft to ferry cargo and crew. Those black holes gave them a small bit of gravity in the ship environment.

"We don't know where Mars is," the Navigator had pointed out, "How do we get there using the ship's drive?"

The Captain had asked the station, "Are there exceptions to the Mars travel ban?"

Bridgestar replied, "*Yes, some ships are allowed based on their registry.*"

The Captain smiled at the time and replied, "Bridgestar, check our registry, you'll see that we should be allowed passage."

At that point the Navigator had transmitted the ship registry data over to Bridgestar.

The Captain knew what the answer would be -- Bridgestar came back with the reply, "*Your registry is quite old, but it checks out.*"

The station then quoted the passage fee, which was for the Captain and his crew to provide a certain quantity of hemoglobin for Bridgestar's nanoassemblers -- a resource the station apparently was unable to produce for itself on the dozens of supply moons it maintained. Most ships drew blood from their crews early in the voyage to build up the amount required for the passage, but the Captain maintained a supply on board for just that purpose.

The Captain had smiled at the Navigator and his other top officers. *Mars, here we come*, he thought. The Captain and Navigator watched on magnified optics as the morphing Bridgestar quickly used those tiny tumbling squares and triangles to construct a massive toroid or conduit just big enough for their gigantic vessel to slip through -- the micro wormhole gate that Bridgestar preserved in its library would be expanded to fit that conduit, and the Captain knew that on the Mars side an identical sized conduit was currently being constructed to allow their exit.

"*Freighter, this is Bridgestar,*" the station had called.

The Captain listened to the playback of himself acknowledging, "Go ahead Bridgestar."

The station then said, "*Freighter, you have an interstellar drive. We don't recommend interstellar drives through the gates.*"

The recorded Captain asked, "Please explain."

Bridgestar replied, "*The singularities used in interstellar drives are sometimes known to influence the function of the wormhole. There have been cases where gates have closed without warning, and the ship did not achieve passage. We recommend that you use your interstellar drive to get to Mars, instead of the wormhole network.*"

The recording displayed a blank as the Captain had considered what to do, then he replied, "We don't know the route or Mars coordinates. Can you tell us?"

The station returned, "*This station does not have the navigational data for routes through interstellar space.*"

"In that case we will take our chances and continue the passage." the Captain replied.

"*Very well,*" replied the station, "*you do so at your own risk.*"

The Captain stopped the recording. The cabin materialized around them and the monitors disappeared. He looked at the Navigator.

"Do you suppose this is an effect of the interstellar drive influencing the wormhole?" the Navigator asked.

But the Captain just stared at his navigator deep in thought. They were interrupted by one of his other officers in the next room.

"Captain, take a look at this!" the Officer exclaimed.

The man floated / leaped into the control cabin and settled at the com workstation. An image was forming on the screen -- a small vessel floated in the void outside among all the others. It was a new type, slightly larger than the probes they had seen earlier. Vessels and probes could be seen moving in and out of bright circles of light.

"Wormholes! There must be dozens of gates out there," the Captain exclaimed, "Capture one of those probes and see how it works!"

"Aye, Captain," one of the crew hurried off.

But the Officer was still fiddling with the video controls, trying to zoom in on one of the larger vessels, "You've got to see this, Captain." he implored.

The image of the craft filled the screen and all three men let out a gasp. They knew that vessel well!

"The *Towa Maru*! But what is it doing here?" the Captain wondered.

The *Towa Maru* was an ancient relic that had been handed down and preserved for many generations. No one knew how many hundreds of years old the legendary vessel was.

"There are lots of identical ones out there, Captain -- must be the same kind of vessel," the Officer proposed.

Without warning the com sounded -- there was a call coming in. The Officer, closest to the controls responded, "This is the bridge, go ahead."

A face came on the screen and again the men gasped -- it was the Captain, or should we say, another Captain. The men looked back and forth at the real Captain standing next to them and the image on the screen, unable to believe what they were seeing.

"Captain, this is the Captain. No time to explain -- permission to come aboard, sir."

CHAPTER 12

Randall Carta had never handled a murder case before. In fact, she didn't know anyone who had. Homicide had always been a fictional mystery from old Earth literature and videos. So it was a surprise when she and Lenny were called to pay a visit to Grindavik on top of all their investigations into the x-ray storms.

"The Grindavik folks may have discovered a way to escape the storms," the chief had said, "so I thought you might be interested."

Escape the storms? How many millions of folks had tried that already? *And if they're so smart, how did someone get killed over it,* Carta thought.

Carta and Lenny arrived at the spaceport and took the loop pneumatic tube around to Grindavik proper. Eva Landerman, the accelerator facility director, was quite congenial as she took the two investigators down the deep elevator to the sprawling underground complex.

"113 kilometers long?" Lenny Chopra whistled in surprise as Landerman described the scale of the facility.

"It's easier to accelerate particles when there's a lot of runway," Landerman explained, "Even though the new magnet technologies allows us to create very small accelerators nowadays."

Lenny was quite interested, "How small?"

"As small as the palm of your hand, so far." came the reply.

Eva and an assistant led the investigators through the double doors into the large chamber where the accelerator observations take place. The main Hyperaperture Mark III facility is this way, they said, pointing down a side tunnel. They walked into another vast chamber that had been hollowed out of the red stone of the mountain, one end of which was under construction. But at the other end a massive toroid stood vertically -- a darkened field of shimmering space suspended in the middle.

Carta couldn't help but stand with a sort of lean, and she noticed all the platforms and equipment were oriented slightly diagonally as if in reverence to the device. Apparently, the *Infinity's Breach* vessel was inside the wormhole on a mission.

"Where were the bodies found?" she asked point blank.

Eva hesitated, and all the technicians within earshot seemed to give a little wince. It was a painful topic.

"Over this way." Landerman indicated.

The farther away from the big torus the straighter Carta was able to stand, until she and Lenny stood among stacks of materials, crates, and construction equipment. There on the floor faint blood stains still smeared across the pavers, and white chalk outlines showed where the victims had lain. *Thank goodness we don't have to actually deal with the corpses*, Carta thought.

"The corpses were completely drained dry of all blood?" Carta asked.

Landerman confirmed, "Yes, except for what constituted stains as you can see."

The small group walked over to where equipment had been stowed away, awaiting later installation in the construction work.

"Some of our new portable Seed Hyperaperture units are missing too, and one of the wormhole tethers." Landerman pointed out.

She and Lenny took an hour or so to make their own documentation of the scene as Landerman conversed with her staff. Carta didn't really want to be there, since she thought it was taking time away from the x-ray storm investigations. When the two had taken all the photographs they needed, Carta walked over to where Landerman was waiting.

"Did you say there were video recordings?" Carta asked.

Eva got a perplexed look on her face as she replied, "Yes, funny thing -- the video shows one of the COSCAPP vessels exiting the aperture before it was scheduled to do so. But the videos from inside the vessel were normal, as if the mission continued."

Carta watched the woman's eyes as she spoke. There was something she wasn't telling.

"If you don't mind, I'd like to see those videos." Carta asked.

Landerman looked a bit nervous as she replied, "Hildebrandt Engineering has all the video and telemetry feed archives."

Eva and her assistant escorted Carta and Lenny through a series of lifts and corridors until they reached Hildebrandt. The factory was bustling, as Hildebrandt engineers manufactured more copies of the portable Seed Hyperaperture device.

A man approached them on the factory floor and Eva made the introductions, "Inspector Randall, this is Tom Hildebrandt, owner and operator of Hildebrandt Engineering."

Carta reached out and shook the man's hand. He had a bedraggled look as if he had been up all night, and seemed to be stressed out over something.

"Tom was close to one of the victims." Eva offered.

Oh yes, Carrie Johnson, Carta thought. The world had dealt him a cruel blow.

"I'm sorry to hear about your loss, Dr. Hildebrandt," Carta began, "We'd like to see if we can apprehend who was responsible."

A nervous Landerman edged in, "She wants to see the videos taken during that time."

What is this woman hiding, Carta thought.

Hildebrandt though preoccupied with the death of his girlfriend also seemed to have a lot on his mind regarding factory deadlines ahead of the x-ray storm. Nevertheless, he agreeably led them to a lab off to the side where the COSCAPP work was being done.

As they settled down in front of the monitors, Lenny excused himself, "Do you mind if I take a look around?" he asked.

"Go right ahead," Hildebrandt agreed, and then called out, "Arden! Give Inspector Chopra anything he needs!"

Lenny left with the acne-faced youth.

Hildebrandt started accessing the videos, and took a while to get to the pertinent sections. On the interior screens, faces of the crew doing their various tasks sped by as he fast-forwarded the video. There were also exterior screens showing fascinating views of small vessels floating through a black void. However, the scene Carta was most interested in was the view of the Hyperaperture lab, that showed large numbers of technicians and construction workers quickly moving back and forth in front of the camera during the day in that queer diagonal slanted walk that was necessary near the torus. When the digital clock showed evening and night, the numbers of active technicians on duty trickled down to one or two, with no one passing in front of the cameras for long periods of time. It was during one of these lulls that something emerged from the aperture and parked for a while, then moved out of the scene. The assumed time of the murders matched the digital clock. Tom backed up the video until the parked vessel was frozen on the screen.

Carta gasped. She had seen that vehicle before.

"Is this one of the COSCAPP vessels?" Carta asked.

Hildebrandt replied in the affirmative, "Yes, but we can't understand it. See how the other screens show us out in the hyperspace bubble doing operations -- which means this could not be the *Infinity's Breach*, at least not from our time."

Carta was still speechless -- the likeness was too uncanny . . .

Just then Lenny rushed in, "Carta, you've got to see this!"

Carta looked up as if in a trance. *I wonder . . .* she thought, and then absentmindedly followed Lenny into the other room. Hildebrandt, Landerman, and the other assistant cautiously lingered behind. The room they entered had several workbenches along one wall, and various high-power electrical transformers at the other end. Several transparent cylinders, presumably pressure tanks, were lined up in the middle of the room, containing complicated arrays of electrical components. Fat cables snaked from the transformers to each of the clear modules, and disappeared inside.

Arden Tuttweiler stood against one of the sidewalls looking guiltily down at what must have been the remains of one of the modules, but no transparent housing was visible. There apparently had been a small explosion that had destroyed the equipment.

"These are our wormhole power tethers," Hildebrandt began, then explained how each of the fat cables slipped through a miniature aperture to connect to the COSCAPP vessels and other test gates they were feeding power to.

"What happened here?" Carta indicated the destroyed installation.

Arden looked as if he were caught with his hand in the cookie jar.

Hildebrandt described the destruction of their earlier SCAPP unmanned probe, "The co-orbiting black holes shot off to who knows where."

Lenny walked over to the wall and pointed out a couple of holes, "This is what I wanted you to see, Carta."

Randall walked over to the wall and saw tiny perfect circles bored into the material. Looking through one of the holes, she could see other walls that had been penetrated beyond as if something cut through soft butter.

"These little singularities are very small, and would have evaporated within an hour. But they stayed intact long enough to penetrate the walls." Hildebrandt explained.

Suddenly it seemed as though the whole world came crashing down on Carta. The room and everything in it faded away as she realized her earlier suspicions were correct. She had come here reluctantly investigating a murder, but had stumbled on perhaps a key to the more urgent investigation of the x-ray storms. The two incidents were somehow related!

Carta herded everyone into a nearby conference room and had them all seat themselves. She brought out her digital note pad and wirelessly sent several photographs to the projection wall. The first photo showed one of the small wrecked spacecrafts she and Lenny had seen among all the gnarled heaps of metal, near those unidentified corpses at the ruins of Novissima.

Hildebrandt stood up suddenly, "That's the *Towa Maru*! I can see the number stenciled on the hull!"

Sure enough, some white, stenciled, alphanumeric symbols were visible on smooth portions of the hull. It was also possible to make out the smashed cockpit and a few portholes, but there were major rents opened up to reveal the underlying Toshige hovercoils.

Another image projected on the wall. Again, Hildebrandt identified it as the missing SCAPP unit, twisted and convoluted in the vast field of wreckage.

A third image showed cleanly bored holes in the red Martian landscape, hundreds of them out to the horizon. Again and again, images showing pieces of twisted equipment that could have been from their labs were flashed on the screen. Carta watched the faces of the folks around the table as they looked at each photo with looks of incredulity. Then she stood up.

"Maybe those little black holes that flew out of the wrecked wormhole tether have evaporated by now. But somehow there are more black holes out there still causing problems. Whether you knew it or not, I think it is perfectly clear -- you folks are responsible for the x-ray storms," she calmly exclaimed, then added, "Whoever was piloting the *Towa Maru* has not only caused a world-wide disaster, but is also guilty of murder."

She glanced over at Hildebrandt, who looked as though he had seen a ghost.

*****

"We have finally have discovered what is causing the x-ray storms." Dr. Jacob Harrison told the heads of departments as they sat around the conference table.

Carta looked at all the faces -- there were some fairly high-profile folks in the group, including Grindavik Colony President Howard Statner. Randall had no idea this group was so highly connected. From their table they could look out and see the vast Hyperaperture lab, with the parked *Infinity's Breach* undergoing preparation for another mission. The sight of the vehicle made her shudder.

Harrison continued, "Apparently some black holes got out of containment and fell to the core of Mars. The momentum of the fall carried them all the way back up to the surface again on the other side of the planet. Since there is virtually no resistance to cause them to slow down, they've been bouncing up and down in a pendulum effect."

Tom Hildebrandt had a relieved look on his face -- Carta could not imagine why black holes in the planet core could have helped the man fight his demons. The whole table broke out in small talk as the scientists and engineers in attendance contemplated the implications of such a disaster.

Hildebrandt asked a question, "But what about the x-rays?"

Harrison explained, "X-rays are a natural by-product of singularities as they devour matter and evaporate."

"Why does it follow a spiral path?" Statner asked.

"Orbital dynamics," Harrison began, "The black holes are still orbiting the Mars center of gravity, but the orbit path is below the surface. In the same way a spacecraft at certain inclinations alternate between northern and southern hemispheres, somehow the black holes had gotten on a slightly eccentric orbit that slowly works its way down the latitudes."

"Is there anything that can be done?" Hildebrandt asked the question on everyone's minds.

Harrison looked discouraged -- the news was not good, "These black holes seem to have been big enough so they don't evaporate quickly. There's nothing we can do to stop it. It will continue to decimate the surface until it reaches the equator, then it will continue up the latitudes again. The holes bored by the singularities will continue until there is nothing left. Of course, the planet will collapse in on itself way before that happens."

The folks at the table began murmuring to each other again. The forecast gave them only two weeks before the storm reached Grindavik, and they still weren't sure if the No Point hole could be expanded or not.

One of the scientists asked, "What about Hughes? Tom says the *Towa Maru* is still drawing power through the wormhole tether."

Carta had been sitting back during the whole conversation, but now slowly stood up. All eyes were on the newcomer.

"I'm sorry to say this," she reluctantly reported, "but all the evidence points to Hughes and his crew as the perpetrators. You all say the *Towa Maru* disappeared through an aperture, but there are videos showing the craft arrive right about the time the murders took place."

There were protests at the table, as no one could believe Hughes and company could be capable of such an act. Carta was beginning to understand the nature of the hyperspace bubble, where events and effects could happen before the cause as long as their local causal path was logically sequential.

Carta continued, "And furthermore, the *Towa Maru* has been photographed at the scene of the Novissima accident that started all this mess. Our evidence lab has gone to retrieve the wreckage as we speak."

The protests got louder until Harrison had to quiet everyone down. He said, "But that doesn't make sense. How would the *Towa Maru* end up at Novissima before it was even invented? The folks at Stockwell Institute down there must have been responsible -- they've always been too secretive. They must have been performing exotic experiments without anyone knowing."

"How, doctor, do you account for the *Towa Maru* being there?" Carta challenged.

Harrison suddenly had an idea. His face brightened as he proposed, "What if there is a second hyperspace bubble. What if that aperture they disappeared in linked the two. Maybe that would explain other vehicles we don't have any clue about, such as the large starship or whatever it is."

Carta wasn't fazed by such a stupid suggestion, "Just be warned. I think there is something going on here and we're going to find out what it is!"

Carta got up and walked out with Lenny in tow.

When they had gotten out of earshot Lenny spoke up, "You were very good in there."

Carta turned and eyed him for a second, then rolled her eyes, "There's more we didn't discuss. Yes this group is involved somehow, but there are still a lot of unknowns. What about those millions of missing colonists? And that explosion or huge wreckage from outer space? I think that Hughes fellow had more deals going than he let on."

Carta and Lenny decided to stay in Grindavik for a while since they were hot on the trail of a potential solution. They visited

Hildebrandt again, and Toshige Enterprises trying to get more information out of the engineers and scientists on the team.

Only two Sol-days later Carta found out the Hyperaperture team had initiated their own investigation and had uncovered some disturbing evidence. Carta and Lenny found themselves in the Hyperaperture facility again talking with Dr. Harrison.

"So you have seen the *Towa Maru*, even after it supposedly disappeared down the aperture?" Carta asked.

Harrison reluctantly confirmed, "Yes, since the *Towa Maru* got lost on her maiden voyage, any other sighting would be after its disappearance. This time we sent out the *Infinity's Breach* with instruments on board that had the sole purpose of tracking hull numbers and identifying how many times the vessel shows up."

"And?" Carta prompted.

"We were skeptical at first, thinking all that we would see would be *Infinity's Breach*," Harrison explained, "But your hunch was correct -- we found several cases where the *Towa Maru* was clearly the vessel observed."

There was something else that Harrison was not saying.

"Tell me what's on your mind, doctor." she coaxed.

Harrison hesitated. He didn't want to say anything that would incriminate the team.

Reluctantly he said, "Like the time of the murder, we've spotted the *Towa Maru* exiting the same hole just after the *Infinity's Breach* enters the bubble -- maybe waiting long enough to not be noticed."

CHAPTER 13

Sixty-five years previously the whole No Point lab was in a state of excitement. Yu Gao and Hai Qi kept vigil by the maintenance station to see what was going on. It was like a New Year's party -- no one wanted to go home. Gao could see Liang Zhou and the other physicists running back and forth as they exchanged data.

"Can you tell what's happening?" Qi asked him.

Gao looked back at his own screen. There was not much he could discern from the meager data piped into his station -- it only showed the health of the combustion chamber and not anything that the sensors might be recording.

"I can see temperature. I can see magnetic fields. I can see holes in your intelligence. Why do you think I could see black holes?" Gao replied.

Qi frowned but chuckled inside -- always a joker that Yu Gao. Without warning Zhou and several others began to applaud. Word came around that another singularity had been achieved for a brief instant.

Gao began to wonder -- what would they do if they had a sustained black hole? Would that help them achieve combustion between matter and antimatter particles?

Somehow, he thought not -- it was likely just a spin-off achievement. And what if one got away?

Qi put into words what Gao had been thinking, "I can see it now -- a pitted interior. I hope the containment fields don't leak any."

They would have to get *Little Pang* to buff all the surfaces again.

Just then Gao saw Xiaoyu Lin with a tray of tea -- she was passing out little paper cups filled with the liquid in celebration. Gao couldn't take his eyes off those voluptuous curves, as Xiaoyu swayed between the workstations of the scientists. Xiaoyu began walking their way, about to set two cups in front of Gao and Qi. What perfect eyes and lips! The girl was right there next to him for a moment as she set the cups down. Gao's heart fluttered with excitement, and then she began to walk away.

"Lin Xiaoyu --" Gao began, but realized he had nothing to say. In Chinese, they actually speak the family name first, and given name last when they address someone.

The girl turned around and looked at him, "Yes?"

There was a lengthy pause as Gao looked at the beautiful woman of his heart's desire.

"What is it?" Xiaoyu repeated.

The pause was getting uncomfortable.

"Um, thanks." was all he could manage.

"You're welcome." she bowed her head and walked away.

That was awkward, Gao thought. Qi looked at him with amusement.

"You've got to be a man! Next time embrace her and carry away her heart like in those Western romance movies." Qi advised.

Just then Zhou and the other physicists began to clap again. "Multiple black holes. They're somersaulting over each other!" someone shouted.

"Would you look at that! Keep it going, keep it going!" Zhou directed.

Whatever it was the team had accomplished, it went on for several minutes as the accelerator and magnets were toggled in some delicate balance. Then suddenly there was a horrible wrenching noise. Gao knew it could not be good -- steel tearing itself apart.

Alarms went off on his workstation as the combustion chamber health monitoring system reported violations and anomalies all over. The magnetic fields were being obstructed somehow.

"Shut it down!" Zhou called out to someone.

Gao looked over at the big chamber and could see it was somehow warped out of shape. To his right Qi was frantically trying to respond to some of the alarms. Gao looked at his sensor readings and at the video screens. The video!

Zhou and several others quickly walked over, "What's going on?"

Gao could not believe his eyes, "Sir, there's something huge in the chamber!"

A frustrated Zhou snapped back, "We've lost containment -- those massive black holes have destroyed the chamber!"

Gao was stunned beyond belief -- it couldn't be! "No sir. There's something large in the chamber -- a vehicle or something!" he managed.

CHAPTER 14

Tom Hildebrandt could not believe his eyes. Only moments before *Infinity's Breach* had been shooting through hyperspace, racing to get to a small hole before it closed. He had watched, as time seemed to stand still. From the right and left multiple versions of themselves had converged on that one point, as if in slow motion. The other copies of the *Infinity's Breach* had rushed toward the hole and one by one veered away and broke off the chase. Briefly Tom had seen another version of himself staring back at him from that other viewport. He remembered that day, doing a practice run toward the hole to make sure the timing would be right -- good luck, he had said to himself across the void, knowing that the future Tom had the responsibility of going all the way and penetrating the No Point hole. Today he was that future Tom -- the day of reckoning had arrived.

From the nose of their small craft extended the Expander Probe (EP) or Eppy, pointing forward like an ominous proboscis. The distance had closed suddenly, and there it was right in front of them. The coils on Eppy had pulsed, activating powerful fields sufficient to melt away the sides of the hole, creating a larger and larger entry cone -- enough for *Infinity's Breach* to pass through.

Eppy had collapsed on impact, as it was designed to do, taking the brunt of the momentum *Infinity's Breach* had built up on its forward thrust. The vessel came to an abrupt stop. Around him Hildebrandt saw scored metal walls just centimeters outside the viewport windows. Hildebrandt's head began to spin. Those walls were from another era, another time -- from sixty-five years earlier. It had worked! The *Infinity's Breach* was now sitting inside the No Point test chamber!

"All stop thrusters. *Infinity's Breach* subsystems health check." Naveen Tandon the pilot called back, "Hovercoils functional. Thermal check. Pressure hull check."

Hildebrandt could see the woman hacking away at her controls as she switched into quiescent mode.

"Air thruster damage -- two clusters, superficial damage." Tandon continued, "Outer hull damage on starboard bow."

Hildebrandt was concerned -- what about power, com? "Are we still connected to Grindavik?" he asked.

Tandon was a pleasant-faced young woman of Indian descent. Tom might have been interested in her if it had not been for his recent loss.

"Yes sir. The wormhole tether is intact and we are still in contact with Grindavik." Tandon affirmed.

An intact wormhole tether meant that a continuous sliver of spacetime spanned across sixty-five years linking them to their home -- they were drawing power, data, and communications from their colleagues in the future.

Tom relaxed, "Welcome to the past."

It was hard to believe they had just created an honest to goodness link between the future and past -- a genuine closed timelike curve, operational right in front of their faces. Hildebrandt turned to check their precious cargo. The Seed Hyperaperture instrument panel showed the unit was powered up, healthy, and ready to be deployed as soon as they could get out of there. He had heard the stories that somehow there were a chronology protection conjecture -- would nature somehow prevent them from leaving this chamber, thus frustrating the loop in time? Hildebrandt didn't think so, as long as they could preserve local causation.

"There's air outside, Dr. Hildebrandt. I think the test chamber imploded." Tandon commented.

Jacob Harrison, who had until that point been quietly looking over his instruments jumped in, "It will be easier to extricate ourselves that way. Who knows how much damage there was to the No Point lab, or if anyone out there is still alive -- we may be prying at metal beams for days."

Tom turned and eyed the hatch that hid pry bars and cutting torches. *Might as well get those out*, he thought. He began to unlatch the door and pile the tools on to floor.

The elderly fourth member of their crew looked out his viewport and sighed, "My, my, I never would have believed it!"

Without warning there was a loud clanging sound. Someone on the outside was knocking on the hull! Harrison looked around and grabbed one of the pry bars that Tom had just taken out.

"Wait, there's a place where we can bang against structure without damaging the hull." Hildebrandt implored.

Harrison relinquished the tool and Hildebrandt took it through the short corridor to the airlock section. He didn't know Morse Code, but likely the folks outside didn't know the old signals either. *Just a few raps to show them we're here ought to do it*, Tom thought.

Sure enough, the two parties were able to acknowledge each other very quickly. *Infinity's Breach* still had her hovercoils working, so Tom could detect the ship drifting slightly in relation to the chamber walls. He opened the outer airlock door and was able to squeeze between the *Infinity's Breach* outer hull and metal wall of the chamber.

Up above he could see the No Point engineers had opened an access hatch of sorts. Hildebrandt climbed the outer plates of the vessel, over the top, and let himself be lifted up by outstretched hands. There they were -- a half dozen Asian faces staring back at him dumbfounded. He knew what they were thinking -- how did this guy appear out of thin air right in the middle of our black hole experiment?

Hildebrandt wished he could leisurely sit down and 'shoot the breeze' with some chaps from the previous century, but unfortunately knew what his well-rehearsed script had to be. He flashed a specially prepared Mars Interim Government security badge, prepared by Stephan Wang's office using a date 68 years earlier.

"Dr. Zhou?" Hildebrandt proclaimed, "I'm part of a government investigation. I need you to get your people out of the lab as quickly as possible. Also, can you allow me to borrow your phone?"

Liang Zhou complied immediately. Tom watched as the scientists filed out, and wondered which one was Yu Gao, the elderly retired professor whom Tom met at Grindavik University years ago. The elderly Gao had settled down in Grindavik with his wife Xiaoyu. There had been several cases of elderly scientists from that era living among the Grindavik colonists, and it was determined that the original No Point staff witness as little as possible to avoid situations that might give rise to a paradox. In interviews, the elderly Gao recalled the 'anomaly' that had occurred so many years before, but could not remember the details -- only that thereafter he had gotten promoted and that the incident had given him the opportunity to pursue and marry his wife.

Dr. Zhou was the last person in the lab after the equipment had been shut down, "Sir, the phone is over here," he said.

From history, Hildebrandt knew that Zhou had disappeared from public view after the incident, so he suspected the chief physicist had been party to the government cover-up somehow. Tom asked him to stay.

"Do you mind telling me what this is all about?" Zhou asked.

Hildebrandt answered, "I'll explain everything. We need your assistance. But first you must swear you will not discuss this with anyone -- not your team, not anyone."

"If this is a legitimate operation, I'll be willing to do that, as long as it doesn't interfere with my research." Zhou acknowledged.

Tom smiled, "Your research will much benefit from our collaboration, I guarantee."

Just then Hildebrandt's three fellow crewmembers climbed up out of the access hatch at the top of the chamber. Zhou's eyes followed Jacob, Naveen, and the older gentleman as they climbed down the scaffolding.

"We need to get our equipment out of your chamber. Can you assist us in dismantling the bulkhead?" Hildebrandt asked.

Zhou hesitated, "The person you need for that just left the lab. Mr. Gao knows the procedures much better than I."

Hildebrandt smiled again. "Well, I think we have some help in that area," Tom paused as he indicated the elderly man on the team, "Dr. Zhou, let me introduce Professor Yu Gao."

CHAPTER 15

Carta Randall was confounded. She watched as crowds of refugees were being escorted to emergency housing set up in schools, corridors, parks, and other public areas in the greater Grindavik area. Mars was being lacerated right before their eyes -- there would be no solid ground within a month, and Grindavik was one of the last remaining untouched areas that would soon also find its own demise. The final sanctuary -- Carta didn't know all the details, but apparently the Grindavik government was working on wormhole gates that would allow the entire population to walk through to escape the destruction.

But that wasn't what bothered the investigator -- try as she might, she couldn't put all the puzzle pieces in their place. All sorts of events were apparently linked together in seemingly impossible ways.

Two small black holes had flung themselves out onto the Martian landscape when the Grindavik wormhole tether had destroyed itself, then quickly evaporated. But there were still singularities loose out there.

Could folks at the Novissima Stockwell Institute have also been researching artificial black holes that were somehow released from their containment by the impact of a large vessel from space? The black holes passed right through the planet in a perverse orbit of sorts, an extreme flattened ovoid orbit that almost bored through the exact center of the world. The extremely dense black holes sliced through normal matter as if nothing was there, and emitted x-rays as they gradually decayed.

But the wreckage at Novissima had included machines not even invented yet by the team at Grindavik. One of those machines was the *Towa Maru*, positively identified by Hildebrandt himself, which had been implicated in the murder of three Grindavik technicians.

Then again how could this be? Hildebrandt and the rest of the Grindavik folks had presented evidence that the *Towa Maru* had been irretrievably lost through an unknown aperture that shut permanently. Harrison had at one point suggested the invading vessel might have been from an alternate reality, but quickly pointed out that the difference would only be slight -- it would not be likely to find one's evil twin in an alternate universe.

But other bloodless corpses kept showing up in odd places around Grindavik and nearby colonies, as if the *Towa Maru* kept coming back on raiding visits from wherever they had holed up out on the harsh Martian landscape.

And now some new evidence had come to light. Lenny Chopra had found in the archives some records describing an identical set of murders in Novissima that had occurred several months before the x-ray storms had even begun. Those bodies had also been completely drained of blood. Carta thought back on that haunting grainy black and white photograph of the *Towa Maru* again showing up in a lab, and all the technicians on duty at the time found tortured, burned, and dismembered.

"I understand that with wormholes some effects could precede their cause, but even so none of this makes sense." Lenny also sat confused, poking at his meal as the endless stream of refugees passed by outside the restaurant, "And you can't go back in time earlier than the invention of the wormhole."

Carta just shrugged, "I just don't know what to think. If your future self killed someone, could your current self be held accountable for it?"

Lenny suddenly sat up alert, "I've got an idea. Instead of trying to fit all the events onto a timeline, let's make up a separate timeline for each element."

Carta looked at him with a confused expression.

"For example, let's take the *Towa Maru* and create a timeline for it that makes sense, no matter how much it skips forward or backward in time." Lenny proposed.

That's it -- it had to be, Carta thought. She lined up all the digital notes regarding the *Towa Maru* on her pad and began putting them in order. Lenny connected to her desktop and the two of them shifted the little rectangles around on the background.

"Okay first event for *Towa Maru* -- invented at Toshige Enterprises, and outfitted at Hildebrandt Engineering." Carta jumped right on it and placed two notes in their correct places.

"Next we have the short test through the Hyperaperture by Beth Kitamura, followed by the maiden voyage with the Hughes's, Kitamura's, and Toshige's. We have full documentation from its manufacture until it disappears in the wormhole." Lenny added three more little rectangles to the timeline.

Carta began looking at the other end, "And over here we have wreckage of the *Towa Maru* well documented. The *Towa Maru*'s causal path goes from here to here."

"Which is backward," Lenny pointed out, "wrecked before it was built."

"Don't let that confuse the issue. As you say, we've got to have a totally different mindset here." Carta admonished.

That left two known events that didn't yet have a place -- the two homicide scenes.

"It's probably not too much of a stretch to think that the *Towa Maru* had been hanging around Novissima from the time of the murders to the time it was smashed." Lenny put a little rectangle just preceding the Novissima wreckage.

"Agreed. So we have two disconnects," Carta began, "One right after it disappears in the wormhole, and another just before the Novissima homicides."

Lenny noted, "The Grindavik murders were chronologically after the *Towa Maru* disappeared, which means it must have come back out of a wormhole again. Then somehow it took a wormhole back in time."

Carta thought about that for a minute. There was no evidence the vessel had gone back through the Hyperaperture to return to the bubble. Which meant . . .

"They're still here!" Carta and Lenny said in unison.

Carta, excited, started outlining a scenario, "The *Towa Maru* got stranded somewhere when that wormhole shut on them, as we saw in the video record. But let's say somehow, they were able to get back into the hyperspace bubble and linger about among all the floating machines waiting for an opportunity. Then when the Grindavik folks opened up a wormhole for *Infinity's Breach*, the *Towa Maru* waited long enough to not be noticed then exited hyperspace at Grindavik as we've seen. Somehow, they wanted to cover it up, so they got rid of the witnesses. Next, they loaded two portable Seed Hyperaperture units and . . ."

Carta tried to envision the Hyperaperture lab downstairs -- half the lab was being used for operating the device while the other half was under construction.

Lenny knew what she was thinking, "They flew the *Towa Maru* through the big maintenance roll-up doors at the back of the lab!"

An hour later Carta and Lenny were slowly making their way through large roll-up doors, maintenance passageways, and storerooms behind the linear accelerator labs. In particular, a rarely used warehouse got their attention. As they had done earlier when the technician bodies had been found, Carta and Lenny were snapping photos and collecting evidence -- especially the big obvious one right there on the floor. A shredded micro torus lay there discarded where the *Towa Maru* crew had apparently hung out for a while and worked on their machine.

"See, there are definite marks on the pavement where the *Towa Maru* set down on landing feet." Carta noted.

Arden Tuttweiler, the lanky teen that Carta had borrowed from Hildebrandt Engineering pointed at the wrecked device and said, "That's one of the mini accelerators that make up one half of the wormhole tethers. Two tori together form a closed wormhole through which we string our power and control cables."

"So, they must have had trouble with their power." Lenny surmised, "They stole some wormhole tether units to replace their faulty one."

Arden had a perplexed look on his face as he got down on his hands and knees to study the twisted object without touching it.

Carta, noticing the boy's expression wondered, "What is it son?"

"This unit is very strange. Despite the fact that it must have torn to pieces when the black hole pair inside lost their containment," Arden paused as if remembering when he had witnessed the destruction of the SCAPP tether, "this one looks all pitted and oxidized, as if it were many years old. I put this very casing together only a month ago and see -- even the torn edges look old."

Interesting, Carta thought. The team moved onward through the maintenance passages trying to guess the direction the crew had taken the vehicle. Even though the tunnels were made for large vehicles, the sight of a floating vessel moving along them surely would have attracted some attention.

The answer came a few hours later. Carta, Lenny, and Arden came across a rarely used staging area for heavy equipment near a large maintenance airlock. A wheeled, flatbed transport vehicle was parked off to one side, with a canvas cargo tarp piled on the floor. Someone had hurriedly ripped off the tarp and unloaded whatever it had been they were carrying on the flatbed. The crew must have carried the *Towa Maru* on the back of the transport under the canvas to keep prying eyes away. Carta began looking over the vehicle and noticed an awful stench -- the smell of death. The murderers had been there alright.

"Arden, stay back. There's something here you shouldn't have to see." Carta warned.

It wasn't long before Carta and Lenny found another body wrapped in canvas stuffed in a cargo box on the vehicle. The poor fellow must have been the vehicle's driver who had been in the wrong place at the wrong time. She could tell there was not a drop of blood left in the body. Carta was certain if they checked local law enforcement files there would be a report of a missing person.

"Hey look at this!" Arden shouted from across the room, "Beamed energy, and a lot of it!"

Carta left Lenny to take care of the body and inform local officials, and walked over to where Arden stood near piles of bulky components. The area was just adjacent to the huge airlock door that led out onto the bare Martian surface.

"See this?" Arden pointed to a round casing next to the pile, "This is a receiver collector for beamed power, and these are batteries. Looks like they really had power troubles."

"What do you mean?" Carta asked.

"I'd say there's enough high-density batteries to stuff the inside of the *Towa Maru*. These units are of a type I haven't seen before, but look at the power rating on the label." Arden pointed.

Carta didn't know much about power issues, but terawatts did not seem normal to her.

"Each of these batteries packed quite a wallop." Arden explained, "It looks like their wormhole tether destroyed itself before they came back out of the bubble. What we usually do by direct dedicated cable to the power plant, these folks had to do with battery power. They needed all this power for a one-shot attempt to operate the hovercoils through the Hyperaperture just to get out of the bubble!"

"They must have dumped these batteries to lighten their load, then departed out the airlock. But why beamed power?" Carta was confused.

"Don't you see? All they had was one shot to use all their power for those few seconds passing through the aperture." Arden continued, "So somehow they had to keep the charge up with beamed power right to the final instant."

Okay, that makes sense, Carta thought. All that coming out of a smarty teenager. But that left open a lot of other questions. Where would beamed power come from in the bubble? How did the *Towa Maru* get outfitted with ultra-high-density batteries? Now were the perpetrators somewhere out navigating the Martian landscape? The mystery only deepened.

"I think we have a bigger problem on hand." Arden frowned.

Carta looked up with a worried look on her face. *What now*, she thought.

Arden continued, "The thieves took two of the new Seed Hyperapertures. If they're clever they might find a way to set up shop anywhere, draw off our power grid, and go in and out of the bubble as many times as they like, starting from clock zero each time!"

Carta was alarmed. That meant the *Towa Maru* could enter and exit through other apertures just as they had done in Grindavik when the murders had occurred. With all those dozens of future and past experiments going on inside the bubble, who would know if a few of those vessels floating around had malicious intentions!

"Lenny, I think we need to watch all the video recorded from inside the bubble, from time zero." Carta concluded.

CHAPTER 16

Tom Hildebrandt, Jacob Harrison, and Naveen Tandon stood back and watched as the elderly Yu Gao reacquainted himself with his former boss.

"This chamber, everything brings back so many memories." Gao waved his arm to include everything in the room, "These tools are just as I remembered them."

Hildebrandt saw that Liang Zhou still wasn't sure what was going on. The chief scientist had been Gao's senior back then, but then Gao had long since outdistanced his mentor in experience and wisdom in the intervening years.

Gao hurriedly walked over to his old maintenance station and exclaimed, "And here's *Xiao-Pang* the little inspection robot. Who was it -- yes, Qi and I had many a joke about *Little Pang* in those days."

Only an hour later Zhou was convinced he was talking with a Gao from the future. Having gotten over his skepticism, Zhou was completely fascinated by the world fifty years hence.

Though the elderly Gao had been coached not to divulge future events, he found it safe enough to explain their power systems, "Our vessel is powered through a 'wormhole tether' that uses tremendous amounts of power -- more than we could possibly generate on board. What that means is that heavy duty power lines come directly from a major power generator, pass through the wormhole tether, and feed into our systems."

Tom listened from the side and watched as Zhou followed Gao's explanation with great interest.

"In fact, we require enough energy to run a dozen cities, just for this one vehicle. All our power comes from antimatter generators." Gao smiled as he explained.

Zhou's eyes widened, "Do you mean . . ."

"Yes, our work here at No Point was successful." Gao affirmed.

Zhou tried to get more information out of Gao but the elderly professor began to stress the urgency of contacting certain authorities from the Mars Interim Government Department of Interior, and the Mars Science Directorate. Zhou knew the two persons personally in his research dealings and was able to set up an appointment for a few Sol-days later.

Tom was worried about the time, since in only weeks Grindavik would be torn apart by the x-ray storms and renegade black holes. But Jacob reminded him that they had well over half a century until those events would occur.

"You've got to think universally on the big timeline. You can't let your own causal path be imposed on it." Jacob stressed.

"I understand that," Hildebrandt said, "But what I'm worried about is the wormhole tether, that is continuously drawing power from our own time in Grindavik!"

The wormhole tethers set up their own continuity of spacetime through the tunnel they formed, which gave a direct access to the tremendous power generation of Grindavik. But this was also their limitation -- when Grindavik's power plants are lacerated by the x-ray storm, all equipment running off that power from anywhere in the wormhole tether power net would be deprived of its source of electrical current. This had actually been a problem Hildebrandt Engineering had been working on already -- how to get past the short deadline imposed upon all their wormhole tethers.

"So far we've constructed two types of apertures -- Singler Gates are those that simply open up into the general hyperspace bubble because they have no destination specified. And the second Dualer Gates are paired gates that create their own private tunnel between them, unrelated to hyperspace." Tom recounted.

"I see what you mean. We're still at the mercy of the two-week wormhole tether shut off, unless we can power up our equipment from here, sixty-five years earlier." Harrison realized.

"But we can't expect these folks to just hand over one of their major power generation plants in three weeks. At Hildebrandt we've been working on another solution -- if we work off the innate charge of the spinning pair of black holes, produce a second pair with an exact opposite charge, they should both fire up at zero clock time and migrate toward each other in the hyperspace bubble." Tom explained.

Harrison gave a deep smile, "Yes it should work -- for anyone observing the activity in the hyperspace bubble it would appear that two holes come together and annihilate. But in actuality the two would begin as Singler apertures, then find each other and kick themselves out of hyperspace as Dualer dedicated tunnel wormholes. That matches what we see when the flashes of light migrate toward each other and cancel out!"

"A 'Kisser Gate' -- one that begins as a Singler and pairs up to become a Dualer. Yes, so that would get around the three-week limit imposed by the x-ray storm approaching Grindavik." Tom agreed.

But Naveen who had been listening in was still confused, "How does that overcome the three-week deadline?"

Tom laid out a simple scenario, "Let's say we do our negotiations a few Sol-days from now, still within the two-week limit -- we set up the Seed Hyperaperture unit stowed away in the *Infinity's Breach*, and establish a dedicated wormhole bridging Grindavik of our time with today, sixty-five years in the past. So our authorities walk through, get permission for us to set up a base nearby, and then we bring a bigger Seed Hyperaperture through that will allow all our construction equipment standing by to drive through into the past."

Tom paused to make sure Naveen was following.

"We're still within the two-week limit. Maybe there's one week left at this point." Tom continued, "Then we bring in a dozen or so Seed Hyperaperture units that are Singler machines, but have their charge values adjusted to match up with another dozen that remain on the Grindavik side. We keep those twelve units in storage until they can be powered from generation plants we build here on this side, sixty-five years earlier. Except that it might take five years to construct such a plant -- we've already gone well past the remaining two weeks of the wormhole death date. The original Seed Hyperaperture unit and all other gates set up at that time are not operable anymore."

"Yes, that's what I don't understand." Naveen replied.

Harrison finished the explanation, "So that's where the Hyperaperture 'Kisser Gate' units in storage come in. Five years from now when we've got all our power plants set up here at No Point, and have constructed all the tunnels and facilities we need to house our people, we simply create the orbiting pairs of black holes and start up those twelve mothballed Hyperaperture units which will begin at clock time zero in the hyperspace bubble. Each of those twelve pairs of singularities will have a unique charge, like a combination, that matches it to the Grindavik gates. As for the Grindavik folks, the next Sol-day after they send their negotiators through, they fire up their twelve matching Hyperaperture gates and twelve new dedicated wormhole tunnels are established to the past."

Tom clarified, "In other words, the Grindavik folks don't have to wait five years for the construction to be complete on this side -- they just turn their machines on the next Sol-day and they bypass those five years before the limit expires and the x-rays come. As it turns out, I have those twelve combinations right here in my brief case."

Two Sol-days later things began to proceed just as Tom and Jacob had outlined. With the elderly Gao's help the team disassembled the No Point test chamber to allow the *Infinity's Breach* to float out on the lab floor. They moved the machine to a remote warehouse, set up the Seed Hyperaperture unit and installed a shielded tunnel to bridge through the torus -- a walk-through wormhole between the future and the past.

As soon as the man-sized gate had been established, Grindavik Colony President Howard Statner walked through from the future with Mars Interim Governor Stephan Wang and his aides. It was a time for celebration.

Tom wasn't sure what happened next as Harrison, Gao, and Zhou escorted the small entourage into a separate room with Eiger Mitchell and Dae-Hyun Myeong who were officials from the contemporary Department of Interior and Mars Science Directorate. Instead, Hildebrandt walked back through to his own time in Grindavik in order to get the larger industrial-sized gates ready to bring through in the event the negotiations went well.

The first thing Tom did after making sure the large industrial gates were on track was to head over to Hildebrandt Engineering to check on the control frequency of the lost nanoassemblers. Fortunately, there was less urgency now that they had discovered the source of the x-rays and lacerations was uncontained black holes, but still the nanoassemblers were a mystery gnawing on his mind that he had to solve. Tom found the nano lab deserted, as the engineers normally working there had been needed on the Seed Hyperaperture production line. He looked through the nanoassembler model numbers -- several generations had been developed, and each had its own control protocols.

The escaped units had been the early test generation, as Tom recalled. He looked up the communication specification and realized they had borrowed direct digital control protocols from the facility environmental system, just for testing purposes until their own protocols could be established. In other words, the same wireless control of lights and air conditioning had been borrowed for control of the nanoassemblers. *Hmm*, Tom thought, *that gives me an idea*. He quickly downloaded the list of environmental control devices used at Hildebrandt and rushed back to the Hyperaperture labs. He would need to make comparisons later when he had some free time.

At one point as Tom wandered in to the Hyperaperture facility from the side, he watched the entire negotiation team walk back through to Grindavik, including the officials from the past, to be shown the facilities and colony from the future -- presumably to prove what they were saying was true. The group was taken out in fliers with multi-spectral viewing apparatus to witness the sobering real-time destruction along the leading edge of the x-ray storms.

It wasn't long before approval had been achieved. Mitchell and Myeong had apparently discussed the matter directly with their contemporary Mars Interim Governor March Addard before approval had been granted on condition that the entire operation remain secret, as had been done in the historical records. The Seed Hyperaperture units and the *Infinity's Breach* were taken under cover to a remote tunnel at the nearby community Pointless and the team from the future was given parameters on where to begin their excavations to build the new power plant and colony. Pointless and No Point were sister cities, connected by underground passageways.

"Why can't we just stay and set up at No Point?" Naveen asked.

Harrison explained, "Because of the history books. No Point was always too small, even in our day. That means we must have set up our colony at Pointless."

The next Sol-day Tom watched as heavy machinery drove through the industrial-sized aperture and began pre-planned operations right away. A steady stream of cargo and equipment poured through and were being stashed everywhere they could find nooks and crannies in their assigned tunnels. Twelve Singler 'Kisser' Hyperaperture units came through and were being stowed off to one side, awaiting the time five years hence when they would be set up to allow the general population of Grindavik to walk through to safety. Naveen also piloted the *Infinity's Breach* back to Grindavik to do some minor repairs when the vessel had forced entry into the No Point test chamber.

Satisfied that things were going smoothly, Hildebrandt walked through the smaller gate back to the future Grindavik facility. Though they wouldn't be able to fire up the 'Kissers' on the Pointless side, they would be able to power the Grindavik mates right away and begin the evacuation immediately, assuming the five-year operation at No Point and Pointless succeeded.

Tom directed the Hildebrandt Engineering crews to finish installing the twelve gates and set up queuing plans for the large crowds and their allowed luggage. Without warning, Teresa Hughes ran up to him.

"Dr. Hildebrandt! Tou-san and Kaa-san came through on the com unit! Come quickly!" she said.

Tom rushed over to observation room, skirting the huge vertical toroid Hyperaperture device. A technician sat waiting for them with earphones on. Hildebrandt snatched up another pair of earphones.

"Hughes! Do you read me?" Tom cried.

A static-filled voice came on the other end, "Tom, finally we get through!"

"Hughes, what have you been up to? The authorities have charged you with murder!" Tom replied.

Masamune Hughes came back with a startled tone to his voice, "How did they know about that? Tom, we couldn't help it."

The signal cut out for a few minutes and Hildebrandt frantically tried to raise his friend again. Murphy! Could it be true? Were those accusations by Randall and Chopra true after all? Tom began to swell with anger -- what does he mean, 'he couldn't help it'?

The noise-filled background yielded Masamune's voice one last time, "Tom, our com is out, but we can communicate through the suit com system. Get a suit com near the wormhole tether in three Sol-days."

"Hughes, get back here immediately!" Tom ordered, "Hughes come in! Come in *Towa Maru*!"

But the line was dead.

What did he mean by getting a suit com near the wormhole tether? As anger welled up inside, Tom tried to put together the fragments of Hughes' message. He couldn't believe that the confounded investigator could be right about his top engineers! Tom looked down as poor Teresa sat longingly by the com unit hoping her parents would connect again.

Another messenger came along just then, "Dr. Hildebrandt, we're ready to start up the 'Kisser' gates. We also have six advance teams that the government wants to cross over a day early."

Advance teams? Hildebrandt hadn't heard about advance teams, but he saw no problem with it. Tom once again skirted the original Hyperaperture device and made his way back to where the 'Kissers' had been deployed. As he rounded the corner, he was shocked -- crowds of people, mostly families, stood waiting in the queues in front of the machines. Advance teams! Those were government folks sending their families to the front of the line. *I can't believe they would be so brazen as to do such a thing*, Tom thought.

Hildebrandt walked into the small control room and started the countdown sequence for start-up. In order to power twelve gates at once, the entire Grindavik Colony had to cut its power usage down to a minimum, mostly for emergency lighting and life support. Hildebrandt had folks that were coordinating with the colony power grid on the timing of the power down.

A half hour later the first gate powered up and Tom could see the usual shimmering where the pair of black holes orbited each other and warped the spacetime continuum so much as to create a hole into another universe. Tom imagined spots of light in the bubble migrating together as the Grindavik gate charge inversely matched that of the gate deployed (hopefully) sixty years earlier at Pointless. One by one the other eleven gates came online and Tom was impressed by the row of shimmering wormholes.

Tom indicated for the technicians standing by to insert the shielded walk-through tunnels that would withstand the tremendous gravitational tidal effects that two co-orbiting black holes would create. It was as the final shielded tunnel slipped into place and Tom looked through into blackness when he realized something had gone wrong. They should have been looking through to the Pointless facilities!

"Sir, we haven't been able to get the holes to migrate and connect with each other." one of the technicians announced, "Each of the gates are just opening up into the hyperspace bubble as plain Singler gates."

Hildebrandt put each of the gates through a series of tests and realized it was true -- a bridge to the past had not been established on the new migrating gates. They had lost to Murphy again. What could have gone wrong? Tom looked out on the group of soon-to-be refugees and saw maybe a hundred children of all ages staring back at him expectantly. It was a view that tore at his heart.

CHAPTER 17

The Captain approached the massive interstellar freighter in the small craft, fully laden with trade goods. He looked out on that strange miniature enclosed universe, where multiple versions of one's self could exist side by side. Traffic crisscrossed the void, many of whom were likely scientists conducting investigations, but who knew what other sort of business was going on. This late in the bubble the numbers of small craft began to drop off dramatically, and holes disappeared one by one all over the place.

This trip had been bad -- the Captain had lost one of his best officers and was obliged to leave him behind on the other side of the aperture.

The Captain nodded back to his Navigator, then thumbed the com unit. Another version of the Navigator came up on the screen.

"Please put the Captain on," the Captain said, referring to the version of himself that currently had the bridge on board the starship.

The shipboard Navigator obediently turned over his shoulder and called for his commander. Immediately the other

Captain showed on the screen. *I'll never get used to this*, the Captain thought.

"Permission to come aboard, sir." the Captain requested.

The commander on the starship granted permission and closed the com link. The Captain flew their small craft toward one of the hangar doors on the large interstellar.

Something seemed wrong. The usual electric arcs, winds, and flashes had ended early on in the life of the bubble, but still there seemed to be a storm brewing. The Captain watched as all the apertures shut down except two -- the one they just came from and one other. It was lonely after all that traffic had disappeared, and the huge interstellar drifted without any other company. Why did it seem there were dark clouds forming just beyond the range of vision?

As the Captain approached the open hangar door, suddenly he noticed that other remaining aperture wink out of existence -- only their gate was the last isolated exit from this dreary void. The Captain gunned the thrusters toward the large hatch but for some reason he couldn't make any progress.

"There's a wind blowing, sir," the Navigator explained, "It's quite strong."

The Captain saw dark clouds billowing in, like a hurricane first slowly, and then faster and faster rotating about the last isolated aperture like the eye of a storm. He raised the power level trying to gain the safety of the hangar but to no avail -- the wind took hold and caught them in a deadly swirl around the hole. A deafening roar could be heard as powerful gusts pounded the hull.

"Give me more power to the gravity drive!" the Captain shouted.

But the Officer manning the engineering station shook his head -- there were not enough gravity wells out there to leverage against. The small vessel was wrenched away from its intended target.

Round and round the wind blew as they spiraled closer to the hole. Each time they passed the interstellar the Captain gave it another try, fighting the wind to try and reach that open hangar. But soon the Captain realized their massive fortress was also being swept around -- the starship was caught in the vortex.

"Sir, they've abandoned ship," the Navigator announced.

The Captain could see another small vessel exiting the hangar door, only to get caught in the storm in turn. The great freighter began to be torn apart as the horrific winds tore at its sides. How could this be? He did not remember abandoning ship before -- he did not experience that timeline -- that other Captain could not have been a version of himself from the past. Was it an alternate universe?

"Hold on! After all we've been through, we may not make it this time!" the Captain yelled over the deafening roar.

The storm only got worse. The Captain began to fear for his life as the little craft was shaken beyond anything he had ever experienced before. He looked out and saw huge chunks of structure break away from the interstellar and get sucked into the aperture. Then all hell broke loose and the last thing the Captain was conscious of was the entire storm rushing through that small hole.

CHAPTER 18

Lenny Chopra pointed at the screen logging all the sorties conducted by the Grindavik scientists. He and Carta Randall had painstakingly matched each of the logs with their video counterparts, and made notes each time one of the COSCAPP vessels appeared on the video. With some effort they were able to cross-reference most of the appearances on the video with their own logs, and confirm which mission they were viewing.

"I don't see this one in any of the logs." Lenny noted.

Carta turned from her own screen and watched the clip being fast-forwarded on Lenny's screen. A COSCAPP vehicle shot in front of the camera and disappeared through an aperture.

"Zoom in and see if there are any identification markings. We have the known flight and trajectory of the *Towa Maru*'s maiden voyage, and this path doesn't look familiar." Carta said.

Lenny selected several frames from the clip and zoomed in on the identifying markings. Contrary to those they had seen on the known vessels, the markings on this one weren't as vibrant -- it was as if the craft had been sitting out in the sun for a few decades, fading the paint to almost nothing. Lenny looked at several more frames, and stopped.

"Look at this," he said, "It's faded but definitely the *Towa Maru.*"

Carta took down a note in her digital pad. There were several of them now -- appearances of the faded *Towa Maru* that didn't correspond with any of the logs. It was as if Hughes' vessel had dropped out for a while and gone through some rough times before making a comeback. The vehicle looked aged somehow, like the shredded wormhole tether component they had found back in the Grindavik storehouse.

"Take a look at this one," Lenny pointed at another sequence.

The captured scene was faint and very far away. The video had been taken right at the beginning of the bubble, when flashes of light drew together and annihilated. This strange phenomenon happened every time one peeked into a fresh wormhole -- numberless flashes of light seemed to migrate toward each other and disappear, after which the regular apertures were the only things that remained. In this video, a COSCAPP vessel darted from the side and disappeared into one of those flashes of light before it could combine with a second flash.

Interesting, Carta thought. Could that be an early recording of the *Infinity's Breach* penetrating the No Point hole mistakenly created some sixty years earlier?

"Where does this video come from?" Carta asked.

"It's one of the very first videos taken by the older APP machines before they had wormhole tethers." Lenny replied.

"Are there any other videos taken at the same time -- in other directions?" Carta wondered.

Lenny looked through the directory and said, "Yes, there are two more wide angle. I think they did a panorama of 120 degrees each to capture all sides."

"Play all three back next to each other." she said.

Lenny set them up in three windows and started them all at the same time. In the one clip, the distant COSCAPP vessel could immediately be seen darting across the picture and falling into the flash of light. A little later and Carta saw what she was looking for, but in a different window. Several COSCAPPs raced for one hole, but all of them veered off except one, which slipped in.

"Hmm, I think we have something interesting here," Carta began, "These craft over here on the second screen are multiple versions of the *Infinity's Breach* doing practice runs on the Chinese No Point hole."

Carta ran all three clips back and forth in a loop.

"See, there's the *Infinity's Breach*, the one that actually penetrated through to No Point," Carta indicated, "But over here on screen one, out of the action happening at No Point, one vessel finds a way to slip into those early combining flashes."

The two investigators watched the clips loop back and forth for a few iterations, and then Carta called up Jacob Harrison to see if the scientist could put any light on the matter.

"*What!?*" was his reaction, "*Someone slipped in before the flashes annihilated each other?*"

Carta hadn't anticipated the surprised reaction, "Doctor, just what does it mean when two flashes combine like that?"

Jacob's voice explained over the phone, "*When two apertures are created together a pairing occurs, and the resulting tunnel between the two is exclusive -- it doesn't share the hyperspace bubble. When you open up only one aperture it tries to connect with something, so all the single apertures ever opened link together to create the bubble.*"

Harrison paused to allow that to sink in, then continued, "*But we've developed a way to charge the gates, or create a quantum code if you like, that tends to gravitate over to a matching hole. We nicknamed these 'Kisser Gates'. This means that decades apart if two groups open up matching apertures, they will migrate toward each other and pair up, kicking themselves out of hyperspace -- an exclusive tunnel between the two is born.*"

Carta asked, "So what are we seeing at the beginning of the clock, when multiple flashes annihilate each other?"

Harrison hesitated as if the concept bothered him somehow, "*That means our gates are connecting different eras of time.*"

Carta was unsure about what Harrison meant by it all, only that it gave her the clue she was looking for. She politely hung up and turned to Lenny.

"I think we have a scenario that connects the two timelines of the *Towa Maru*," she confidently stated.

Carta outlined what they knew already, that the *Towa Maru* was designed and built after the x-ray storms began, then went missing through an unknown aperture on her maiden voyage. Apparently, the vessel then reappeared in hyperspace, presumably entering in through another aperture, and made multiple trips in and out of other gates killing crews and stealing equipment as they went.

"So far this is all taking place after the Novissima disaster, because you can't go back prior to the first wormhole." Carta pointed out.

Lenny jumped in. "But when the Grindavik team forced open the No Point black hole experiment, a way opened up to a time before the disaster."

"Yes," Carta confirmed, "And when the Grindavik folks create their pair-coded gates connecting the future and past, the *Towa Maru* must have taken advantage of the brief time those gates appear in the bubble and jumped in, propelling them into the past."

"So that's how the *Towa Maru* could be destroyed before it was even built." Lenny acknowledged.

CHAPTER 19

"Okay shut everything down. We've got to see what's wrong on the Pointless side."

Tom Hildebrandt made his way over to the Grindavik industrial staging area and saw that the operation was still underway -- forklifts were going in and out of the large aperture taking supplies back to the Pointless excavations. His mind began spinning as he wondered why the other sets of gates weren't connecting. Murphy! If those twelve 'Kissers' weren't successful, they would still be fighting the x-ray storm collision with Grindavik only days away -- all their wormhole tethers would suddenly go offline even at historical Pointless. And on top of that it was hard to concentrate wondering what Hughes and his crew had been up to.

Tom walked back again through the small man-sized gate connecting to the past. The gate was still running off the future Grindavik power grid, in continuous causal connection through the wormhole tether. Again, he found himself right in the middle of a busy excavation operation, and not far away the large industrial gate was getting loads brought in by the forklifts he had seen earlier -- that large gate was also running on future Grindavik power. So, the operation sixty-five years earlier was going according to plan -- what about five years later? Did something happen in the intervening five years that stopped the operation to prevent the deployment of the twelve gates on the Pointless side? Unfortunately, there was no short cut wormhole connecting the end of the five years -- the only way to find out would be to wait that long, which would go well beyond the one-week limit on the wormhole tethers. This was something that needed Jacob Harrison's attention and maybe even higher up the authority chain.

An hour later Harrison frowned as he heard the news. Too much depended on those gates working -- there should have been wormholes established between Pointless and Grindavik already to keep their evacuation schedule.

Grindavik Colony President Howard Statner, who was also standing nearby was confused, "I don't quite understand what the issue is. Don't we already have wormholes back to the past?"

Harrison explained the problem once again, "We're on our own back there. If we try to involve any of the locals the information will leak out -- who knows what kind of paradox it could make. All we have is about five hundred meters of red rock tunnel and borrowed light bulbs overhead. We don't even have a power source back there."

"You mean there's no place to send our families?" Statner asked.

Jacob tried to explain how five years back at Pointless equaled a few hours at Grindavik, "It's all history to us. Sixty-five years of history between us. Our construction crews working sixty-five years ago can take all the time they need to construct places for us to live, then switch on the gates and let everyone go through. On our side our timeline doesn't pass linked to their timeline -- we can just pick anywhere in that sixty-five years and skip over the rest, as long as there are tuned gates waiting to pair up with those we have on this side."

Statner understood, "That means something happens to stop our crews before they can build the power plant and set up their gates."

"Exactly." Hildebrandt confirmed.

"Okay we've got to start one of the Pointless gates up now, while we still have power to draw on from the Grindavik power plants," Jacob decided, "I'll arrange to get singularities loaded up into one of the Pointless gates. Tom, get that set up as soon as you can. In the meantime, Howard, we've got to meet with Governor Wang and come up with an emergency evacuation plan in case no facilities are waiting on the other side!"

Early the next morning Hildebrandt stood by at Pointless as a fully loaded gate hummed in readiness, powered by a wormhole tether. They had taken one of the twelve out of storage status to test if it would connect with one of the Grindavik gates.

"Power it up." Harrison directed.

The technicians got the miniature accelerator primed and guided the co-orbiting pairs of black holes into the circular path at blinding speeds. The center of the torus revealed a reddish hue as the aperture opened, and when the technicians inserted the shielded walkway, they could see red rock tunnel walls and crowds of people on the other side. *It appears to be working*, Tom thought.

A man and a woman walked through whom Tom did not recognize. They didn't even stop to talk, but just nodded and headed for the Pointless exit leading toward the main town. Another small group of men emerged from the gate manhandling a hoverpallet loaded with a compact Seed Hyperaperture unit. But Hildebrandt had never seen that model before -- these were not from Hildebrandt Engineering! Tom's technicians just stood around not knowing what to think.

Jacob also looked perplexed as a steady stream of folks promptly walked out of the gate and headed for the exit.

"Excuse me, sir," Harrison stopped an authoritative-looking elderly man, "Where are you from?"

The man looked back in a matter-of-fact way and replied, "Bonestell of course."

The man looked around as if seeing the Grindavik-Pointless team for the first time and asked, "Isn't this the Bonestell return point?"

Hildebrandt and the others were in shock and couldn't say a thing so the man continued to walk on with his fellows.

An hour later Hildebrandt, Harrison, Statner, and representatives from Governor Wang sat at a dusty conference table tucked inside a temporary job shack at the Pointless diggings. Behind them through the shack windows could be seen a steady stream of refugees coming out of the gate from Bonestell.

"So our gates may still be connecting, but not to our Grindavik mates?" Tom asked, "I thought Bonestell was deserted."

"There must have been a paradox," Harrison proposed, "Somehow connecting with the No Point folks in the past must have changed the future somehow."

Statner thought he understood what that meant, "Do you mean there are two timelines coming from this point?"

"Yes," Jacob affirmed, "I'm guessing there was a pristine timeline that leads to our future, and we've changed that by our presence here. Who knows what sort of changes have taken place, until we corner one of those Bonestell fellows and grill him on their history."

"But our people are still in trouble in Grindavik!" Statner stressed.

"Yes indeed, we still have our people to bring back here, and no facilities available." Jacob returned.

Everyone paused and stared out the window as a team from Bonestell began to set up a large-scale Hyperaperture gate for industrial equipment. It was as if those other folks were just taking over!

"Whatever we do, I think we need to turn off the faucet and concentrate on getting our own people back here." Statner recommended.

Tom and Jacob agreed, and Harrison ran outside to tell the Bonestell crew to set up somewhere else. Tom watched out the windows as an argument broke out and one of the Bonestell crewmembers looked angry. Statner and the others followed Tom out to back up their colleague.

"We've done this before many times," a more calm-faced woman stood up to Jacob as the others held the angry man back, "As soon as we bring in our transports we'll be on our way."

"We've got an operation in progress here, you can't just set up your gate right in the middle of things." Jacob returned.

The angry man started shouting, "Grindavik! I should have known you were a Grindavik! I'll tear him apart!"

Several others came up and began to calm the man down.

"Let us unload our equipment and we'll be on our way." the woman negotiated.

"Destroy the planet and then you try to drive us out! I'll kill you Grindavik!" the angry man was heard to say.

Jacob turned to Statner and the governor representatives who nodded their assent.

"Okay, you've got one hour to be cleared out of here." Jacob said to the woman, and the Bonestell group turned and continued their setup.

The Bonestell team took two hours to clear out. Several large pressurized transports came through their gate and paused long enough for the group to pack up and leave to who knows where.

By that time word had come through Wang's office to start setting up emergency hygiene stations and begin evacuating Grindavik anyway, through the little man-sized and industrial-sized gates still running off the future power grid. Trying to get the 'Kisser Gates' working before x-rays destroyed the wormhole tether network did not appear to be an option any longer. Operators were frantically creating CAD models of tunnel cavities, and high-speed Kajima numerical control Continuous Miner machines tore into the rock. Hildebrandt watched displays as animated grinder heads worked through the CAD volume representing actual cut out cavities. The massive excavators carved high-bay chambers in short order, sending the loose rock back through the industrial gate to be dumped somewhere in the future Grindavik. Meanwhile, a steady stream of evacuees trudged back in time single file off to the side. It was mayhem back home, and the empty rock haulers always had a full load of refugees hanging on when they returned to Pointless.

It was a terrible unorganized mess! At this rate, and with only one industrial-sized and one man-sized gate in operation, it was doubtful the entire population could be moved before the x-ray storm struck.

CHAPTER 20

How could it have come to this? Masamune Hughes lamented at the mess they had gotten themselves in. Slowly, through the suit com system, Hughes made his report to Tom Hildebrandt beginning with the events that had occurred after the *Towa Maru* had disappeared into that distant aperture from which the massive spacecraft had emerged.

Hughes had been dumbstruck and the crew was in disarray. He was still feeling motion sickness from the zero-g flight. In just about every direction it was pitch black -- Hughes got the impression of vast distances. The *Towa Maru* was definitely not in a hyperspace bubble anymore.

"I'm reading vacuum outside. I think we're in space." Beth Kitamura reported.

From ahead of them one lone point of light shown as a star pierced the gloom. The glowing orb was close enough to illuminate Kasei had it been in the vicinity. Yet all the spectral indicators were wrong -- those were the feeble rays of an alien sun.

The crew pondered in silence. Was there some mistake in the instruments? No human had ever reached another star before.

"Rotate the camera around. Can we see the aperture?" Hughes asked.

As the craft thrustered around on its axis, all six of them gasped as an artificial space station came into view. The majority of the structure was cast in shadow with highlights where the distant star illuminated it. The bright beams of *Towa Maru*'s spotlights pierced the darkness and swept across a strangely active surface. Hughes couldn't describe it -- what shape could a continually morphing entity be classified as? Hundreds of small robotic triangles and squares tumbled over a lattice structure to various destinations, causing the lattice to grow or shrink organically. It was as if the intricate machines were cells in a large organism, performing self-maintenance and repair. Hughes was confused as ever -- what sort of alien technology was this? How did they find themselves in such a strange environment?

Beth slowly flew around the space station, while Masamune Hughes and Jiro Kitamura snapped photos and videos of the fascinating operation. In one instance, a square panel that had tumbled to a certain location parked itself on the lattice and a robotic arm unfolded from its middle. After performing some sort of repair, the arm folded itself in again and the square panel tumbled away end over end to a new destination, as grippers along each edge alternatively grasped and released the underlying structure. In another instance, several panels came together to form a small shape that thrustered away from the main station on its own power. Hughes thought he could watch the strange choreography for hours.

"What's that?" Hiroyuki Toshige exclaimed as he pointed to the port side.

Hughes rushed over and peered out a porthole. The station had taken on the shape of a long appendage that formed a loop or torus. There was a shimmering in the middle, in what Hughes had come to recognize as a live aperture.

"It's a gate -- maybe we can get back through!" Emi proposed.

But Hughes frowned. They had seen their entry aperture shut -- who knew if this hole would get them back home. Hughes never felt so powerless in his life -- they were in a strange environment with unproven technology. He half wanted to wait around here and see if they could find out for certain how to generate a passage back to the hyperspace bubble.

"Why isn't com working?" Beth asked, "If only we could get confirmation from Carrie and Tom."

Hughes was alarmed for a second, "Aren't we getting any power? Is the wormhole tether still connected?"

Beth responded with a shake of the *Towa Maru*, as if she were tipping her wings to say hello to someone on the ground.

"I've got plenty of compressed air for attitude control." she pointed out, "Our compressors are back in the Hildebrandt Engineering lab -- we're venting jets of air out in space."

Beth paused a moment then spun the nose toward that distant star, "Hold on! I'm going to take us for a spin with the gravitic pulse drive."

Hughes and some of the others who had released their acceleration straps scrambled back to their seats and hung on. There was a punishing press as the *Towa Maru* plunged sunward for a few minutes, and then Beth turned around and retraced their route back to the strange morphing station.

"We've got plenty of power," she noted.

Masamune said, "I think we should go for it -- there's an aperture right there waiting for us. We can always reverse ourselves."

Beth moved them toward the center of the torus and again steered the *Towa Maru* through the aperture. Again, they found themselves in a dark, featureless void. It was clear they had not made it back to the hyperspace bubble -- behind them the strange morphing space station was still there -- had they gone anywhere at all?

Hughes began to get anxious -- *where the heck are we*, he thought. He looked over at Sachiko and could tell she was worried about their children Ichiro, Teresa, and Sabby.

Beth set the *Towa Maru* into a parking orbit about half a kilometer out from the morphing station and powered down all inessential systems. She disconnected the data feed from her helmet and floated out of the pilot chair.

"I'm going out," she proclaimed as she made her way back to the airlock, "We've got to see what happened to the com systems."

The woman was still decked out in the metal pressure suit, helmet under her arm, brushing up loudly against the walls as she moved.

Hughes watched her squeeze past, "You're going to need a buddy, and someone who knows the systems -- I'll go with you."

Hughes wasn't all that proficient in extra-vehicular activity, and certainly had never done an EVA in zero-g before. But there were only two pressure suits on board, and he was quite certain the second suit would fit him better than the other passengers. Hughes still felt a little queasy with space sickness as he followed Beth into the airlock. The second suit stood to one side of the exit hatch facing across the way toward Beth's empty suit stand, still connected to umbilicals for recharging all the consumables like air, drinking water, and power. Hughes began to feel nervous as he realized what he had volunteered for. It had only been days, it seemed, since he had put on a suit like this back in Delaware Heights and had followed Sachiko out to hit balls. But that had been a protected environment with lots of safety protocols in place -- there wasn't a possibility to drift away and get lost in deep space.

At least Hughes knew how to get the equipment on. As he slipped into the rear entry port and struggled with extending his arms and legs into the proper openings, the lightweight hard-shell joints passively rotated back and forth following his movements. Beth helped him seal the backpack and check the equipment to make sure all life support systems were functioning properly.

Beth pointed at his radio and switched hers on to do a suit-to-suit com check, and suddenly jumped back as if she were startled. Hughes switched on his radio and was in turn jolted by the com traffic already in progress.

". . . *do you read? Can you hear this transmission? Please acknowledge,*" a digitally produced voice was saying.

The quality was bad, as if the frequencies didn't quite match. The signal would momentarily get clear, then degrade into garbled static, and then cycle back to a clear voice again. Also, Hughes was a little confused by the accent -- an unfamiliar pronunciation he hadn't heard before. Beth looked at Hughes through the helmet, as if waiting for him to make the first move.

Hughes got himself ready to transmit and said, "Uh, hello?"

The digital voice came back on, "*Yes freighter this is . . . trouble with radio?*"

The transmission dropped in the middle as the signal went out of phase.

"This is the *Towa Maru* -- we're not getting a clear signal." Hughes replied.

". . . *turn on shipboard data telemetry* . . . " the voice scratched through.

Hughes was getting a bit worried, "Who is this? Why do you need our telemetry?"

". . . *station. We need to see what went wrong,*" the highly fractured voice explained.

Beth had been watching Hughes the whole time and abruptly jumped on the line, "It's the station with the aperture gate -- they're trying to troubleshoot our passage -- they think we are a freighter." she said.

Hughes looked at her and considered a reply to the digital voice. It was all very bizarre -- who would have the capability to create an aperture out here when Hughes' team had just invented the technology?

There was a bigger issue at stake that began to dawn on him. Humankind had yet to venture beyond Sol's solar system, and yet here was this alien station orbiting some unknown star and communicating in English.

"Who are you, and why do you have the ability to create wormholes?" Hughes asked.

The digital voice replied, "*We will download an information package . . . data connection.*"

Hughes lost the middle of the message, but was fairly sure the station wanted to wirelessly download some instructions.

"We only have working radio in our suits -- there is no data connection," Hughes began, "We intend to do repairs."

"*Thanks freighter, keep in . . .*" the voice concluded.

Hughes followed as Beth depressurized the airlock, picked up some tools, and opened the outer hatch. She clipped on one of two safety tethers and began pulling herself hand over hand toward the stern of the vessel.

Hughes slowly poked his head out the opening and was briefly struck with terror. All that blackness -- as if he could fall toward eternity. He became conscious of his own breathing inside the confines of the helmet and somehow took comfort in the protective shell. Hughes clipped himself in and kept his eyes on the hull as he worked his way from handhold to handhold, alternatively setting and releasing every other clip as he went along. Up ahead, Beth could be seen with the bundle of tools drifting out to the extents of their tethers. She stopped and waited for him to catch up.

As Hughes got closer to where Beth was waiting, he began to see the damaged surface of the hull scorched by an electric arc that had struck them before they had plunged unto the aperture. A maintenance hatch had been sheared down the middle leaving a finger wide crack. Beth got to work right away and began removing the pieces of hatch and stowing them in a specimen bag. Underneath, hover coils lined the opening that centered on the com avionics.

"*Look at that -- one of the beryllium tuner blocks has been damaged.*" Beth noted as she broke open the electronics box.

Beryllium! That would be very difficult to repair. Beryllium's dimensional stability in large temperature swings had made it the material of choice for tuning blocks, but there were no spares on board.

Hughes reluctantly pointed out, "We'll have to make repairs before we give it another try through the aperture -- I want to make sure Tom has a say in this. They might have figured out a way to get us back by now."

Beth reeled in another tool and began removing the damaged tuning block. They pulled out an intact one as well for comparison. Hughes thought back on the nebulous station, and the tumbling robotic panels with all their protruding implements -- *surely the station should be able to manufacture some parts*, he thought.

"Um, excuse me, station." Hughes sought the digital voice, "We need to make repairs on some parts. We'll need some manufacturing capability. Can you help us?"

The familiar station voice came online in the helmet com, "*There are manufacturing and repair facilities at Everwebber Port up system.*"

What does that mean, Hughes thought. He followed Beth as she made her way back to the airlock carrying the two beryllium parts. They sealed the outer hatched and re-pressurized the airlock. By the time they had gotten out of the suits and set the various batteries and tanks for recharging, Jiro came back with an announcement.

"The station gets periodic supply ships from a small planet orbiting the star," Kitamura said, "We watched a few arrive and take themselves apart, all the pieces contributing to the station maintenance."

Jiro described how the supply ships were made of the same square or triangular robotic panels. Each time a ship docked with the station, all the panels comprising it would tumble over the station structure until nothing was left of the ship -- as if it dissolved on contact.

"We need to repair this beryllium tuner block," Hughes brought Jiro up to speed on the repair efforts, "I wonder if those supply ships come from Everwebber?"

Hughes and Beth described to everyone the strange conversation they had had with the station, and they all agreed to follow the supply ship route back to the planet of origin. They all strapped in and Beth again confirmed that they had power and pneumatics through the wormhole tether. Once Beth and Emi had set their course with the gravity drive inward toward the planet, they were free to move about, prepare meals, and do various chores as needed.

The trip took several days, during which time the six of them got to know each other a little better. Masamune, Sachiko, Jiro, and Beth had had social interaction before through their ward activities, but there had been only professional interaction with the Toshige's until that point. Hughes wasn't even sure which ward the other lived in. At first Hughes felt a little awkward, but after a while the mutual appreciation for humor and similar technical interests brought them all together. Masamune learned that Toshige had been his Home Teacher for a couple months way back at the beginning of the Hughes' move to Grindavik, but he had totally forgotten about it. In Grindavik, Home Teachers usually oversaw the smooth transition of new move-ins, and helped them integrate with the ward.

In spite of all the camaraderie, there was still need for private time-outs that posed a problem, since the bunks were quite narrow -- and it was difficult for each couple to get alone time together. On the one hand they were all grateful Toshige had outfitted the galley with its demonstration food supply, but on the other hand they all felt somewhat ruffled and haggard as Beth brought the *Towa Maru* into an orbit around the planet.

Hughes looked down on the desolate world with some reservation. It was pockmarked and cratered similar to Earth's moon, and certainly didn't have any atmosphere to speak of.

There was evidence of sparsely settled built-up areas, but there didn't seem to be much activity on the ground. If they had to go down there for repairs it probably mean more suit time for him. They detected several artificial satellites in orbit and at one point a small automated spacecraft followed them around for a bit before giving up and heading back to where it came from. Hughes thought about getting one of the suit com units out to see if there had been any radio traffic, but the little craft had already gone before he could put the plan into effect.

"Mas, take a look at this," Beth called out as she looked over her instruments.

Hughes floated over to where Beth indicated a radar image and magnified camera view of a massive structure orbiting the planet.

"Do you think it's another station?" Beth asked.

Hughes studied the object -- there was something familiar about it that he couldn't quite place. As he watched the perspective change suddenly it dawned on him -- the huge structure was identical to the machine or spacecraft they had observed in the hyperspace bubble! For a few minutes Hughes was confused -- were they back in the bubble again? He had observed the view of that ship many times as they had done experiments and sorties with the SCAPP and COSCAPP vessels. But no, there was that planet surface below them.

"I think we were correct about it being a spacecraft -- it must be a twin to that massive machine we saw in the bubble," he concluded.

Hughes hoped some of the curiosity he had experienced upon viewing the huge vessel might be answered -- was that ship built by future versions of themselves as all the other SCAPP and COSCAPP vessels had been, or did the ship carry other unrelated explorers?

Just then Jiro, who had been trying to locate the origin of the supply ships spoke up, "It looks like the robotic vessels are lifting off from the vicinity of an active mining operation. It's mostly automated machinery. Wait -- I can see people moving around down there!"

Kitamura put the view on the screen and everyone gasped in unison. Up until this point, the severity of their situation had kept Hughes' mind on the operation of the COSCAPP vessel. Suddenly the alien star, morphing station, and tiny figures loping around in space suits on a dusty surface brought to his mind the startling reality of where they were -- in a distant solar system far away from their home on Kasei. Were those beings walking around down there human or something else? How did life find its way to this distant corner of the universe -- a thousand questions ran through his mind.

"We --" Hughes managed to mumble, "we have to go down and talk to them."

Hughes looked over at his wife. She was still worried about the children, but he could tell the fear of some unknown alien intelligence was back. *Too bad there are no golf balls nearby*, Hughes thought.

Beth also had a worried look on her face as she turned to Emi, "Can the gravitic pulse drive take us down to the surface?"

"I don't think anyone has actually used it that way on Mars before, but we've done tests pulsing the hovercoils. It should work." Emi confirmed.

The two women got to work on the drive while Masamune and Jiro worked out a coordinate system for the new planet. It wasn't entirely obvious at first, but after a few observations they identified the poles and mapped out longitude and latitude. The gravitics didn't work intuitively the way orbital mechanics said two proximate masses should behave -- the craft was able to slow down and hover over a specified spot on the surface even though they weren't at geostationary altitude. Beth took them on a gradual descent that used gravity to break their orbital speed and quickly got them situated above their target. They aimed for the little suited figures that Jiro reported had by that time all piled into a vehicle of sorts.

The *Towa Maru* lightly touched down on the top of a dust-covered hill. Hughes could see mirrored faceplates of four bulky aliens looking their way -- humanoid at least. He could feel his own heart beat as he thought of first contact with inhabitants on a world distant from his own. Hughes and Beth went back to the airlock and suited up. After depressurizing the airlock, Hughes went first and stepped outside, followed by Beth.

The surface was very similar to that of Earth's moon, Hughes thought. He had visited the moon early in his life but had watched from a porthole window as colleagues stomped around in the thick gray powder outside. This time he was the one to step out into that desolate environment. He looked down slope and carefully chose his steps toward those others. The four strangers continued to look up at them and readied what looked like a weapon. Hughes was not sure what to do -- were the aliens hostile? He tried to show empty hands, slightly raised in the universal sign of 'we come in peace', and eased himself to a point about four or five meters in front of the others.

Hughes faced the group in what seemed like an endless lapse of time. The suits they wore seemed a bit primitive to him, constructed of soft material that might have been fashionable in the early days of Earth's space exploration era. *How quaint*, he thought -- it must take hours for them to get ready for an EVA. Then Hughes realized his mirrored visor was in place and he reached up to expose the clear bubble of the helmet so the others could see his face. It appeared to him that the action must have relieved the strangers, because each of them pulled up their own visors to reveal perfectly human faces looking back at him. Asian! *What fascinating tales these folks could tell*, he thought. There was a woman who appeared to be acting as leader of the group.

Hughes took a chance and decided to use Japanese instead of the more universal English -- he could always repeat himself later.

"Hello. We have need of repairs on our ship. We back traced the departure point of the cargo crafts and saw your mining operation and thought you might be able to synthesize a part for us." Hughes said through the suit radio com system.

At the sound of his voice the woman tensed up again. Could she understand him?

Hughes could see her lips move as she replied, but the actual voice must have been generated by a translator because it sounded electronic, "*We are just visitors here too, observing the robotic operation. However, we do have the ability to synthesize some types of parts. What do you need?*"

Hughes caught some movement out on the pockmarked plains and saw the robotic mining machinery building a tower-like structure in the distance. The four strangers turned to follow his gaze as the tower suddenly transformed itself into a rocket and shot off into space -- another supply ship on its way to the alien morphing station.

Hughes replied, "We need a beryllium alloy part machined."

"*Beryllium!*" the woman's voice exclaimed, "*We don't have any beryllium. Could you use titanium instead?*"

Hughes considered that for a moment. Titanium would not have the dimensional stability that beryllium had, and would surely shrink and expand depending on whether that side of the COSCAPP was in sun or shadow -- it would surely not be able to keep the system tuned in a consistent manner. On the other hand, perhaps Beth could tune the thing simply by rotating the *Towa Maru* ever so slightly until resonance was achieved. It was worth a try.

"Titanium may do temporarily I suppose, enough to get us back through the gate." Hughes mused, "Please follow us."

The woman hesitated for a minute or two, apparently not sure she could trust them. Then she turned to the others and left a brief set of instructions before following he and Beth up the hill. The woman's suit was so bulky she obviously labored to pull all that mass up any elevation gain. Hughes reached the *Towa Maru* and stepped up onto the small staging platform that deployed whenever the airlock was in use. Since the lock was only big enough for two persons, especially when one of them was wearing a suit so large, Beth waited outside for the next repress cycle.

When the woman stood with him in the airlock, Hughes asked, "What is your operating air pressure?"

The woman hesitated a bit, but showed him a pressure gauge that allowed her to monitor the atmosphere external to the suit. Hughes could not make heads or tails of the units on the gauge, but assumed she would be wise enough to avoid any dangers that could come from pressure sickness. As they waited for the airlock pressure to equalize with the *Towa Maru*'s internal cabin air, Hughes could see the woman speaking to her people through some private channel. After a while, as if acting on some command from that unseen conversation, the woman explained that she intended to keep her suit sealed to maintain biological containment -- after all, history was full of examples where isolated cultures had merged, decimating one or the other because they had not built up the correct antibodies in their population. *Smart girl*, he thought -- no need to start a plague here.

Hughes opened the inner hatch and led the woman to the *Towa Maru*'s control cabin where three of his colleagues were waiting.

Through a hand mic (so she could hear through the helmet) Hughes introduced himself and pointed to the others, "And this is Dr. Hiroyuki Toshige, his wife Dr. Emi, and Jiro Kitamura. You are on the *Towa Maru*."

Masamune showed her a bit of the control room, explaining some of the equipment, "We're so glad to find you! We've been wandering all over and have seen nothing but robotic systems," he said.

From the direction of the airlock a partly suited Beth wandered back, followed by Sachiko who had been back in the hygiene unit.

"This is Dr. Kitamura's wife Beth, and my wife Dr. Sachiko." Hughes introduced.

The woman appeared quite excited at the sight of Sachiko and began a silent, animated dialog inside the helmet.

Jiro jumped up and switched on the speaker so they could all hear her.

"*My name is Sochiko!*" she exclaimed, "*I can't help but feeling we are cousins somehow.*"

Interesting, thought Hughes, a stranger of Japanese descent in another solar system with a name similar to his wife. It was a pleasant surprise indeed.

Hughes suddenly realized the woman might have need of recharging her air and batteries, "We have extra air that is quite sterile. Can we service your suit while you are still in it?"

Sochiko thanked him and showed him the umbilical connectors. Beth pulled out a universal fitting and they began to replenish the woman's gases.

While that was being completed, Masamune brought two small metal parts, one of which was cracked in half, "This one was broken, and you can see it is a mirror of this intact piece. Can you scan in the geometry and cut a new one for us?" he asked.

Sochiko took the piece and turned it over in her hands, then turned to Hughes and asked, "*Can we get to orbit? Our mother ship has the right equipment.*"

Hughes answered in the affirmative. They somehow got Sochiko into one of the accelerator seats and in no time the *Towa Maru* had reached significant thrust from the gravitic pulse drive. The instruments found more and more artificial satellites that they had not seen before, including another large spherical station, and Sochiko's mother ship, the *Soarer*, that had been parked in orbit. Once again one of the smaller robotic craft approached the *Towa Maru*, and Sochiko explained that it was an automated tug trying to contact them via radio.

Hughes and the others had been talking to the woman in Japanese, but somewhere during the conversation Sochiko showed that she had a native proficiency in English, even though her accent was a bit butchered. From that point on they spoke in English because the translator missed some things.

The *Towa Maru* pulled within a few meters from the *Soarer* hatch. In the airlock, Sochiko clipped on a tether and jumped across the short gap to the other open airlock where a suited colleague was waiting. Sochiko handed over both the intact and broken pieces that Hughes had given her. The other crewmember took the pieces inside and Sochiko followed the tether back to the *Towa Maru*. Hughes had been in his pressure suit with her in the airlock, and brought her inside the cabin again.

"*Who are you? Where do you come from?*" the woman suddenly asked.

Hughes had wanted to ask her the same thing. The feeling that they were somehow distantly related was too uncanny.

"We're from Kasei." Hughes began, "It's a long story, but I'll just say that we've been trying to prevent a planet-wide disaster from destroying our home. But we went through the gate and got lost. We've been wandering ever since."

Before Hughes could return the question Sochiko asked, "*Have you been sending us messages?*"

"No, we saw you for the first time near the mining operation and thought you were overseeing it." Hughes replied.

"*What about Bridgestar. Have you ever been to Bridgestar?*" Sochi queried.

Hughes answered truthfully, "I don't know what that is. Is Bridgestar a planet?"

"*We don't know either, but there is evidence of extremely hostile pirates that may come from there. Do you know anything about pirates?*" she asked.

Masamune was surprised, and answered in the negative. Suddenly it all made sense -- the weapons, the cautionary stance, the mistrust of strangers.

Sochiko asked, "*Tell me more about the 'gate'.*"

Hughes explained, "You don't know? It's an orbital facility out on the edge of your solar system that allows ships to pass through a wormhole to distant stars. Kasei is far away, my dear, orbiting around a star named 'Sol'."

The woman showed astonishment at his explanation when she asked, "*How did you engineer the gate?*"

Us engineering the gate? Hughes had been thinking all along that he and his crew had intruded on the civil works and infrastructures of these people, when in fact they seemed just as lost as he. He couldn't really say they were part of the team that invented Dualer Gates upon which the morphing station was based -- someone else may have invented the technology on their own.

Hughes replied, "We just stumbled on it. And unfortunately, we have no idea how to aim it or get back."

"*How long does it take to get out there from here?*" she asked.

"The *Towa Maru* can get there in just a few days -- she's quite fast." Hughes noted.

Sochiko seemed intrigued by the aperture, as if she had some agenda in mind, "*Do you have any video of the gate?*"

Hughes brought her over to a monitor, and she bumped around in the heavy suit until she could see the screen through her clear faceplate. He played back the video they had recorded only days before. The woman stared on in fascination.

Hughes narrated some scenes until the video came to an end, "Then we were here again. We keep going between two solar systems as though the mechanism is stuck. We can't get back to Kasei."

Still bundled up in her suit Sochiko explained to the six *Towa Maru* crew members a little about her world, which apparently was located exactly opposite the host star. She and her shipmates had come exploring the dusty planet, with the intent of mining it's resources since their own world consisted entirely of water!

"*The official name used to be 'Sado' and it was a prison world. Now we call our planet 'Mother' because it gives us our sustenance.*" Sochiko explained.

"There was an island on ancient Earth named Sado. That was also a prison. What a strange coincidence!" Jiro mused.

Sachiko and Sochiko seemed to have developed a friendship closer than the others. They smiled at each other as if they were old buddies.

"But where did your people come from?" Sachiko asked, "We didn't think humans had left Sol -- and here you are speaking our language! "

Sochiko's native tongue, though unintelligible at first, had proven to be some derivative of Japanese. And her English was pretty good too. Unfortunately, the woman couldn't explain where her people had come from, only that they had been on Mother for many generations, even before any of their historical records.

If they had had some method to compare dates, Hughes and company would have realized they were displaced in time by hundreds of years. Unfortunately, no such clues were forthcoming.

Sochiko delivered the machined parts about an hour later, and the *Towa Maru* took her back to her lander on the surface. There were many more questions that could have been asked, but Beth kept hurrying them up -- no one knew how long the wormhole tether would continue to remain connected.

"We'll visit Mother if we can learn to aim the gate, and if we solve our planetary dilemma." Hughes promised.

They waved goodbye and the *Towa Maru* followed another one of those strange morphing station supply ships as it blasted off into the black sky.

Again, it took several days on the outward journey as the *Towa Maru* made its way to the station and aperture. Beth and Masamune did one more space walk enroute, taking the new manufactured part out to the com system for installation. Hughes was relieved when they finally got back inside, with all parts safely installed in their proper place.

"Let's try this out for size." Hughes suggested.

Beth got at the compressed air thruster controls and began to make hair trigger adjustments on *Towa Maru*'s attitude. The trick was to get the side with the new titanium tuner block with just enough sun and shadow so the thermal expansion of the metal would cause a signal to get through. And the only way to do that was by trial and error.

Jiro got on the communicator, "Hildebrandt Engineering -- Grindavik this is *Towa Maru*, come in. This is *Towa Maru*, come in.," he repeated over and over again as Beth slowly spun the vessel.

It was several hours later when a static-filled response came through. No one could understand what the other party was saying at first, so Beth jockeyed the orientation until the signal cleared up a bit.

It was a recording -- an unknown voice authoritatively demanded, "Hughes you and your colleagues are under arrest. Return to the aperture immediately!"

*****

"Station, this is the *Towa Maru*." Hughes called over the suit com.

There was very little pause as the station quickly responded in the digital voice, "*Freighter, this is Bridgestar. Have you completed repairs?*"

Hughes was taken aback. So, the station was called Bridgestar after all. What about Sochiko's warning of pirates? Suddenly the name 'Bridgestar' made sense -- everything fell into place. Bridgestar must have been a facility constructed in their own future for the purpose of conducting ships safe passage in a network of wormholes between planets. The station would look identical as counterparts orbited multiple worlds. And materials for repairs could be mined and gathered on some worlds, and distributed through the wormhole network to where they were needed. Since Bridgestar used the same wormhole technology as their own Hyperaperture, if there was a problem when one gate fired up and it couldn't find its mate in the other system it might dump the poor ship into the hyperspace bubble, like what happened to the huge freighter.

"Yes, repairs are complete, but we still don't have a digital connection for telemetry." Hughes answered, "Can you tell us how to get back to where we came from originally?"

Bridgestar answered, "*Your passage to Mars is paid for, but the singularities in your interstellar drive have caused problems in the wormhole conduit targeting calibrations. We are trying to adjust the conduit to correct the target.*"

Interstellar drive? *We don't have one of those*, Hughes thought.

Jiro detected his confusion and suggested, "Maybe it's referring to the black holes orbiting inside our wormhole tether?"

Hughes countered, "I think Bridgestar thinks we are the great spacecraft drifting in the bubble. It's passage to Mars must have gone wrong so the station is trying to get the freighter -- us -- back to Mars."

Toshige's eyes widened, "By all means we should allow it to deposit us at Mars!"

Hughes frowned. If they wanted to get home, Mars would not be good enough.

"I'm afraid the Mars Bridgestar is referring to is likely from our distant future," Hughes voiced his concerns, "Which will not be back to the bubble."

Did that mean Mars did have a future after all?

"And another thing," Jiro added, "In order to get a trouble-free passage, it looks like we would have to shut down the wormhole tether."

Hughes got back on the radio with the station, "Bridgestar, we cannot shut down our singularities without catastrophic consequences to our vessel. Can you remind us how payment is made for passage?"

Bridgestar explained, "*Passage is one hundred grams of hemoglobin for every ton of mass of your spacecraft. The hemoglobin is a resource unavailable on our mining worlds and is critical for use in the nanoassemblers in Bridgestar's maintenance chain."*

All six crewmembers aboard the *Towa Maru* gasped. Such a payment for passage would require more blood than the crew had at the moment, even if they were to drain themselves dry. Then a chilling thought occurred to Hughes -- if the passage for the freighter had been paid for, how much blood had been required for that massive spacecraft? Somehow, they had to get back -- that spacecraft might not have been what it seemed.

"Bridgestar, you say passage has already been paid?" Hughes asked.

Bridgestar replied, *"Freighter, the passage to Mars was paid for but unsuccessful. Bridgestar guarantees passage until a successful transfer is achieved. Your vessel is the beneficiary of the transfer, and Bridgestar will make as many attempts as needed to succeed, regardless of the presence of singularities in your propulsion system. Please try again, and Bridgestar will attempt to compensate."*

If what Hughes suspected was true, he was not sure if he wanted to benefit from such blood money. Nevertheless, they were in a quandary, and if they didn't get back, they may never be able to investigate that star freighter or warn their colleagues.

"Okay, let's give it another try." Hughes concluded.

Once again, the *Towa Maru* headed for the morphing station. The great appendage framing the temporary gate torus loomed out in front of them and Beth guided the vessel right through the middle. Hughes closed his eyes, hoping they would find themselves once more in the bubble.

"Space again," Beth broke the hope, "Spectral data indicates it's the same system we just came from."

Hughes snapped up the suit com head phones and listened for any traffic.

"Freighter," Bridgestar's digital voice came on, *"The last calibration was still off -- the transit to Mars was unsuccessful."*

The news was disheartening, even though they figured as much already.

Hughes was getting nervous about the wormhole tether time limit, "I'm not sure what the latest estimate is for when the x-ray storm will hit Grindavik, but it can't be more than a week or so away. This going back and forth is going to leave us stranded without propulsion."

"It's strange -- we could be hundreds of light years from Sol, thousands of years into the future, and still our energy source is causally connected to Grindavik through that small wormhole tether conduit." Jiro frowned.

Sachiko, who had not been feeling well due to the unusual combination of weightlessness and pregnancy, suddenly looked up to Hughes with a concerned look on her face.

"Mas, can we do something?" Sachiko asked, "You know, in case we can't get back before the wormhole tether ceases to function."

Toshige spoke up, "We're still in the same solar system as before, maybe we can enlist the help of that young lady and her crew. Konna tokoro Nihon no kata ga iru to anshin shimasu yo."

Toshige had suddenly jumped into Japanese, mirroring all of their feelings: 'finding other Japanese in a place like this is quite comforting.'

"But it's three days up system from here -- that's at least six days out of the way. We'd be nearing the time limit for the wormhole tethers." Jiro pointed out.

Hughes was also doubtful, "We'd have to have a plan, like ask for an onboard compressor and batteries to hold a major charge. We can't just ask them to install chemical rockets that will do us any good!"

Hughes and Jiro tried hard to talk some sense into everyone, but in the end the four others prevailed and once more the *Towa Maru* followed her previous path toward the dusty planet.

It was two days later when Beth discovered something was wrong -- the airless world was nowhere to be found.

"I'm not picking it up on any of the telescopes." Jiro confirmed.

"Try scanning along the orbital path," Sachiko suggested, "Maybe our passage through the wormhole wasn't instantaneous."

Masamune was getting irritable. Even though he too wasn't against seeing the delightful Sochiko again, they had already used up two precious days of their limited time. If that last jump had taken them to a different date again, those folks may already have been long gone.

"Whoa! There's another planet I've never seen before, somewhat behind where the other one should have been. It's got cloudy swirls, sort of like those old pictures of Earth." Jiro said excitedly.

All six crewmembers looked at each other in puzzlement.

Sachiko was first to figure it out, "Remember Sochiko told us her world had the same orbit, only on opposite sides of the star. I think we've jumped in time as well."

Emi agreed, "If this is their native home, it will be more likely that they will have the resources to help us."

Beth adjusted course to bring them into orbit around the new planet.

"I see a major station in orbit. Very large. Maybe we can dock there for repairs." Jiro announced.

"Excellent idea." Hughes agreed.

However, when they got closer to the huge spherical structure, there were obvious signs of disrepair. Hughes could see an aged curved surface contrasting with the cloudy swirls below, and the absolute darkness of space beyond. The nearer they approached, the more the spherical horizon looked like a small planet with a terminator dividing the light and dark shadows.

Beth approached a tall structure towering away from nadir direction -- like a gigantic eyeball with the optic nerve still attached. Bunches of spherical modules clustered about the tower, and Hughes realized that they might have once been garages for small spacecraft. In numerous locations doors could be seen cracked open slightly, as if the mechanisms were too rusted to complete the job. The skin plates were pitted from micrometeorites, some likely having penetrated the interior.

"I don't think we'll find any help here," Jiro noted, "There are no power signatures. I think this station has been abandoned for a long time."

The crew watched in silence a bit longer as Beth piloted the *Towa Maru* around the entire girth of the sphere. Hughes listened in on the suit com earphones just in case there was any traffic, but could only hear a faint static from galactic cosmic ray background noise.

Beth turned their attention to the planet below and moved their vessel away from the derelict station. Unlike his memory of Earth, Hughes saw constant cloudy swirls below -- it was not possible to see continents or oceans through the swirls like one could on Earth. Kilometer after kilometer passed below without a break.

Suddenly Toshige cried out, "I see a land mass! There's an opening in the cloud cover near the pole."

Beth adjusted their orbit to pass over the break, which showed healthy green landmass and wide rivers or bays. The ocean storms beat right up against the continent but seemed to stay away from the inland portions.

"Take us down," Hughes nodded.

Again, the gravity pulse drive took them into an unnatural dive that ignored orbital dynamics or trajectories used for centuries to slow one down using atmospheric drag. Below them appeared a forest of magnificent proportions.

"Do you see anything that resembles a city?" Sachiko asked no one in particular.

"It's all just forested rolling hills." Emi replied.

Beth's flight path slowed to a crawl as all six of the passengers stared in wonder at a fantastic landscape, familiar yet alien in so many ways.

"Reminds me of the redwood forest back on Earth." Sachiko blurted out.

"Or Sequoia." Beth called back from the cockpit.

"Or Aokigahara, or Kamikochi," inserted Toshige.

There was silence for a while, and Masamune knew more than one of his crew mates fought back tears -- no matter how many years one grows to love the red rock vistas of Kasei, Mother Chikyu (Earth) always beckons one home.

"Now I understand why Sochiko calls this world 'Mother'." Hughes said in a soft voice.

The silence continued for a while longer.

All of a sudden *Towa Maru* passed over a copse of trees and below them could be seen several people standing in the shadows.

"Back it up Beth, down there!" Hughes shouted.

The *Towa Maru* descended in a lazy spiral until it hovered just above the ground, but kept a distance away. Jiro zoomed in with telephoto and put the scene on the screen.

"Over there. You can see several of them crouching behind trees." Hughes pointed out.

Jiro panned the camera around and got a lock on the position. Hughes grasped as he made out a grotesque facemask and blood-red helmet and armor. The person, or creature, was readying a high-powered compound bow fitted with a barbed arrow. Jiro began a target search with a second camera to see what the thing was aiming at.

"They're primitives!" Toshige remarked.

Sachiko was repulsed, "Sochiko came from the same planet as these?"

Jiro zeroed in on a face in the distance, picked out of the foliage. It was an Asian face, and there was almost an audible sigh as it was apparently someone with a technological background -- a series of instruments could be seen attached to a harness over a black suit.

Suddenly the one screen showed the arrow let loose, and just as suddenly the poor Asian fellow went down with the arrow stuck through one eye. Sachiko and several others turned away in horror.

"It's a battle, or something --" Toshige remarked.

All eyes were on the screens as two fellow black-clad figures lifted their wounded colleague between them and rushed off through the undergrowth. Jiro tried to keep the cameras aimed correctly and follow the progress of the skirmish in spite of all the vegetation blocking the view. Beth eased the *Towa Maru* along hovering just above the ground, trying to both keep their vessel out of sight and also to allow the cameras to target in on the two groups using telephoto.

Soon the black-clad trio was lost from sight. Jiro focused on the two pursuing hunters as they zigzagged through the trees with their bows ready. The red-clad figures walked into a cavern of sorts, and after some hesitation on the outside Beth eased the *Towa Maru* into the dark opening.

"Those barbarians may have trapped Sochiko's countrymen." Hughes spoke aloud.

There was no reason to think that Sochiko was related to the black-clad people, but by the look on everyone's face, Hughes could see they were all thinking similar thoughts.

"What can we use as a weapon?" Jiro wondered.

"We don't want to hurt those poor primitives, just shake them up a bit. Mild electric shock?" Hughes added.

By then the *Towa Maru* was fully enclosed in darkness, with spotlights blazing. Anyone further down the tunnel would not be able to miss the approach of the vessel. On the left was a curved wall, but the tunnel wall on the right abruptly came to an end opening up to a wide, liquid-filled cavern. The floor of the tunnel continued on past the range of their spotlights as a beach of sorts.

"I've got an idea --" Toshige announced, and quickly began to gather various items from the cabin, "I'll need a spare hovercoil."

Hughes, Emi, and Sachiko scrambled to help Toshige with his homemade weapon assembly. By the time they finished, using rolls of tape to keep the various pieces from falling apart, the weapon looked quite impressive. The unit could be held like a rifle, but had an extension cord coming out the back that was needed to power the hovercoil.

Masamune asked, "This is not really lethal, is it?"

"Well, we haven't had a need to test a hovercoil pointed at a person before, but I don't think so," Toshige replied, "The hovercoil needs to be pointing in the direction of your enemy, and should deflect projectiles. You can adjust the strength of the field with this knob, and have instantaneous power with this button -- I recommend you keep your back against a solid surface because it could have quite a kick. You could knock someone down for sure."

Hughes wished there had been time to try it out -- he had no idea what the setting should be on the field strength. All he wanted to do was to scare the armor-clad primitives so they would run away and give him a chance to talk with the others.

"One more thing," Toshige added, "The spotlights are added for theatrics -- every time you push the power button the lights will flash full intensity. The combination of field pressure and bright lights should scare them a bit."

Hughes made his way back to the airlock and, with a little help from Sachiko donned the environmental suit. Beth had her suit com headset on and gave him a warning that they were close to something up ahead. The *Towa Maru* came to a stop.

The atmospheric pressure outside was a little off from the cabin pressure, so Hughes went through the whole sequence of using the airlock, ultraviolet light for disinfectant, and air shower to remove particulates -- he remembered Sochiko's precaution against biological contamination and kept his suit completely sealed.

As he stepped outside, he could see several black-clad figures sitting against the cave wall, illuminated by the *Towa Maru*'s headlamps. He walked along the beach, excited for the chance to speak with more of Sochiko's countrymen, but suddenly he stopped. Something was wrong -- the men lined up against the wall were contorted in unnatural positions. It didn't take long before he realized the arrows protruding from the bodies. There was no one alive.

Movement over to the side startled Hughes. Two blood-red barbarians eased out of the darkness with their bows drawn. Panicked, Masamune adjusted the knob all the way to maximum and backed against the hull of the *Towa Maru*. In one quick movement Hughes aimed the weapon and fired two shots at his attackers. Searing lights flashed and one by one the armored barbarians were swept back and slammed against the cave wall. Then -- nothing.

If all had gone according to plan, two primitives would have been running for the tunnel mouth by then. But there they were motionless against the cave wall. Hughes slowly walked toward the still bodies with the weapon drawn. What he saw made his stomach turn -- the armor had been clearly cleaved in two and each of the men had bloodied burn marks on their chests. Masamune had killed two living, breathing souls!

*****

"And you see," Hughes described emotionally to Hildebrandt through the suit com, "I didn't mean to kill anybody."

Speaking on radio through the wormhole tether was so much easier than maintaining a delicate orientation for the titanium tuner block. Jiro, Toshige, Sachiko, and Emi gathered around as Beth raced out to rendezvous with Bridgestar.

Hildebrandt was silent on the other end. There had been no time to tell Hughes what had transpired at Grindavik, or that Tom's heart had been wrenched out of him when Carrie had been taken away.

Hildebrandt brushed that aside, "Never mind about that. The x-ray storm will hit Grindavik in three Sol-days -- the Grindavik power plants will be decimated and all our wormhole tethers will go offline. Get back here immediately!"

CHAPTER 21

It had happened before -- generation after generation knew what had to be done. First it was the colonists from No Point. Someone in the government couldn't keep his or her mouth shut -- there would be a worldwide cataclysm that would start in Novissima on a certain date. The No Point folks had fifty years to search secret government files and technical specifications, and had an accelerator that could be modified to manufacture singularities for Hyperaperture gates. The gate codes were also on file, and it was no trouble to spend extra time figuring out how to hijack Grindavik gates once they came online back in the past.

Those Grindavik devils! The cursed Mars Interim Government! They had invented a technology they couldn't understand, and let loose black holes into the planet core. Over the years No Point folks withdrew themselves from contact with Grindavik whenever possible, and shied away from participation in the Mars Interim Government. Grindavik had destroyed the planet!

The No Point residents weren't stupid. Only a small number knew what was going on at first. When the time came close to where the x-ray storms would be released, they built a gate and hijacked the Grindavik operation sixty-five years earlier. They built massive underground cities and power plants, and evacuated all their citizens back in time, just as the Grindavik folks had planned to do. By the time the x-ray storms came along no one was there to experience the cataclysm. Sixty-five years earlier the No Point residents from the future lived safely in their underground bunkers, unknown to even their former selves living in the surface community.

History repeats itself, especially if you own a time machine. The underground No Point folks lived out those sixty-five years again -- this time in extensive bunkers bored into the mountains of Pointless -- and knew they would have to go back once more. This time they began thinking about their unfortunate neighbors -- what about Novissima where the Grindavik devils release their horror? The underground No Point folks brought Novissima into their circle, and provided them with their own gates that had their causal beginning with the Grindavik engineers. Those evil Grindavik scientists!

Who knows how many times the loop ran its way before Perepelkin, Bonestell, Trud, Aktaj and many other colonies, who right from the beginning had no love of Grindavik and her allies, joined the secret circle. At the end of each loop, entire populations would escape back in time through multiple gates, then disassemble each unit until there was only one machine left. Well-placed charges set on a timer by the last man would blow all evidence of that last gate to smithereens. Then the loop began all over again.

One would think that it would begin to be quite populous back there. But after several generations that was not the case -- sometimes, through low fertility rates or disease, the population heading back to the return point would be less than in previous generations. At other times feuds or skirmishes kept a check on the population size. Each turn of the loop added folks going back, but somehow, they all got integrated somehow, and Mars was a big world with room to expand -- new underground volumes and infrastructure would be added as needed. No one considered what would happen if Mars suddenly became full one day.

Does history change? Do all those closed timelike curves exist from the beginning in a single causal history, like a tapestry that eliminates paradoxes? Or are there alternate realities? No one could keep track --

The one consolation was that each time the loop ran its course, those evil Grindavik scientists met their doom in that monster they unleashed on the world.

CHAPTER 22

Tom Hildebrandt stood back and scratched his head -- what to do with all these people? The Grindavik colonists and refugees were streaming through to the Pointless excavations as fast as their legs could carry them. Only two gates were operational, and some folks complained that they had to stand several hours in the long queue waiting to get out. Hygiene stations were unable to keep up, and already there were water and food shortages.

Harrison and Statner's negotiations with Mitchell and Myeong had gained them a few additional tunnels, but got nowhere with water supplies -- how could they keep the migration a secret if they couldn't account for large amounts of the precious liquid?

And then there was the harassment. Groups of Time Colonists, as they came to be known, would pause in their own shelter-building and pile into rovers and aircraft -- crossing half of Mars in some cases -- just to pick fights and hinder the Grindavik operation at Pointless. Hildebrandt was amazed as the story unfolded, and he couldn't fathom the looping existence the Time Colonists went through every sixty some odd years.

"Wouldn't you meet multiple copies of yourself?" Hildebrandt wondered, "What about paradoxes -- seems like they would come about pretty easily."

Tom, Jacob, and Howard Statner found themselves sitting together in the windowed job shack at Pointless watching the evacuation unfold.

"It's not quite so simple as that. Sometimes you just need to get used to having a twin or two around, but sometimes entire cultures progress from generation to generation, no matter if their causal path zigzags back and forth in time." Harrison explained.

Hildebrandt was not satisfied, "But this is something that has bothered me ever since that SCAPP experiment where our Sachiko and the alternate Sachiko painted different colors. I can't believe a small decision like that is enough to split the entire universe in two."

Harrison apparently had also given the concept much thought, "I don't think it's a case of splitting a universe in two. Have you ever heard of Everett's Many Worlds theory? Everett explained that on the quantum level, every particle exists in many states at once, maybe all possible states. That being the case, all possible scenarios are played out at once, but only the observers attuned to one particular state will be able to observe that state. That would mean observing one Sachiko or another would be linked back to our consciousness somehow. And by the way, personally, I don't think all possible states are there, but only the most probable states are observable. That's why we don't see hundreds of Sachikos out there painting hundreds of colors."

Statner wondered, "But what does that mean to have two versions of oneself. Apparently, they began as one, and because of the choice made, observers in both cases saw a different outcome, thus two different Sachikos."

"I don't have all the answers, but assuming the observation of any particular state is due to consciousness, it might be that those separate individuals are still linked somehow -- a person may be able to run through a variety of scenarios in one's head that are somehow being acted out in an alternate universe. That may be the very definition of consciousness and our ability to visualize or anticipate events that haven't actually happened." Harrison explained, "Think of it this way. What if you went back in time to meet your younger self? We crossed paths with other versions of ourselves in the bubble. Each of you benefits from the other's experience -- one from the younger man's perspective, and the other from what he may become. It's still the same individual. So perhaps consciousness is a single person extending not only forward and backward, but sideways too."

"So how do we get to a state where two individuals exist at the same time, and are observable by more than one universe?" Hildebrandt asked.

Harrison scratched his chin, pausing to think, "Well, that is the nature of paradox I suppose. We've invented a traversable wormhole which makes such things possible, and the bite is taken out of the paradox by understanding those two individuals each have their own causal path, and each have their own alternate state, or causal destiny."

Hildebrandt still wasn't sure he understood the logic of it, but Harrison's explanations made more sense than anything else he had heard. However, neither of the three would have a chance to discuss the concept further -- a ruckus outside drew their attention away from the matter.

Hildebrandt stood up and went over to the window. A crowd was forming, and shouts could be heard. Without warning the crowd parted and a pressurized armored military vehicle drove up and stopped right in front of the shack. Dozens of armed soldiers, weapons drawn, marched into place clearing a circle about the vehicle.

Howard and Jacob rushed out of the shack to see what was the matter, followed by Tom. A pressure door opened on the side of the vehicle and three people stepped out -- Department of Interior manager Eiger Mitchell and two others Tom had not seen before. Mitchell stood facing the floor, as if he didn't want to look the Grindavik folks in the eye.

One of the new persons spoke with a loud voice so everyone present could hear, "You people of Grindavik, you are all under arrest for the destruction of private and public property, and for the endangerment of Mars biosphere and habitability. You will be allowed to pack up your belongings and remove your equipment. In one hour, you will be escorted to your permanent internment camp."

Statner jumped out to protest, but the cowardly Mitchell and the others returned to the tank and shut the hatch. Statner and several others rushed the armored vehicle but soldiers fired their weapons and the Grindavik governor went down, causing the crowd to back up.

Tom stared in horror at the crumpled body of the governor, slowly bleeding away life's precious fluids. Murphy had gone way overboard this time!

Several hours later Tom marched along in a daze. The Grindavik refugees were taken through a maze of soldier-lined red rock tunnels to a location in No Point where several large industrial-sized gates had been set up -- again Tom didn't recognize the designs, assuming them to belong to the Time Colonists. The refugees were sent through the gates, which apparently led on to the 'internment camp'. It fell to Tom and some of the others to walk the line and make sure the folks freshly arriving from Grindavik in the future immediately fell in step and made their way to the No Point internment camp gates.

Fortunately, it looked as though all the refugees from the future would get out before the x-ray storms hit Grindavik. Tom only hoped that once they got to their internment camp, they would be able to negotiate a deal and get out of this trouble. On the one hand, an internment camp meant there might mean hygiene facilities and adequate living quarters for all the people for the time being at least. But on the other hand, it was clear there would be a challenge fighting against the Time Colonists.

Tom stepped back between two rifled soldiers as a string of transports drove past. The trucks were still loaded with Grindavik equipment, there not having been time enough to unload before the move had been ordered. Moreover, a dozen or so refugees sat on top and ducked their heads every time the vehicle passed a location with reduced ceiling height. When the last truck drove by, Tom saw that it carried several stowed 'Kisser' gate units -- now worthless hunks of metal and electronics. It was a bit of irony -- highly advanced torus accelerators without access to any facilities that could breed black holes!

When the transports passed, the stream of marching refugees continued. There in front of Tom walked Stephan Wang himself, Mars Interim Governor, surrounded by his office staff and family members. Tom gave a short salute and watched the group make their way to the gates.

A little while later Eva Landerman walked by with her husband. On and on folks who had been movers and shakers in his world walked by as refugees, just glad to be alive. Other vehicles came and went. Without warning Hildebrandt felt a pang of regret -- there walked Ichiro, Teresa, and Sabby Hughes who had finally been able to speak with their parents, though forever inaccessible. Tom gave Teresa a hug and sent the three on their way.

During his wanderings along the refugee march, Tom found Naveen piloting the *Infinity's Breach* through the red tunnels. The vehicle hovered a meter or so above the floor and gave out blasts of compressed air occasionally for course correction. Tom thought about the compressors back at Hildebrandt Engineering, faithfully supplying air through a small wormhole tether torus that framed a zero-length tunnel across time and space to this point, allowing those jets of air. He also saw in his mind's eye the great antimatter power generators strewn across Grindavik crater sixty-five years in the future, piping raw electrical power back through that same wormhole tether to give the hovercoils their lift.

Only two Sol-days -- the x-ray storm would hit Grindavik in two Sol-days, and the generators and compressors would be destroyed, forever cutting them off from their power source.

Hildebrandt followed the *Infinity's Breach* and saw it safely through the internment camp gate. Late that evening Tom rode in a small electric vehicle with Harrison as they tailed the last of the refugees to the camp gate. Tom followed the last marcher and drove through for the first time into a well-lit hall with plenty of room -- all Grindavik refugees safe and accounted for.

CHAPTER 23

Masamune Hughes could not have felt more frustrated. He knew it, and Jiro Kitamura knew it -- the trip back to that water world was a waste of time. Perhaps if they had been able to meet up with Sochiko and once again request their assistance it might have been worthwhile, but there had been no way of knowing how far the chronological offset was. The gamble didn't pay off. Beth Kitamura had set them on the fastest acceleration possible back to Bridgestar, but the wormhole tether had only one more Sol-day of functionality before they lost all power and attitude control. The crew scrambled to charge every battery they could think of.

"I'm going to set the compressed air reservoir tanks to 1.5 times their design pressure." Beth announced, assuming there had probably been that much safety margin built in anyway.

Hughes got on the suit com and called for Bridgestar, "We're coming in. Have you compensated for our singularity?"

"*The wormhole has been adjusted again and is waiting for your transit.*" Bridgestar replied.

"Bridgestar," Hughes tentatively began, "This may be our last opportunity to pass through. Our power will fail in a matter of hours. I have a request to make in advance."

"*Go ahead freighter.*" Bridgestar waited.

"We may not have enough power to reach Mars, or whatever habitable planet is on the other side. Can you allow us to pass through at high velocity?" Hughes asked.

"*Bridgestar will match your speed and vector, and will be able to aim the exit as needed.*" was the reply.

Hughes made the final request, "Aim us to achieve a low circular orbit."

"*If such a solution is possible it will be done.*" were the final words Hughes heard from the station.

It wasn't long before the station could be seen through the viewports as a single bright point of light.

"I've got the station on screen." Jiro announced.

The screen showed a grainy image of the morphing Bridgestar. As one watched the image, it was clear that the large torus appendage was being realigned to match the vector the *Towa Maru* followed as it screamed through the heavens.

In no time the station was upon them, and Hughes had to wince as they passed through the torus one last time. Hughes hoped this time would be successful -- after all it was Hildebrandt that had assured them that they had spotted the *Towa Maru* again in the hyperspace bubble, though the chief engineer was strangely silent about the details.

The words that came out of Beth's mouth buried all hope, however, "Space again -- it's still vacuum outside."

They had tried, and failed.

"Bridgestar has aimed us up system. There's a star there but it's not Sol." Beth added.

The hours whiled away. All they could do was wait until that final moment when the wormhole tether lost power and containment and spewed its little black holes out into the void. They couldn't even tell anyone about it, because the Grindavik folks had all evacuated already.

"Let's set up distress signals in case there's someone out there that can help us." Sachiko suggested.

Hughes set up a repeating mayday signal using the suit com, and Jiro set the spotlights to blink out an SOS signal off of battery. The assumption was that if humans like Sochiko were around, that universal cry for help would likely still be valid. Finally, Beth set the craft into a slow roll in respect to the sun so they wouldn't get stuck with one half freezing and the other half burning up.

The end came suddenly. A loud explosion could be heard and all the lights went out and only a single weak battery-powered emergency bulb flipped on. Beth lost all control over the air thrusters and gravitic pulse drive.

The six humans so far from home drifted silently through the void.

CHAPTER 24

Tom Hildebrandt sat in the small electric car in that large well-lit hall and smiled -- it was over, or at least the escape from the x-ray storms had succeeded. It would only be a matter of time before they could negotiate the terms of their freedom. Surely the Grindavik colonists could not be held responsible for the disaster!

Tom got off the car and turned to give a final greeting to those on the other side of the gate. Eiger Mitchell stood there apologetically and watched the chief engineer.

"I'm sorry!" Mitchell called out, "I couldn't do anything about it."

Then, the scene in the other side vanished as the gate on the other side was shut down. Hildebrandt continued to stare at the torus as their own gate just showed a blank dark background meaning it had opened up to the bubble again.

For the first time, Tom looked around at the hall and took in the detail. Leading up to the gate were long rows of stanchions for crowd control that wound around in a long queue. Next to the gate on both sides were scars on the floor where apparently more gates had been mounted and then removed. More stanchions stretched out from those as if to form many parallel lines and queues. *Strange*, Tom thought. If only one gate was used to bring us here, why the need for parallel queues?

Scattered around the hall were small piles of items, as if those waiting in the queue got tired of carrying something and just decided to move on without it. A small group of people stood off to the side examining the wall nearby. Tom would have gone over to see what they were doing but he got distracted as Teresa Hughes ran up.

"Dr. Hildebrandt, there's plenty of room for all of us! Ichiro and Sabby and I found an apartment just for us, already stocked with food." Teresa said.

"Nice!" Hildebrandt responded.

Teresa wandered off again as folks could be seen going about the place exploring.

Tom walked over to where Jacob Harrison had joined the folks inspecting the wall.

"What do you mean this was the scene of a homicide?" Jacob asked incredulously.

For the first time Tom recognized who the two persons were that Jacob was talking to -- Carta Randall and Lenny Chopra the two government investigators.

"I tell you, Lenny and I have seen photos of this place. Several technicians were murdered and dragged over here -- see, they didn't even bother to clean up the mess." Carta pointed.

Tom looked over and saw dark stains on the wall and floor. It wasn't clear whether the stains were blood, but if they were blood, Tom could imagine bodies piled up hidden behind the gate that was once there. Suddenly it all came back -- stepping out of the *Infinity's Breach* near the Hyperaperture, only to find Carrie . . .

"Are you sure it was here? We're sixty-five years in the past. How could you have seen photos of this place?" Harrison asked.

Then Carta said something that shocked Tom right out of his wits, "The *Towa Maru* is here somewhere. Doctor, if I'm right, we're not at an internment camp sixty-five years in the past. This is Novissima right before the x-ray storm hits!"

Hildebrandt and Harrison frantically ran from room to room to find some indication of date and place. The signs were all over the place -- Time Colonists vacating the place leaving entire infrastructures and towns with the lights still on, only to send the Grindavik refugees to their doom just before the onslaught of the destructive x-ray storms. The proof was easy enough to find, and it became clear that though they had found refuge only hours before the failure of the wormhole tethers, it was only days before some gigantic space vessel would crash in this location and deadly black holes released into Mars' core. The relief faded from Hildebrandt like a puff of smoke.

Only hours later the wormhole tethers exploded right at the predicted time. The *Infinity's Breach* and other machines that used the tethers suddenly became inoperable. They were stranded in a strange, vast underground labyrinth, far away from their own time and home.

And still the clock was ticking down the final hours.

The next Sol-day Hildebrandt sat with Harrison, Landerman, Carta, Chopra, and several folks from Wang's office in a newly discovered conference room. The table showed signs that it had been in use most of the night, with empty mugs, stale snacks, and pitchers with varying levels of water.

"Okay, so now we're on a mostly uninhabited world waiting for the moment of destruction," Harrison noted.

"Our counterparts are still this very minute in Grindavik. No one up there knows anything is going to happen." Hildebrandt pointed out. *And another me is up there struggling with escaped nanoassemblers*, he thought.

Harrison frowned, "We can't contact them for help. They haven't even invented the Hyperaperture yet. And what would it gain us? A few months down the road we'd still be in this same quandary, only with two Grindavik populations to worry about."

There was silence around the table, as each person likely wondered what it would be like to meet an earlier version of themselves.

"And besides, none of us have any memories of getting contacted," Harrison continued, "We're caught in the loop just as much as the Time Colonists, only we have the bad end of the deal."

There was another pause in the conversation.

Eva Landerman tried a new tack, "What do we know about the crash and subsequent events?"

Lenny spoke up, "It was centered here in Novissima, right around the Stockwell Institute."

"That's up in the surface town." Hildebrandt thought out loud -- *or at least it wasn't in the hidden colony.*

"So, what I'm thinking is that we still have a few Sol-days -- maybe we can try to prevent this thing from happening." Eva proposed.

Everyone looked at her with a stunned expression -- why didn't I think of that, they seemed to say. Others began to jump in with similar ideas.

"There seems to be two events that, when combined, brought about the storms in the first place." Hildebrandt said.

Eva was nodding, "Yes! Has anyone checked Stockwell Institute for how they are containing their black holes?"

"And we can get on the network and com to see if there are any large ships in the area!" Mark Tomes from Governor Wang's office suggested.

Hildebrandt noticed that Jacob was shaking his head. The physicist had a frown that was getting deeper and deeper. Suddenly Tom knew what his friend was thinking, and no matter of checking would help deter the disaster.

"Don't even bother." Harrison said quietly.

Everyone else looked in that direction and the room got silent.

"What do you mean?" Eva asked.

"I know exactly what happened." Jacob said in a matter-of-fact way.

That got everyone's attention. The frown started to spread among all who were present.

"It has something to do with the hyperspace bubble," the physicist began, "The entire reason the bubble exists in the first place is because two or more wormholes connect together. In our case dozens, maybe hundreds, of wormholes all started their existence in the bubble from zero."

"But what does that have to do with black holes passing through the planet, or giant spacecraft --" Eva began, but stopped when she realized what he was referring to.

"What happens when each of the wormholes begin to shut down. What have you got when there are only two wormholes left -- a tunnel. Then what happens when one of those shut down -- what is left?" Harrison asked.

"Nothing --" Eva replied.

"Exactly," Jacob nodded, "The volume that was in the tunnel reverts over to the last standing wormhole, along with anything in it." (**Figure 6**)

Again, silence reigned around the table.

Tomes thought he understood part of it, "So you're saying the massive spacecraft drifting in the bubble, which entered using a giant aperture appropriate for its size, gets sucked through the last hole which blew it to shreds up the canyon? What about the black holes tearing up Mars?"

Harrison frowned even deeper, "The big ship in there was our biggest gravity well when we used the gravitic pulse drive on *Infinity's Breach*. I'm not sure how the thing works, but there's enough mass on that ship to equal a small protoplanet. It's my guess that they have some fairly hefty singularities to drive their propulsion."

"So, the big ship squeezes through the last wormhole, which is a comparatively small aperture, dumping its black holes in the process." Tomes stated.

"Exactly." Harrison confirmed.

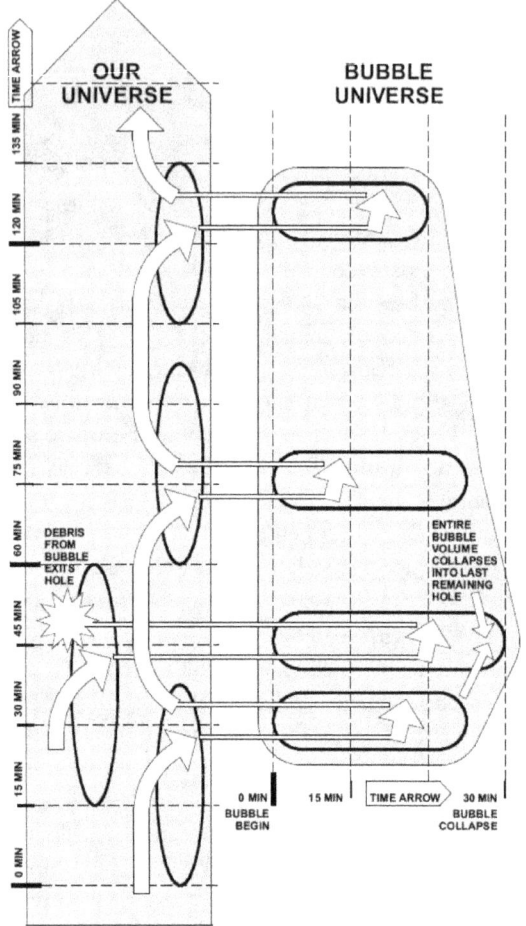

Figure 6: Collapse of bubble universe: entire bubble volume collapses into last remaining hole, and all debris exits from aperture into our universe.

"So, instead of black hole containment, or massive ships in orbit we need to find an open wormhole at Stockwell Institute." Tomes concluded.

But contrary to what Tomes had been expecting, Harrison replied, "That is true, but it's not that simple. What do we do if we find it? Shut it down? If we shut it down the other wormhole would still be open -- the Hyperaperture that is in our Grindavik lab! Remember Mission Prime A? There were only us and one other wormhole open that long. No matter what we do the massive ship would be torn through a small hole and dump its singularities into Mars' core."

There was silence again as the folks in the room considered this new information. Murphy had won. There was nothing they could do about it -- no matter how advanced a warning they had, the problem seemed to be hard-wired into history.

CHAPTER 25

It was cold, very cold. Masamune Hughes could see his breath turn to vapor every time he exhaled. There was a layer of frost on all the equipment.

Sachiko Hughes huddled in the insulated bedding, and snuggled up against Masamune's back. He had to keep her as warm as possible to protect the unborn baby. Since the hovercoils had shut down, they were all being exposed to galactic cosmic radiation at alarming dosages -- Hughes wondered if the baby would even survive at all.

"We're running low on consumables," Beth Kitamura croaked from across the cabin in a hoarse voice, "The scrubbers aren't functioning well and there is very little oxygen left."

Hughes reached over and scraped some frost off the viewport. He peeked through the resulting gap at -- nothing. He never dreamed he would end his life drifting among the lonely stars in the cold void of space.

Hughes faded away and began to dream. The spirits from another realm drifted as lights bobbing on a gentle sea, coming closer to take him away. There were dozens of them -- so beautiful. One got close and Hughes became alarmed --

it had the face of a man with a fierce gleam in his eye. There was a pounding as the fierce eyes bore into his soul and looked straight through his heart.

Beams of light crisscrossed the void. One pointed right at him and blinded him.

"Are they alive?" he heard a voice say.

*****

Hughes woke up later wrapped in warm blankets and restraint straps. He was still in weightlessness, but there was plenty of light filling the cabin.

Across the way Sachiko smiled at him, "I thought you'd never wake up."

"Where are we?" he didn't remember a cabin like this on the *Towa Maru*.

Sachiko smiled again and said, "We've been rescued. A group of salvagers found our vessel just as the air ran out."

Hughes sat up suddenly, or as close as one could do so in zero-g, "And the others?"

"All safe. They're taking us to their outpost. It's quite nice apparently, and they can always use some good engineers." Sachiko soothed.

Hughes remembered his dream, "So we're not dead?"

"Masamune Hughes, you still have a bright future in front of you. It just may not be where we thought it would be." Sachiko assured.

"I miss the kids. I wonder if they're alright." Hughes mused.

"I do too. I miss Ichiro and his unique perception of the world. I miss that smarty little Teresa. And poor little Sabby. But they're in good hands, Mas." Sachiko reflected.

Hughes relaxed a bit -- his wife was in a good mood.

"One of these days I'm going to fly out to Bridgestar and figure out how to rebuild a gate." Hughes concluded.

But Hughes never passed through an aperture again.

CHAPTER 26

The most important task was to find that open wormhole. Tom Hildebrandt found himself walking the main streets and tunnels of Novissima with Carta Randall and Lenny Chopra.

"This is really spooky," Lenny noted, "Carta and I explored these same corridors after they had been struck by the x-ray storm."

Hildebrandt looked over at Carta who seemed to be in deep thought. They passed several empty restaurants and turned the corner.

"I think I know where that wormhole came from." Carta said.

"It was Stockwell Institute, right?" Tom asked.

Carta shook her head, "No, it's one of your gates."

"What? How could that be?" Tom asked.

"The *Towa Maru* is loose somewhere. Several of the Seed Hyperaperture units were stolen from the Grindavik lab, along with wormhole tether hardware. The *Towa Maru* slipped through one of the flashes of light in the bubble just before it paired off and annihilated. I think this is where the vessel came." Carta proposed.

"But that's impossible," Tom protested, "The wormhole tethers have all gone past their limit. Those seed units were powered from the tethers."

Carta stopped and turned to look straight at Tom, "I don't know the details, but whoever is in possession of the *Towa Maru* knows a lot about rigging their own power."

"So, you think the *Towa Maru* is here in Novissima, now?" Tom asked.

"Perhaps," Carta confirmed, "We've come up with a scenario that has the *Towa Maru* going in and out of gates, making raids. What better way to have clear access to all the open gates, or to have a good escape route, than to keep your own gate open."

Hildebrandt was skeptical. Hughes would not do something like that -- their story of getting sucked out of the hyperspace bubble from air rushing to the vacuum of space made more sense -- the *Towa Maru* simply exchanged places with the massive spacecraft when the latter's interplanetary transportation system had a glitch.

Carta must have read the look on his face when she said, "Take a seat in here for a moment. I have something to show you."

Tom looked up and saw the name of the eating establishment that had several tables conveniently located on the street -- 'Burning Boat Pub' -- and was struck with some forgotten memory. Somehow, he knew that name!

The three of them sat down and Carta pulled out her digital pad. Tom had difficulty concentrating as he thought about that name. On the screen, a video began to play. First Carta showed raw footage taken on one of the SCAPP or COSCAPP missions (Tom couldn't tell which). The video showed vessels crisscrossing the hyperspace bubble with that big ship in the background. Next, she showed a portion of the video zoomed in on the ship. Tom couldn't believe it when he saw one of the COSCAPPs fly right into a gaping hangar in the side of the massive vessel. Again, and again the COSCAPP passed in and out of the spacecraft hangar.

"Is this the *Infinity's Breach*, or the *Towa Maru*?" Carta simply asked.

Tom didn't know what to say, except that he knew they had kept operational records of the *Infinity's Breach* right from the beginning to this day. The image had been zoomed in farther than the digital resolution could support, but it was indeed clearly one of the COSCAPPs. If that vessel showing on the screen were the *Towa Maru*, how could it have gotten from Hughes' lost in space scenario back to the bubble again?

"So, you see, Doctor Hildebrandt, the crew of the *Towa Maru* have been conducting raids, and are using that giant spacecraft as a warehouse of sorts to stash the goods!" Carta concluded.

Hughes what is happening, he thought. If Carta was right, then someone had likely rewired the *Towa Maru* and was using a gate set up in Novissima as a base of operations. Rewire the *Towa Maru*?

Suddenly Hildebrandt had an idea. As he racked his brain to figure out where he had known of the name 'Burning Boat Pub' he remembered something he had heard once. Quickly he looked for a network portal and began a search using the name as key words.

Three entries came up: Morioka Funekko Nagashi festival in Japan, Donggang Wang Yeh festival in Taiwan, and the Sayville Halloween Boat Burning in New York. They each appeared to be a festival of sorts. Tom wished Hughes were around to give his thoughts on the Japanese event. Apparently, each of the festivals involved sending evil away on a burning boat. The solution hit Hildebrandt like a ton of bricks.

Carta and Lenny looked up in confusion as Tom rushed over to the pub's phone. He wasn't sure this would be the right thing to do, but in the same way he took a chance with the SCAPP colors, he knew he had to warn himself somehow.

Remember to preserve the causal path, he thought. No information can begin within a loop. He had to think of some way of giving warning without explicitly saying what the issues are.

Tom dialed his own number in Grindavik -- what time was it anyway? Someone answered the phone -- it was an earlier version of himself.

"Hello?" his former self sounded as if he had just woken up.

All Tom could think of saying was, "If you're ever in real trouble, remember me."

Then he hung up. Tom knew that his former self would be curious enough to trace down the origin of the phone call and find it coming from Burning Boat Pub. And when the time was right the information would spark an idea. He had left all the work to his former self and violated no causal paths for the information.

"I've got to talk to Harrison." Hildebrandt explained, and left Carta and Lenny to themselves.

An hour later Hildebrandt had gotten Jacob Harrison and Eva Landerman in the conference room.

"When I was watching the marchers back in those tunnels at Pointless, I saw some gate units still loaded on a transport. How hard would it be to start up an aperture?" Hildebrandt asked.

Harrison scratched his head in mock annoyance, "Well, Novissima has a power plant, and Stockwell Institute has a small accelerator of sorts, but when I went to look at it I was disappointed in its scale -- it certainly won't be enough to breed black holes."

"What about the Time Colonists' 'Kisser Gate' -- the one they sent us here in? Isn't that still operational?" Tom wondered.

Jacob answered in the affirmative, "I think so, and it uses some form of wormhole tether technology. I'm not sure where the power source is, but I assume it uses Novissima's power generator."

"Okay, I think I may have a solution." Tom smiled, and began to describe his idea.

Harrison and Landerman were in complete agreement. Tom gathered his best engineers, including young Sally Averman and Arden Tuttweiler, and got to work.

Early the next morning there was commotion down the hall. Carta and Lenny brought in a stranger who was all tied up. The fellow was Asian in appearance but had a violent demeanor.

Mark Tomes rushed in as well and exclaimed, "We saw the *Towa Maru*! It was right in front of us before they put distance between us."

Lenny explained, "Some folks were up in the town and came across several men who were looting abandoned stores. They tackled this fellow but the rest got away in the *Towa Maru*. They sailed right down the boulevard as if it weren't a pedestrian throughway."

The man was getting a little rough, so Carta braced herself like a lithe feline and threw him to the floor. Not waiting for him to recover, she pulled him up by the collar and pushed him into a chair.

"What is your name?" Carta demanded.

The man kept silent. Carta asked several more times but to no avail. Tom knew Carta was getting frustrated when she pulled him up on the table and strapped him down. Lenny brought out a kit with several wires attached that she patched onto his temples. A turn of a knob brought a blood-curdling scream so haunting Hildebrandt vowed he would never get on the wrong side of the law.

This time the man started talking, using a strange sort of butchered English.

"My name is Davo."

Carta through a series of questions brought out an interesting story. Davo was the member of the crew of the starship drifting in the hyperspace bubble. They had come from a time in the distant future from an artificial satellite named *Blister* -- which was a massive zero-g garage of sorts. He and his crew were farmers that grew crops on rotating artificial gravity centrifuges inside the vast volume. But on the side, they had a more sinister occupation -- to steal ships and raid ports.

"So, tell me -- how did you get a hold of the *Towa Maru*?"

Davo's eyes brightened at the name, and he said, "The *Towa Maru* belonged to our grandfather many generations ago. Masamune Hughes crashed and built the Salvage Empire, eventually constructing *Blister* itself."

Hildebrandt looked at Harrison. The story was fantastic, but seemed to jive well with what Hughes had explained himself.

Hildebrandt couldn't resist, "So the vessel you have been using is hundreds of years old?"

Davo replied, "We're not sure how old it is, but it is highly prized among our people. We wrested it from the Tensakians, who in turn got it from who knows where."

Carta continued, "You've been using the *Towa Maru* for your illicit activities!"

"Captain Kret and Torga have been restoring it for years." Davo replied, "Then Dagoth captured the probe and figured out how it got its power. We've been using the wormholes to expand our business."

"Where is your gate in this city?" Carta asked.

Davo looked at her with pure hate. Hildebrandt stepped back a few paces -- the prisoner had been talking like a normal human being but suddenly there was an evil there that Tom could not fathom.

Carta turned the knob but this time Davo resisted with an iron will.

"You'll never -- get -- it out -- of me!" the sweating prisoner said between labored breaths.

Suddenly Davo tore free from the straps and caught Randall by the throat. Everyone else in the room reached for the prisoner and tried to pull him away, but with a single twist of the neck the investigator fell down limp. Hildebrandt didn't know what happened next as he was thrown against the wall. The engineer couldn't believe a single man could have so much strength. But in a moment it was over -- Lenny pulled out a weapon of sorts that shot out a lightning-quick projectile, which pinned Davo to the wall by his throat. The prisoner gasped for breath for a few seconds then also went limp. A fierce Lenny stared at the dead man for the longest time, undoubtedly fighting the urge to tear his body apart with rage.

The pirate's gate was found only two hours later -- there are only so many places one could set up a wormhole for free passage by a COSCAPP vehicle. The gate was active, and it had been apparent that the *Towa Maru* had just recently entered the bubble again.

No time left, Hildebrandt thought. The time for action is now!

*****

Even Governor Wang showed up for the burning boat sendoff. Crowds of people gathered around the *Infinity's Breach* with its ungainly cargo. Hildebrandt's engineers had taken the Time Colonists' gate and mounted it to the top of the COSCAPP vessel so that it resembled a huge toroid antenna. The Hildebrandt Engineering team had also rigged up an onboard attitude control system to replace the lost functionality of the compressed air jets. It didn't take much to scavenge parts from their own inoperable gate units, and reroute power in such a way that *Infinity's Breach* shared the connection through the gate's operational wormhole tether. They searched for the other mouth of the wormhole tether at Novissima's power plant but couldn't find it -- apparently it got its power from a plant some sixty odd years earlier that the Time Colonists had set up.

Hildebrandt had gone over the mission again and again with Harrison and Landerman. The burning boat would carry the live gate up out of Mars' atmosphere to a benign orbit around the sun. If both the pirate and Time Colonist apertures were kept open there would still be balance and the bubble would continue to exist. When the burning boat reached the proper orbit, they would shut down the pirate aperture and allow the wreckage from the interstellar freighter to blow out the Time Colonist gate along the orbital path out in space. That way, any singularities released by the explosion could take their time and evaporate at a safe distance away from any planetary body.

There was only one catch -- they couldn't do it on automatics. The ability to remote control the *Infinity's Breach* died when it's original wormhole tether popped.

"I'll have to pilot it myself." Tom insisted.

There were few people who knew how to pilot the COSCAPPs, and even though he was not as skilled as Naveen, he knew he had to do it for Carrie, and Hughes, and all those who lost their lives in this mess.

Tom clanked over to the hatch in his hard plate environmental suit and allowed Arden to place the helmet and secure the fastenings.

"Don't give yourself a hard time." Tom gave parting words of advice through the helmet com.

Arden had vowed to eventually travel back to Grindavik and work for Hildebrandt Engineering there, undoubtedly bumping into his younger self at some point.

"I'll still be here -- it's only a matter of consciousness." Tom had explained when his employees begged him not to go.

"I'm sure the Tom Hildebrandt in Grindavik will somehow feel this experience, and I will live on through him." Tom comforted, "Oh and by the way. Tell my other self to take a look at the light switch in Hildebrandt Bunker -- it matches the command codes for those runaway nanoassemblers! Thank goodness they are only in the pipes."

Tuttweiler looked up at his boss astounded. It was so simple -- the direct digital control scheme for the lighting of the environmental control system worked off a wireless bus system. A command to turn lights on or off would be broadcast out on all the nodes, but only the light switch with the proper address would respond to the wireless signal. As it turned out, every time someone turned on the light in the rarely used Hildebrandt Bunker, the shared signals told the missing nanoassemblers to self-replicate down in the pipes and clog the plumbing. When the light turned off, the self-replication would end. Tom's counterpart would know what to do.

And there was another Carrie, alive and well. Suddenly Tom had a revolutionary thought -- how many Toms had sacrificed themselves in parallel realities (whether perishing in x-ray storms, runaway nanoassemblers, or industrial accidents), to allow this Tom to enjoy everything he had accomplished so far? Did each scenario in his imagination somehow represent a connection to those other possible universes? Would his decision here and now allow another Tom in another reality to live a long, fruitful life with another Carrie?

The refugees in Novissima would eventually contact Grindavik and the truth of what happened would become widely known. It would be a very interesting world to live in!

Tom entered the hatch and shut it behind him. He moved his way to the cockpit and settled into the pilot's seat. In no time the gravitic pulse drive got the vessel moving on a steady rise that would take him out of Mars' atmosphere.

"Com check." Tom spoke into the suit mic, which fed through to a high-power communications system that had been rigged into the vehicle's subsystems.

"*Loud and clear.*" came back the reply.

Hildebrandt thought back on the timing of this mission. He remembered the time he himself had kept the Hyperaperture open as long as they could after the *Towa Maru* on its maiden voyage had been blown through that other hole into vacuum. They called that mission Prime A because it was the longest ever recorded. That was the other competitor here.

All the other apertures had been shut down leaving only that one and the pirate's aperture open in the end. All he needed to do was to keep the Time Colonists' gate open longer than Prime A and they would win.

Tom set a course away from Mars orbit and roared up into the sky. To hell with you, Murphy!

Two Sol-days later Hildebrandt got word that the other aperture in the bubble was about to shut down. He had been riding the solar orbit for a few hours now, and had already aimed the Time Colonists' gate in such a way that any material released from the collapsing hole would stay on the correct vector.

This is it, Tom thought. This is the decision point. I have two choices right now. I could wait past the tipping point and change the fate of Mars, but sacrifice myself in the process. Or, I could save myself, shut down the gate, and history would follow exactly as we remembered it -- the pirate gate would release the black holes and the cycle would begin all over.

Murphy's true colors finally showed themselves -- no matter how much trouble there seemed to be, there was still a way out. Murphy wasn't destiny. Nor was it just engineering. *It's still a matter of free will after all*, Tom thought.

I could die for Mars. I could die for Carrie.

Or I could simply fly away with my own gate and interplanetary vehicle powered with a sixty-year time limit --

What does it feel like to split a universe?

Dear reader, it's your choice:
1) Shut down Time Colonists' gate, save Tom: go to Prologue
2) Keep Time Colonists' gate open, save Mars: go to Epilogue

EPILOGUE

Ichiro Hughes and Tina Fatjo struggled up the faintly marked path. The route was not particularly steep, just that any slope is always harder to negotiate in an environmental suit, even at one-third gee, and they were carrying equipment. As Ichiro neared the top of the slope, he could hear himself breathing in the narrow confines of the helmet, almost overwhelming the sounds of life-support fans working to keep his faceplate defrosted.

Ichiro let his gaze wander over the reddish rocks ahead of him, trying to get a glimpse of what lay beyond. He took the last few steps as the distant valley began to reveal itself over the top of the eclipsing ridge -- it was one of those breathtaking views that were so common on Mars, framed by towering stone and icy cliffs of enormous scale. Reaching the highest point of the climb, he paused long enough to catch his breath, but kept his eyes on those far away low lands that he had come to see. There was a city down there, the one that had become his home.

"*We can see Novissima from here.*" Tina said through the helmet com as she came up beside him, then she froze.

"*What day is this?*" she asked, "*I've been here before, long ago and far away.*"

Ichiro smiled, "Today is when the x-ray storms swept across this valley, in that other life."

Tina continued to stare down into the valley as haunting images reached up deep from her memory. Ichiro studied her face and began to worry.

"*This -- is when it happened.*" Tina said silently.

She could almost see Drake and Mei-Hua reaching up to her for help. It was the same exact Sol-day the tragedy took place, and Tina was living it all over again. Ichiro and Tina gazed down at the valley in silence.

Behind them another person climbed up to join them.

"*What's up guys? Is this the place?*" the freshly arrived woman asked.

The two turned to face the third person. It was Mei-Hua.

Tina became animated again, "*It happened right down there. You couldn't get away in time -- it was horrible!*"

"*Thanks for saving us guys,*" Mei-Hua acknowledged lightheartedly, "*Race you down!*"

The three made leaps and bounds as they descended toward the bustling town, taking advantage of low gravity and highly articulated suit joints. It had just been by chance that Reuben Drake and his two assistants had been in the area and had run into the Grindavik refugees. Tina recalled that was why they had been asked to observe the x-ray storm in the first place -- in that other reality. Now there were two Tinas, one of which was a year wiser.

It had only been a day since history had changed, and already there were grand plans for the future -- a future that everyone had been granted at great price. They would never see another Time Colonist again, caught in their recurring loop in the past. Consequently, all opposition to the Mars Interim Government suddenly vanished as the detractors had exiled themselves in history -- there would be no more anti-technology movements, no more distorted science, mystic reversion, or clandestine sabotage. Out there on the red landscape entire deserted cities sat waiting for the taking.

But Ichiro had wider horizons. He and Teresa had just attended a meeting outlining a new age of space exploration. First Liang Zhou, the physicist from No Point who had followed them into the future, proposed to establish large scale power plants in orbit around the sun, using the difference of potential in the sun's magnetic field, and pipe it back to Mars via wormhole tethers. Such a power generation scheme required little maintenance and was scalable around most heavenly bodies. And perhaps eventually even those natural massive singularities out in the galactic core could be harnessed as gigantic power generators. It would establish a power grid of astounding proportions.

Next, small robotic spacecraft would be launched, each mounted with a Dualer Gate connected directly back to its twin on Mars -- tremendous thrust and continuous acceleration could be achieved just by piping unlimited fuel through the wormhole directly to the exhaust nozzle, without having to lift the great fuel tanks and infrastructure required. Using this technique, at any milestone location such as passing a planet or moon, humans could simply step through the gate and perform their observations in person for a few hours, then be back on Mars for dinner. And Ichiro couldn't wait to see how the gravitic pulse drives would be developed, perhaps eliminating the need for chemical fuels.

In the next step colony ships would be sent to distant stars as robotic probes equipped with Dualer Gates -- no matter how many centuries it took to reach the star, the population back on Mars would not need to be involved until the probe finally reached its destination -- then colonists could simply step through onto the surface of the new world.

And then finally there was the 'Bridgestar' concept described by Ichiro's father. A self-maintaining network of wormhole gates could be established in orbit around every star with planets in the habitation zone. The 'Bridgestar' could connect to the ever-growing power grid, utilize resources found in the various systems, and export unique resources to all the other systems depending on need. The day would soon come where a ship could take a weeklong trip to Alpha Centauri or even farther away.

Contrary to what the Time Colonists thought, it was apparent that the wormhole technology would open opportunities no one could even imagine.

Ichiro followed Mei-Hua and Tina to the nearest Novissima surface airlock and entered the city. There was a bright future in store for them, and Ichiro knew his parents were already there.

ABOUT THE AUTHOR

A. Scott Howe is a senior engineer at NASA Jet Propulsion Laboratory and has two PhDs (in architecture and robotic construction systems). He is on the NASA development team building long-duration human habitats for deep space, and permanent outposts for the moon and Mars.

Look for these other science fiction novels by A. Scott Howe:

Waterball (2012)

Blister (2013)

Theoloop (2021)

Replicycle / Retrocause (2023)

www.ingramcontent.com/pod-product-compliance
Lightning Source LLC
Chambersburg PA
CBHW071852220626
47052CB00002B/78